The only people Ren had shown affection to, in Lina's memory, were herself and the old ladies—and with the old ladies it was just a grandchild variety of affection.

Which left herself. Lina smiled and wriggled down against the cushions. Just imagine Ren settling down on top of her now, on this elegant living room sofa—planting a knee on either side of her hips, twining his fingers into hers and pushing them into the cushions, bending to press warm lips to her mouth and taste her tongue—no, she and Ren would never do such things.

Unfortunately, she drifted into a dream in which they were doing exactly such things. His hands coasted along her breasts, caressing them through her sweater; his hips sank heavy against hers; his mouth tasted of roses, odd but alluring. She murmured and sighed to him, inviting and pleading for more.

He pushed himself up then, his weight lifting from her body. "Why did you stop?" she protested.

She opened her eyes. Her heart failed her for a moment.

Ren himself leaned over her. He stood behind the sofa, resting his elbows on the back of it and leafing through *Pride and Prejudice*, which he must have picked up from her chest. Her face felt hot. Lord, she hadn't moaned in her sleep, had she?

Ren smiled. "Sorry. Didn't want to wake you up, but George was looking for you."

"How long have I been asleep?"

"I wouldn't know, but it's 11:30 now." He turned a page, smile still pressing a dimple into his cheek. "Sounded like a vivid dream."

Kill me now, she begged the powers above.

The Ghost Downstairs

by

Molly Ringle

Ringle
cl

The Ghost Downstairs

Contact Information: info@thewildrosepress.com

Cover Art by *Rae Monet*

The Wild Rose Press
PO Box 708
Adams Basin, NY 14410-0706
Visit us at www.thewildrosepress.com

Publishing History
First Faery Rose Edition, 2008
Print ISBN 1-60154-447-2

Published in the United States of America

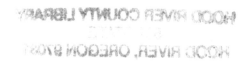

Dedication

For my son, who often slept on my lap while I wrote; and for the houseboys I have known.

I owe thanks to a multitude of people for help in revising this story. I thank my family members, notably Kate, Greg, and Steve, for pinpointing the strengths and weaknesses in the first draft; and Bonny and Rob for letting me bounce medical related plot ideas off them (even though I probably still got some of those details wrong).

I also thank my workshop reviewers from TheNextBigWriter.com: Kim, Doralynn, Payge, Tom, Derone, Rory, Parallel, Wayne, Laurie, Treasure, Wordsmith, and everyone else who dropped in at some point with a useful idea. Thank you all for encouraging me and providing direction!

Chapter One

Lina Zuendel blamed the loss of her job on Stephen King. If she hadn't been reading *Salem's Lot* that night in the nurses' lounge, she wouldn't have been so spooked and jumpy, and she wouldn't have screamed when she turned a hallway corner at two o'clock in the morning and collided with Sara, another nurse. Sara carried a half-full dinner tray and wheeled an empty IV device, and when Lina smashed into her the result was spectacular. Sara fell, knocking over both the IV and Lina. As Lina sprawled on the hall tiles she saw the dinner tray go airborne.

A crescent of burger bounced off her forehead while an apple core hit Sara in the eye. Jabbering apologies, Lina rose to help Sara, planted her foot on a pudding cup, and slipped again, whacking her forehead on Sara's chin. At that point Sara started to hit Lina to keep her away. Lina crawled aside, wiping ketchup off her ear and still apologizing, while two grinning orderlies helped Sara up and led her to the lounge.

Lina admitted in her heart that the moment had been a perfectly executed piece of slapstick. She understood why people laughed. None of them knew at the time Lina would kill a patient because of it.

"I went to get sodium chloride for Mr. Ambaum, to flush his catheter," she explained to the doctors and the hospital administrator who called her in after Mr. Ambaum's death. It was five in the morning; Lina still had a chocolate pudding stain on her white sneaker. "I was rattled after, um, running

1

into Sara. I took what I thought was the sodium chloride, and went to his room and injected it, but..." Her hands still trembled. "It turned out to be potassium chloride. I somehow grabbed that instead; I don't know how."

"You injected potassium chloride into his central venous line?" The administrator took notes as he spoke. He hid his emotions well, but his voice was gruff. He couldn't have been pleased to learn that a nurse had accidentally given a patient a lethal injection.

Mr. Ambaum had been receiving chemotherapy for liver cancer. He had a wife and two grown sons.

"Yes." Professionalism had to be upheld; Lina would not cry in front of everyone. She blinked against the tears and controlled her voice. "I thought I checked. I saw the word 'chloride.' I should have..." She stopped. She should have checked better; end of weak defense.

The hospital already explained to Mr. Ambaum's family that he had died of cardiac arrest after a medication error. Though the family members were merely in shock right now, the administrator told Lina to expect anger and press coverage, though probably not legal action, as the hospital would do everything it could to settle with the Ambaums out of court. In the meantime, the administrator sent Lina home and told her to take tomorrow off. Lina nodded, gathered her shreds of pudding-splashed dignity, and left the hospital.

A fresh September dawn bathed the eastern sky. Lina stumbled along the sidewalk, blinking at buildings and citizens and seagulls. Salmon-colored sunlight gleamed on the cars; roasting coffee filled the salty air with its scent; a beeping bread truck backed into an alley.

Seattle's First Hill bore the nickname "Pill Hill" for the numerous hospitals dotting it, and Lina's apartment sat in the middle of them. When she had moved into it as a fresh young nurse with a bright white lab coat, she had counted herself lucky to live among so many potential workplaces. Now, five years and three lab coats later, she doubted she would stay at Everglade Hospital even if they did forgive her. They had been too kind; she had killed a man. In her own mind she had committed manslaughter. She did not want to give up nursing, nor go to jail, but she felt she deserved both those fates, and suspected she would never touch a syringe again without shuddering. *But this is only the first morning*, she thought in desperation. It would improve with time and sleep. Wouldn't it?

Lina unlocked the iron security gate of her building, trudged up the stone steps, and shuffled inside. She needed someone to talk to, someone close, but she had no one. The other nurses were friendly, but not the sort of people whose blouses she would cry upon. Her brother was probably stoned. Her mom never paid attention to nursing concerns unless they concerned herself. Her dad might actually be dismayed with her for her mistake. Really, Lina had no one.

Except maybe Brent.

In the stairwell, she paused at the landing between the second and third floor, where a window faced Elliott Bay. Deep blue water and evergreen-bristled shores cozied up to the metropolis; a white ferry trundled toward Bainbridge Island. Desperate love for the city swelled beneath her ribs. Seattle had seemed the promised land when she had been growing up in her ugly Tacoma neighborhood, and since she had moved here not a day had gone by when she didn't love it still. Brent had invited her to come with him to Atlanta. Because of her ties to Seattle she refused, and they broke up and said all those cruel things to each other. But would he be kind to her now if she called him and spilled the whole awful story? He knew her better than anyone else did. He was her strongest hope for sanity this morning.

In her apartment she thumped *Salem's Lot* onto her desk, pushed newspapers off her chair, and plopped down to check her email. Like magic, one from Brent appeared. But it wasn't addressed just to Lina. In fact, it appeared to be addressed to everyone Brent knew; the "cc" list went on for about fifty names.

Hi friends and folks! Atlanta is treating me great. In fact, you're never going to believe this, but I'm getting married! Her name's Joanne and we met at a biomed research conference, and well, it had to be fate. I'm too slammed right now to give the whole story, but I'm really happy and wanted to let everyone know, and I'm sure some of you will be calling me anyway for details when you get this. Have a wonderful day!

That was all. Lina checked again, but he sent no separate email for her alone, no kind words for the woman he left behind in Seattle just five months ago. She checked the voice mail on her cell phone. Nothing there either.

She rose on shaking legs and looked at the answering machine on her land line. The blinking light signaled a message. She dove forward, knocking a dictionary off the desk, and pressed the button.

"Hey Lina, it's your mom," drawled the recording. Lina sank back into the chair and put her head in her hands. "I've got these cramps again; they're making me miserable, honey, and I wanted to ask you what that tea was you told me about. 'Cause I swear, sugar, the Midol ain't cutting it anymore. When the hell is menopause going to get here already? Well, at least I got a nurse for a daughter who I can call and complain to. Call me back. Also, Lina, your brother has a thing on his face again. Talk to him about it, okay? Bye, honey."

With dried ketchup in her hair, pudding on her shoe, and shackles of love and cowardice chaining her to an unforgiving Seattle, Lina sat at her desk and wept.

****

Lina quit a week later. The doctors, nurses, and administrators all pleaded with her to stay, but she declined. Every patient visit tormented her, and not just the ones involving IV medications. Every hospital room reminded her of the thousand things she could do to endanger or destroy the trusting folk who had come here to be healed. The newspapers and local TV stations had run the story of Mr. Ambaum's demise. Though Lina had been shielded from having to talk to reporters, and her name hadn't even been printed, she felt her coworkers watching her wherever she went. Even if it was pity and not reproach, she wanted none of it.

There would be no court trial. For Lina's mistake the Ambaums were willing to take a $500,000 settlement from Everglade Hospital, which, a hospital lawyer confided to Lina, was nothing. Families had been awarded millions for similar incidents. Mr. Ambaum, though only fifty-seven, had been an alcoholic his entire adult life, leading to the liver cancer, and Lina got the impression his wife and sons were weary of dealing with him. They wanted to close the case, pay the medical bills, and move on.

That thought depressed her. A person's spouse and children should be the ones who cared the most and fought the hardest. How many mistakes did you have to make before the world washed its hands of you? How far down that path was Lina herself, with such a colossal mistake on her record already at merely thirty-two years old?

She didn't tell her family what happened. She didn't even plan to tell them she quit until she got a new job, and then she would only tell them she wanted a change of scene. That at least was true. Paradoxically, she felt herself unqualified for anything but nursing, while unable to go on being a nurse at Everglade. Her plan, her final hope, was to try being a nurse somewhere else, somewhere with fewer opportunities for lethal error.

On a windy morning in late September, Lina put on mascara and her lab coat, gave up the valuable street parking space she'd held down with her Impala for a week, and drove to the University District for an interview. The ad in the *Seattle Times* sought a live-in nurse for "Drake House, elegant retirement home." Lina's current apartment now oppressed her—in addition to its hospital-central location, it bore too many memories of Brent—so she emailed her résumé to the address given. Marla Drake, the landlady, called her the same day and set up an interview. All Lina had to do was not screw it up, assuming she could stand the place.

No problem there. She fell in love with the house upon sight: a red-brick, three-story mansion with a spiky iron fence and a steep black roof. Marla, a short middle-aged woman with a seemingly permanent grin, let her in, pumped her hand, and beckoned her to follow. Lina crossed the thick white carpets, gaping at the furnishings: a grand piano, wavy old windowpanes, hardwood floors in the dining room. The ground floor smelled of lemon cake and freshly vacuumed rugs. Her spirits wobbled upward. In such a place, she might stand a chance at practicing qualm-free nursing again.

Marla brought Lina to a small parlor where a

thin man in his fifties with bushy gray hair hopped up from the sofa and smiled. "My husband, Alan."

"Welcome, Lina." He shook her hand.

"These are our quarters." Marla settled herself into a polished wooden chair with green cushions. "Couple hundred square feet to hide away in. Have a seat."

Lina sat in the indicated chair, which matched Marla's, and Alan relaxed onto the sofa again, twiddling a pencil between thumb and finger.

"I'm an RN myself," Marla said, "but God knows I need helpers. Best case would be someone who can move in. Makes the shifts more flexible. Room and board come with salary, and the rent is real cheap. Especially for this town."

Lina smiled. "Sounds fine to me. I'm happy to move."

Alan scratched his nose with the pencil. "Don't mind leaving that commute behind, huh?"

"Not a bit."

The interview flowed as smooth as small talk. Then came that inevitable question. "Why did you leave your last job?"

Lina had undergone two other interviews in the last ten days, in facilities like this one—though nowhere near as beautiful—and at this question she launched into an account of her collision with Sara and the subsequent medication mix-up. No matter how she tried to downplay it, the story could only end with, "The man died." After that, both interviews had turned chillier, and Lina went home knowing she wouldn't be called back.

Everglade Hospital had agreed not to mention the incident if anyone called for references. Disclosing the truth—or not—was Lina's choice.

The lemon cake smelled so good. The carpets were so clean.

Lina cleared her throat. "Hospitals can get very

depressing. Very hectic, impersonal."

Marla and Alan Drake nodded in commiseration.

"I love nursing," Lina said, "but I really wanted a more home-like environment, with patients I could get to know and stay with longer."

The very next day, Marla called to tell her she got the job.

On the first of October, during a rainstorm, she moved into Drake House as the new resident nurse. After unpacking her boxes in her third-floor room, Lina took a notebook and went to see each of the eleven senior citizens. She wore her white lab coat to look professional and her hair loose to look friendly. She hoped the result wasn't mere contradiction.

The residents' quarters comforted her, with their potted plants and wallpaper and large-print book collections. In such an environment she felt relaxed, or at least more relaxed than she had been since her involuntary manslaughter. Encouraged by her mood improvement, she talked half an hour with each resident, learning and writing down their habits and ailments, and what they liked and disliked about Drake House.

"The meals are wonderful," at least half of them said.

Cook very good, Lina jotted down in her notebook.

"Marla and Alan set up such lovely activities for us," some added.

Fun times, Lina wrote.

"We're all such good friends; we're like a big family," nearly all said.

Happy place, Lina recorded.

The dislikes were minor. The radiators needed replacing; they clanked and took a while to heat up. "But Alan or Ren lights a fire for us in the living room, and we sit down there and have a grand time," said Dolly Tidd, her third patient. "Have you met Ren? Our houseboy? Oh, you will! He's just darling. Do you have a boyfriend? No? Then you will *love* Ren."

Cute coworkers, Lina wrote, then crossed it out. She was too much of a wreck for romance right now. Besides, with a title like "houseboy," this Ren was probably still in high school.

The residents' other dislikes included the lack of an elevator, though there was a wheelchair lift on the front staircase; the difficulty visitors had in finding parking; and, oh yes, the ghost.

Lina's pencil paused the first time someone mentioned it. "The ghost?"

"Yes," said Betty Carter, cutting an article out of a newspaper at a pace of about five snips per minute. "But it doesn't really hurt anyone, and we're all used to it."

"Then I hope to hear some good stories around that fireplace."

And Lina wrote *Haunted house believer* on Mrs. Carter's page.

Then George Lambert, who was hard of hearing but didn't let that stop him from flirting with every woman he met, shouted at her, "Did they tell you about the ghost?"

"Not much. What does this ghost do?"

"Don't worry!" He winked. "I'll protect you."

She dropped the topic and moved on to his medical history. But her last patient brought up the ghost yet again.

Augusta Beltrayne, who everyone called Mrs. B, had the room next door to Lina's. Mrs. B, a tiny, brown-skinned lady, eighty-nine years old, had advanced macular degeneration, arthritis, and a stunning number of magazine subscriptions. They overflowed her shelves, filled four crates, and lurked in piles under the lavender armchairs.

"Not much point, the way my eyesight's going," Mrs. B said. "But I love the smell of them. Especially these." She lifted an issue of *Vogue*, and flashed a smile full of teeth so straight they had to be dentures.

"I'd be happy to read to you once in a while, or find you some audio material."

"That would be marvelous. Then I could just turn up the volume if that poltergeist starts knocking on walls." Mrs. B laughed.

Lina lowered her notebook. "Okay, you're the third person to mention a ghost. Is there anything I should know?"

"Don't you worry. All it does is rearrange things and walk up and down the stairs."

The clouds darkened outside. Lina told herself the chill up her spine was really still Stephen King's fault. "People see it?"

"With my eyes I'm hardly the one to ask! But no, I gather nobody sees it. They just hear it—footsteps and so forth."

"Have you heard it?"

"My door swung open one day and tapped against the wall, three times, like someone was standing there playing with it. Only there wasn't anyone."

Stupid to get goose bumps from a dubious anecdote, Lina scolded herself. "Was that the only time?"

"Not exactly. I could swear things end up in different places than where I laid them down. But then, I'm not exactly young anymore!"

A burst of static and a loud voice from the open door made Lina jump almost out of her chair. "Good evening, everyone," said the voice, Alan Drake's. "Dinner is served! Please come on down." The intercom clicked off.

Lina let out her breath.

"Oh, good!" Mrs. B flung aside the *Vogue* and reached for Lina's hand. "Let's go down."

Mrs. B squeezed her arm as they walked down the corridor. "I'm so glad you're my new neighbor. That last nurse hardly stayed a month. She was such a jumpy thing."

"Why did she leave?"

Mrs. B gestured as if sweeping cobwebs out of her face. "Oh, she said her computer keys kept tapping by themselves in the middle of the night. Honestly, can't some people get earplugs?"

While Lina digested that remark, Marla Drake bounded into view at the staircase's second-floor landing. "Hey, Lina!" Perhaps because she lived with the elderly, Marla seemed to be in the habit of shouting. "How's your room?"

"Fine. I haven't spent much time in it yet, though. I've been talking to my new housemates."

"Well, you got one more. Our twelfth room just got filled. Jackie Clairmont. You can meet her at dinner."

"My!" said Mrs. B. "What a busy day. Two new people."

"First of the month." Marla led the way down the stairs to the main floor. "I reckon people's leases are up." She laughed, a single-note bray.

They stepped into the dining room, onto the shining hardwood floors Lina had admired. Four tables, with six chairs each, gave residents and visitors plenty of seating choice at mealtimes. Lina helped Mrs. B into a chair and sat beside her. The Drakes, George Lambert, and Gertrude Brown (age eighty-six, high blood pressure, bluebird motif in room) rounded out their table.

Two young women burst out of the swinging doors to the kitchen, pushing carts of food. In their wake appeared a young man, probably a student at the nearby University of Washington, his white sleeves rolled up, a pitcher in each hand. His dark eyes took her in as he glanced across the room. Realizing this must be the Ren she heard about, Lina averted her gaze. The kid had to be ten years younger than she was. Wouldn't that be a lovely way to get back at Brent when she finally answered him? *Nice to hear from you,* she could write. *I've taken a new lover too. He just turned twenty-one and does dishes in a retirement home.*

Lina turned to Alan. "So, when was the house built?"

"Nineteen oh-five. It was actually a sorority until the sixties."

"My grandma was the housemother," Marla said. "She bought the place when the chapter closed."

"The ghosts are old college kids," hollered George Lambert, "trying to party with us." He winked a milky blue eye at Lina. "Kids your age!"

Lina spread her napkin across her lap. "Hardly my age."

A shadow fell over their table. She looked up to find the young man standing beside her.

"Hello, Ren!" Mrs. B said. She turned to Lina. "Now, Ren's the best part of living here."

"Ren Schultz is our houseboy," Marla said. "This is Lina, our new nurse."

"Aren't you lucky!" George boomed to Ren. "New girl moved in for you!"

A dimple formed in Ren's cheek and he glanced at Lina, who was squashing her toes together under the table and wishing to dissolve. "Welcome," he said. "How about some coffee tonight?"

God save her; now he was asking her out in front of everyone. Lina fussed with the cloth napkin on her lap. "Um, I'm too busy. But thanks."

Marla burst into her raucous laugh. Alan and the residents grinned.

"Well..." Ren lifted one of the pitchers he held. "We've got tea too, if you prefer. No strings attached, I promise."

"Oh." Lina was blushing so hard she felt likely to get an aneurysm. "Sorry. I—yes, coffee, please." She pulled her hands out of the way to allow Ren to pour coffee into her mug.

Marla wiped her eyes. "Oh, Lina. We need to eat with you every night. You're a hoot!"

"Be nice to her." Mrs. B held up her mug. "I'd take Ren out for coffee myself if I were sixty years younger. But I'll have tea tonight, please, Ren dear."

Ren reached across, still wearing that dimple, and poured it for her. Before he withdrew he nodded at Lina in a manner she would have labeled 'formal' with a splash of 'impish.'

She considered asking if they had any arsenic handy to stir into her coffee. Instead she addressed the Drakes again. "So, 'houseboy.' That seems like an old-fashioned job title."

"In the sororities they're still called houseboys," Mrs. B said. "My granddaughter is an Alpha Phi. She talks about them all the time."

"What do they do? Dishwashing and serving?"

George guffawed. "That's not all they do! Lock up your daughters!"

Lina glanced at the next table to see if Ren heard. If he had, he was pretending he hadn't. He went on pouring water for someone without so much as a smirk.

"Oh, George!" said Marla. "Well, I don't know about the sorority houseboys, but ours does practically anything in the house, and the yard too. He's a godsend."

"U-Dub student, I imagine," Lina said, calling UW by its familiar abbreviated form.

"No, just working," Marla said. "Oh, Gertrude, here, let me get that salt for you."

While the topic of dinner conversation turned to the role of salt in one's diet, Lina glanced again at the houseboy. He stood in profile to her. A sharp, slender nose; dark hair trimmed short and tending to curl; firm lips that did not part except to speak. She easily imagined Ren featuring in some daughter's daydreams, especially those who liked the pale poet type—and those who didn't find him too young. If she had to choose a man to succeed Brent today, she would have chosen a bookish fellow in his thirties or forties, unaffiliated with medicine, maybe British, definitely fond of wool sweaters—cardigan or pullover; Lina wasn't choosy, as long as the colors weren't obnoxious.

She twirled beef stroganoff around her fork. She didn't have to choose anyone today, though, and a good thing too. Witness the mess she already made of an innocent remark about coffee.

"Who are the people over there?" asked Mrs. B.

Marla blotted her mouth with her cloth napkin. "The new resident, Jackie Clairmont, and her family. Widowed lady."

"Well, aren't we all."

Lina looked over her shoulder to see the one senior she hadn't met yet. Mrs. Clairmont had a mass of curly white hair and wore an emerald-green pantsuit. A wooden walking stick leaned against the wall beside her. A man and woman in their fifties, presumably her children or children-in-law, sat with her.

"Said she was a sorority girl here," said Alan, "back in the thirties."

"She remembers my grandma," said Marla. "How about that?"

"Oh, a fellow University woman!" said Mrs. B. "I shall have to make friends with her."

"What did you study, Mrs. B?" Lina asked.

But Mrs. B did not get to answer, for at that

moment someone shouted in a hoarse voice straight out of a horror movie, "You! What are you doing here? Where's Julia?"

Lina and all the other diners turned and stared. Jackie Clairmont rose to her feet, gaping at Ren, who had just arrived at her table. He, understandably, seemed quite taken aback. Mrs. Clairmont pointed at him and repeated, "What are you doing here? What did you do with Julia?"

Ren stepped backward, cheeks pale, clutching the carafe of tea against his ribs. He didn't take his eyes from Mrs. Clairmont except to dart occasional glances at Marla Drake.

Marla looked scandalized. Her short red hair, which always stood on end, now appeared to be doing so out of shock. She jumped out of her chair and rushed to Mrs. Clairmont, whose relatives were trying to get her to sit down. "Now, Jackie," said Marla, "you don't know this boy. This is Ren Schultz. This is our houseboy."

But apparently Mrs. Clairmont possessed more strength than the average nonagenarian, for she threw off Marla's hand, seized the walking stick, and raised it in the air. "Where's Julia? Why are you here? Where is she?"

The walking stick whipped down and struck Ren on the arm. Everyone gasped. The carafe clattered to the floor; tea splashed on the hardwood. Ren ducked and retreated into the kitchen. The door swung shut behind him. People murmured and exclaimed; Marla and the Clairmont relatives tried to calm and scold Mrs. Clairmont at the same time.

"Did she hit him?" Mrs. B squinted at the place where Ren had been standing.

"Right on the arm!" answered George Lambert with relish, as if he was watching a boxing match.

"Well, for goodness' sake, I don't care who she is, that's just unwarranted!"

Lina rose from the table, activated into motion by her nurse instincts. "Maybe I should..."

"You should go make sure Ren is all right." Mrs. B winked.

Lina struggled not to look flustered. She nodded and set off toward the kitchen.

She found Ren pacing alone in the pantry. He rubbed his forearm, which bore a dark pink mark.

Lina thought this was one of those rare moments when the phrase "He didn't know what hit him" was especially apt, and she had to clench her jaw muscles to keep down a smile. "Is your arm all right? Can I get you some ice or anything?"

He kept pacing. "It's okay. I'm a quick healer. It probably won't even bruise."

He didn't seem okay. Lina stood in the doorway, watching him take three steps toward her and three steps away, over and over. "Kind of scary when people lash out like that," she said. "I once had a woman get so upset with me for trying to take her temperature, she stomped on my foot."

"Hm." It was a quick sound, exhaled through his nose. "So that's the other new woman. What's her name?"

"Jackie Clairmont, I think. I haven't met her yet."

"Jackie Clairmont...her married name, I suppose?"

"Probably. They said she was a widow. Do you think you know her?"

His eyebrows lifted. "Doesn't seem likely."

"I wouldn't worry about it. Old folks sometimes, you know how they are. Supposedly she lived in this house when she was in college. She's probably just getting her memories confused."

"Did she?" Ren still paced. "Interesting."

Marla Drake rushed in. "Oh, Ren, there you are! I'm sorry; so, so sorry! Lina, dear, could you go help

Alan with Mrs. Clairmont?"

"Of course." Lina turned back to the dining room.

Behind her, she heard Ren ask something in quiet tones, and heard Marla answer, "Yes, but I didn't think it would be any trouble."

She heard no more of their exchange once she pushed through the swinging door. She went to the table where Alan and the family members were soothing Mrs. Clairmont.

"I know," Jackie Clairmont said, in her loud, creaky voice. "I know and I'm sorry. It just rattled me to see him. A houseboy, there."

Lina poured her a glass of water, not sure what else she was supposed to do. After a few more minutes of Mrs. Clairmont insisting she was all right and that it wouldn't happen again, everyone returned to their seats, and dinner resumed.

"Is Ren all right?" Mrs. B asked her.

Lina nodded. "Just startled, I think."

"Goodness, I am too." Mrs. B set down her fork. "I tell you, Lina, I'm going to get to the bottom of this."

She sounded like someone in a formulaic mystery novel. Lina had to smile. "Bottom of what, Mrs. B?"

"Who's 'Julia,' for one thing? And why does it warrant smacking our poor Ren with a cane?"

"Good questions." Lina glanced at Mrs. Clairmont. Alan Drake was escorting her and her two family members out of the room, all of them balancing their dinner plates. Jackie Clairmont wanted to eat the rest of the meal in her room tonight. Small wonder.

Ren did not come out for the rest of the meal either, not even to clear the dishes. Lina didn't see him until she went down to the kitchen later to get a mug of herbal tea for her neighbor, Mrs. B. Ren stood at the sink, washing the larger dishes, the ones that wouldn't fit in the dishwasher. He did not turn around or say anything.

She wanted to apologize for being an idiot when they had been introduced. She wanted to sympathize with him for the way Jackie Clairmont had humiliated him. Somehow her mind associated her own slapstick disaster with Mrs. Clairmont's attack. And on her first night in a new house she wanted someone to talk to, someone who was neither her patient nor her employer, someone to replace the other nurses or interns who had always been around in the staff lounge and who could be counted on for a friendly word.

But, faced with his silent back, and feeling drained from such a weird first day of work, she said nothing and went upstairs again.

She brought the tea to Mrs. B's room. "What with me and Mrs. Clairmont, I imagine poor Ren is thinking about a change of job right now."

Mrs. B smiled at her over the mug, her brown eyes crinkling. "I doubt he'd leave, with a pretty new girl like you in the house."

"Pretty! Well—no, I'm sure he doesn't think..." Lina stopped spluttering, aware it was only making things worse. "He seems nice, but he's too young for me."

"He couldn't be that young. He was here when I got here, and that was five years ago."

"Maybe he started as a teenager."

"I suppose. Anyway, you probably have a man already."

Lina's smile wilted. She turned to brush dust off the edge of a shelf. "I'm...between relationships."

"Oh, I'm sorry. What happened to the last one?"

"Moved to Atlanta for a fancy hospital job. I didn't want to go."

"Careers these days." Mrs. B shook her head.

"It's for the best. I love Seattle too much to leave it, too."

Lina straightened a row of large-print *Reader's Digest*s. "I told him how I felt. Lots of times."

"Then it wasn't meant to be. You'll find someone else." Mrs. B sounded perfectly certain, the way old ladies could.

"Maybe someday." Lina moved to the door. "Goodnight, Mrs. B. You can leave the mug beside your bed. I'll take it down for you in the morning. Ring if you need anything."

Back in her own room, Lina unzipped her jeans and wriggled out of them in preparation for bed. She grimaced at the stubble on her legs—gone too long without shaving again. She fell behind on her beauty treatments when she didn't have a boyfriend, although maybe now with this Ren in the house...

She rolled her eyes at herself and tossed her jeans into the laundry hamper. *Pretty*, Mrs. B had said, but you had to remember this was from a woman with failing eyesight. At five-feet-nine Lina was taller than she wanted to be, and felt awkward for it. Her hair lay flat and straight no matter what heating and curling implements she tortured it with. Her mouth, nose, and chin, all taken together, had a duck-like look in her opinion, though one past boyfriend had been sweet enough to call her mouth sensual. She thought her light amber-brown eyes were her best feature, and therefore accentuated them with mascara. But beautiful? Hardly.

Still...she stepped over to the mirror above the vanity, holding her nightgown against herself for warmth and cover. Under these gentle incandescent lights instead of the hospital fluorescents, her skin already glowed a healthier hue. She'd get more sleep in this job than she used to; that would help as well. And maybe with some lip gloss, yes, perhaps then pretty wouldn't be out of the question.

The lamp snapped off. The room went dark, except for the filtered city light through her blinds. She thought the power had gone out, then noticed the red glowing numbers of her alarm clock; it was still functioning. A faint glow seeped under her door from the lights in the corridor too. Nothing else had gone off, only her lamp. And it had sounded like the click of the switch, not the tiny contained explosion of a bulb burning out.

Her heart pounded. She saw well enough in these bluish night-hues to know nobody was standing in the room with her. Everything was where she left it, nothing moved.

She advanced to the lamp and turned the switch. The light came back, regular as you please. She tried this a few times, turning the lamp on and off, and left it alone a few seconds each time to see if it changed state by itself. Finally she decided she was being ridiculous. Once in a while switches did that. You pushed them farther than you realized, or not far enough, and they gradually slipped back into the "off" mode. It happened. It didn't have anything to do with ghosts.

She tugged her flannel nightgown on at last, and sat down at her computer.

I made it through my first day, she typed in an email to her mom, dad, and brother. She paused to add the addresses of a few people back at Everglade who had left "Hang in there" messages on her machine after she had quit.

Definitely a change, she wrote, *but I think I can manage. Still, it's quiet here and they say the place is haunted—yeah, sure—so for those in the Seattle area, let me know if anything fun is going on this weekend, and I'll try to come.*

She included Brent's email address. Just one of the group. It was the first thing she sent him since his engagement announcement.

But as she shut down her computer, she knew she was unlikely to drive across town to do anything 'fun' if invited, and doubted anyone would invite her. She was forgettable. Brent had demonstrated that.

"Just me and the old folks and the college ghosts," she said aloud, then wished she hadn't, despite not believing in ghosts.

But to be on the safe side, she left the lamp on when she climbed into bed.

Chapter Two

Lina had read it took at least two months to feel at home in a new job—besides, where else would she go?—so she stuck it out at Drake House even though it often felt like a foreign culture. They called things by pet names or ones she wasn't accustomed to. The room adjoining the dining room was a 'parlor,' a term she never encountered except in Victorian novels. The 'living room,' in contrast, was the large room at the front with the grand piano. 'Firesides' were the casual gatherings at the fireplace in the living room on cold evenings.

"Having a fireside tonight!" Marla or Alan would tell her. "Come on down!"

The iron fire escape on the house's back exterior wall was 'the smoking lounge,' since no smoking was allowed in the building and therefore smokers had to step outside. As far as Lina could tell, though, none of the residents or employees did smoke, so the term must have been a holdover from the sorority days, like Ren Schultz's job title of houseboy.

Lina didn't talk to Ren much during the first two weeks. She figured he was avoiding Jackie Clairmont and her vicious walking stick, and he was always busy cleaning or fixing something when Lina did stumble upon him. Though he kept to himself, he did seem to be around a great deal, and Lina wondered if he ever went home. When she remarked on this to Mrs. B one day, she learned he already *was* home.

"Comes with his job," Mrs. B said. "Tiny room in the basement. I've seen it when I'm down there for laundry. I don't know how he can stand it. That basement's eerie if you ask me."

Lina eased Mrs. B's bare foot out of the basin of warm water and toweled it dry. "Considering Seattle rent prices these days, he probably thinks it's a bargain. By the way, have you made friends with Mrs. Clairmont? She doesn't say much when I visit her."

"Dolly and Gertrude and I have gotten her to play gin rummy with us. Haven't asked her yet why she whacked poor Ren, though. Those ugly warts looking any better?"

"I think so. Just going to apply a little more of this stuff." Lina dabbed wart-remover ointment onto Mrs. B's heel with a gloved pinky. "She probably has some interesting sorority stories about this place."

"I expect so. All we've talked about in regards to U-Dub was what we studied and what we wore. And how hard it was to get a decent drink during the Depression!" Mrs. B laughed.

Lina smiled and taped a small bandage over the warts. "I wonder if the U Library has any history on the house. Might give us theories on our ghosts."

"You should go look! And I'll see if I can't sweet-talk some clues out of Jackie."

Sounded like a good hobby, and Lord knew Lina needed one. She still got nervous thrills in her stomach when she checked her email, thinking Brent might write to her, though she had no good reason to be nervous. What could he say?

A spell of self-analysis during an afternoon walk in the cool October sunshine showed her the pathetic truth. She hoped he might write, *I was wrong to leave. I love you and only you. I'm dumping Joanne and coming back,* or at the very least, *I'll never love her the way I loved you, but if you and I can't be together I suppose I have to take the second-best option.*

She thwacked a mailbox post with her rolled-up umbrella on her way past. He was never going to write that. She was acting like a fatuous young girl. A mature woman would forget the jerk and embark upon a spicy new relationship. Say, with a twenty-something coworker.

Unworkable idea, but at least it made her smile.

Anyway, until she answered Brent in a personal email and actually addressed the subject of his engagement, she wouldn't know what he'd say.

At the end of her second week at Drake House, Lina typed out a message that underwent several drafts before she considered it acceptable.

Dear Brent:

I've been so busy with my new job, I haven't had the chance yet to congratulate you. I didn't want you to think I was sulking. Of course it was a surprise, but I wish you and Joanne all the best. I hope to meet her someday. Please stay in touch.

Take care,

Lina

His answer, the next day, was:

Thanks L. Glad you're doing good. Never thought I'd get engaged so fast but this thing with Joanne knocked me off my feet! You'd like her; she's really great. Thanks for writing. Makes me feel better about the bitter goodbyes. You take care too.

- B.

She re-read his email four times, feeling offended and breathless, like he had casually grabbed her head and stuffed it into a pile of wet leaves. She turned off her computer and staggered down to the kitchen. Ren and the cook were preparing the house's lunch, but she ignored them and steadied her hands by making a cup of coffee.

Knocked him off his feet. How very nice for him. Nothing at all like his tame, ho-hum relationship with Lina, she supposed he meant to say. She edged past the cook and put two slices of bread in the toaster, tapping her fingers on the counter as she waited. *Bitter goodbyes*—right, did he mean the part where he accused her of having no spine, no sense of adventure? Or the part where she accused him of having no regard for what she valued? Or the way he answered she must not really love him; and her retort that maybe he was right?

Her toast popped up. She slapped it onto a plate, attacked it with peanut butter, and thumped the plate onto the breakfast bar beside her black coffee. The *Seattle Times* lay in a heap on the bar; she pulled it over and flipped through it. She could go to her room and cry, but that would be continuing to act like a fatuous young girl. She could write him a nasty email and never send it, but that would be feeding the fire.

Most infuriating of all, she realized she didn't even want him back, and was upset over him anyway. What she wanted was that whole year and a half of her life back, since it had come to nothing. She had failed at a relationship, as usual, and hated the fact. She knew she had to get on with life, jump back into the saddle and so forth, but how did people do that?

The crossword puzzle in the newspaper was about one-quarter filled in by someone with a tentative pencil. Lina found the pencil in a cup on top of the microwave and sat down to finish their work. She didn't have to be on call until after lunch; might as well burn off some steam by throwing herself against the mighty wall of the *New York Times* crossword.

It didn't help. After twenty minutes she still got

no satisfaction from filling in the easy clues, and the hard ones just made her want to stab the puzzle creator with a number two pencil.

For instance, what was she supposed to do with *Munchies, his 'n hers*, six letters, beginning with C-R and ending with E? Her mind stalled on 'crepes,' but that didn't end with E, and while crepes might have been considered munchies, there was nothing particularly his-'n-hers about them. Adding words and crossword puzzles to the list of things hell-bent on vanquishing her, Lina reached for her toast without looking.

Someone took a sharp breath. A hand caught her wrist; she lifted her head. Inches from her fingers, a hairy brown spider skulked on her plate, two probing feet right there in her peanut butter. She yelped. Counting leg-span, the thing must have been three full inches across.

Ren, after stopping her from putting her hand straight on it, let her go and clapped a dishtowel around the spider. Spindly legs emerged from the cloth, and the creature skittered toward her edge of the counter.

"Look out!" Ren said.

"It got out," Lina said at the same moment. She leaped off her stool.

When the spider crawled over the edge, lost its footing on the smooth Formica surface, and fell to the floor, Lina was ready. She smacked one sneaker-clad foot down on top of it, and felt a crunch through the rubber.

She retracted her foot to view the crushed brown shape on the floor. "Got it." She took a napkin from the dispenser on the counter, and bent to collect the dead spider. After dropping it in the trash, she allowed a moment for a deep breath. The adrenaline was the first thing to dispel her gloom today.

"Thank you," she said to Ren.

"No problem. I'd hate to see anyone get bitten. Hobo spiders are venomous."

"I know." Lina shuddered. "I saw a case once at the hospital."

"Nurse. That's right. You would already know."

"Maybe Alan and Marla should call an exterminator."

Ren shook his head. He sorted out the newspaper, peeking under each section. "We have some traps in the basement. I'll replace them. Best way, really, is to encourage other spiders to live here. They prey on the hobos."

"You study entomology or something?" Lina picked up her cup of coffee, glancing around for anything small and moving.

"No. Hobo spiders show up in the news now and then." Ren smiled. "Anyway, entomology is about insects. Does it cover arachnids too?"

"I'm not sure. Good question."

Ren picked up her plate. "I assume you don't want this anymore."

"You're right. I don't."

"Can I get you another one?"

"No, I think I'm off toast for a while. Maybe forever."

"All right." Ren glanced at the one section of the paper he had left undisturbed. "Going to finish the crossword?"

"No. It's giving me a headache. I can't work out the last few clues."

Ren turned the paper around toward himself. Three seconds later, he picked up her pencil and filled in *C-R-O-Q-U-E* for the *Munchies, his 'n hers* word.

Lina leaned over the counter to read it. "Croque? Oh. Croque monsieur..."

"Croque madame," Ren finished, saying it with her. "Types of sandwiches. Croque, meaning munch."

As he spoke, she caught the unmistakable scent of grape gum. Ordinarily the snaps and chomps of gum-chewing irritated her, but he was so subtle with it she hadn't even noticed until now. She found the smell comforting. It took her back to her childhood when she and her brother would buy gum and candy at the AM/PM and climb up to the cul-de-sac to watch cars zooming by on I-5 below.

"Wow," she said. "You know about French *and* arachnids."

Ren bowed his head, as if he thought he had been too boastful. "Well. Leave it to the kitchen help to come up with the food ones."

"Would have taken me all day." Lina stepped back. "Thank you again. See you at lunch."

"See you." Ren didn't glance up; he was immersed in another clue.

He had dark brown eyes, and dark brown eyelashes to match. From that angle, when he was bent forward over the breakfast bar, they appeared to be sweeping his cheekbones. Which was a stupid thing to think, because everyone's eyelashes were situated close to their cheekbones. Lina marched away.

She had enough time before lunch to start some laundry, so she carried a basket of clothes down to the basement, using the back stairs, which happened to pass the kitchen. Before she reached the ground-level landing, she made sure her underwear and dirty socks were tucked out of sight beneath a towel. On the landing she met Ren coming up from the basement, his apron dusty with flour, arms laden with institutional-sized cans of peaches.

"Finished your crossword," he said.

"Already? What was the river in Estonia?"

"Narva. N-A-R-V-A."

"Don't tell me you just *knew* that."

He shifted the cans. "I think I'd seen it in

another crossword before."

"Too modest." She started down the stairs to the basement. "You're good. I'm coming to you next time I'm stuck."

His voice floated after her. "I'll do my best."

His footsteps moved into the pantry over her head as she reached the basement. Her limbs felt lightweight. She switched on the water in a washing machine and scattered powdered soap into it.

What was that, then? Flirting, that's what. She hadn't tried that for over a year, since getting together with Brent. As she remembered him, the gloom resettled itself around her. Irrational, really. She would have to get over Brent, yes, and flirting with Ren might be good practice, but it could hardly be anything else. She knew nothing of Ren except his name, his aptitude with vocabulary, the fact that he wasn't in college, and the way his hair narrowed to a curling point at the nape of his neck.

And she hadn't even realized she knew that last thing until now.

The laundry room door slammed shut, startling her. She was alone in the room and hadn't seen anyone in the basement. Drafts and strangely-weighted doors were common enough in old houses, but she still felt uneasy. The basement had no pet name, and Lina saw why. Low ceilings, inadequate light from bare bulbs, half a dozen small rooms with solid doors, and jumbled storage boxes stretching into far dark corners would only have inspired nicknames like 'the crypt' or 'the mortuary.' Time to go back upstairs.

She turned and almost tripped over her laundry basket, which was lying upside-down behind her. She may have put it there—unlikely a place though it was—but she was pretty sure she did not turn it upside-down.

A chill shimmied up her spine as she

29

remembered the lamp turning itself off her first night.

You were supposed to talk to ghosts, she had heard. Let them know you were friendly. She had been known to murmur hello to dead patients' bodies in the hospital when alone with them, telling herself it was a courtesy to the deceased person, but also because secretly she hoped it might keep them from turning into vampires and attacking her. She had worked long, late hours and her mind, with Stephen King's help, devised some bizarre horrors. But nothing in the hospital had ever moved by itself, corpses or otherwise.

"I don't have anything against you," she said aloud to the laundry room. "Please don't try to scare me."

Nothing answered, of course.

Lina flung her clothes into the machine, picked up her basket, and escaped from the laundry room. She considered stopping on the way up to ask Ren if he had ever noticed anything uncanny around here, but vetoed the idea. She may have selected him as her latest flirtation practice, but running up and saying, "Something just shut the door and turned my laundry basket upside-down!" won the prize for pathetic conversation openers. Even the names of Estonian rivers beat that.

All the same, she was determined you couldn't pay her to stay in that basement overnight. No, sir.

****

She wanted to forget her wrecked love life and her potassium chloride nightmare, start up new flirtations, and focus on her new job and surroundings. Really, she tried to. But her brain stayed stuck in its pessimistic groove.

That afternoon, as she visited her elderly housemates and checked blood pressures and answered medication questions, she found herself thinking that this was it. This was where she would live out her days. She'd be a nurse here for the next fifty years, then break her hip and get transferred into a room and become a resident, and die in her sleep not long afterward. It was hard to see how she would ever meet a decent man and fall in love. Her choices here were practically nonexistent, unless some resident's great-nephew was visiting. The only eligible bachelor in the house—aside from George Lambert—was Ren, and she could do better than a boy in his early twenties who tidied up an old folks' home for a living. Even if he did happen to be a crossword genius, magnificently well-mannered, and delectable as a dish of coffee ice cream.

That night, brushing her teeth in the bathroom down the hall from her room, she stared into the mirror and observed her eyelids succumbing to gravity; and was that another gray hair over her ear? She plucked it out, flicked it into the trash can, and let the toothbrush go slack as she gazed at her reflection. Fine. She knew the truth. She didn't think of herself as too good for Ren. Rather, she feared he wouldn't be interested. Not that she was interested in *him*, but it would have been comforting to think herself desirable. He certainly didn't go out of his way to talk to her. She passed him on the way up tonight while he mopped the kitchen floor; she remembered glancing in approval at his strong shoulders and lean waist. She frowned. *I can't even get the houseboy. I've become old and boring.*

She spat out the toothpaste. Enough of this. Brent may have gotten knocked off his feet and engaged before his last box was unpacked in Atlanta, but that didn't mean she had to follow suit. Her only task right now was to make the best of her situation and build a new track record to be proud of.

However, forgetting her love life was difficult

when the elderly ladies, who made up eleven of the twelve residents, considered it their favorite discussion topic. For instance, at lunch the next day, Betty Carter produced a photo of her youngest son, who was forty-two and divorced and wore a handlebar mustache. "Coming to see me next month!" she said. "He's a hit with the single ladies. You ought to drop by."

"I'll see if I have time," Lina said.

"Marla's nephew Gary is closer to her age," said Ethel Barker, who, in Lina's medical opinion, needed to lose sixty pounds or she'd succumb to diabetes within the year. "He's a sweetie."

"But he lives way out of town, doesn't he?" said Dolly Tidd. "I think she should hook up with Ren here."

Lina shot a look around, but Ren was at a distant table arranging food on a tray.

"That would be my vote too," said Mrs. B.

"I'm not sure I'm in the market right now," Lina said.

The way Ren's hands moved displayed a grace that reminded her of a heart surgeon she'd had a crush on a few years ago. The surgeon had been twice Lina's age and married, of course, but there was no harm in admiring people.

Ren turned, caught her eye, and smiled. Lina twitched and dropped a forkful of cornbread into her lap. Ren walked over with a plate of orange and black frosted cookies. "Would you ladies be interested in tasting these for me before I do the big batch?"

Mrs. B leaned to squint at the plate. "Ren, that's lovely of you!"

Lina folded her napkin around the fallen cornbread, took a crescent-moon-shaped cookie, and peeked up at Ren. "Thanks."

"I want a cat." Dolly took a cookie that, to Lina's

eyes, was actually shaped like an owl.

"Hand me one," said Ethel. "I don't care about shape, just make it a big one."

Lina bit into the moon while Ren handed cookies around. Orange-flavored frosting melted with buttery shortbread in her mouth, and she nearly melted as well. Her sweet tooth would send her the way of Ethel Barker one of these decades. "Very good," she mumbled to Ren as she chewed, one hand covering her mouth.

"Delicious," said Mrs. B, and smiled at Ren. "You're such a sweet boy. You must have a girlfriend. Are you seeing anyone?"

The other old ladies tittered. Lina felt blood rush to her cheeks. She carefully took another bite.

Ren smiled. "No, Mrs. B, I'm not."

"Oh, what a shame! Well, I promise you I won't set you up with my granddaughter, though I'm tempted to."

"Thank you for the thought, anyway." He picked up the plate. "I'll get to work on these cookies." He returned to the kitchen.

The old ladies broke into laughter. Lina glanced at Mrs. B and shook her head.

"Well, now you know!" Dolly said.

"I didn't need to know."

"He never used to offer us special cookies before you arrived," said Mrs. B. "You just think about that."

The trouble was, she did think about it. Ren didn't have a girlfriend—what was the story there? Could he be a comrade in bad breakups? Might they commiserate with each other some late night in the kitchen? His reticence made him interesting. She suspected he was bright, and obviously he was kind, so what else was under the quiet surface? He was still undoubtedly too young, but Lina considered it good that she was even thinking about another man.

It showed she was moving on with life.

On the other hand, she didn't want to be like her mother, who went rather overboard when it came to moving on to the next guy and being devil-may-care about his age. Lina's parents had been divorced for fourteen years, and her mom had gone through at least ten boyfriends, and possibly as many hair colors, in that time. Most of the men were either too young or too old for her—not that Lina actually said so to her mother.

But Ren wasn't like those men. He clearly had *some* class. It wouldn't hurt to get to know him, would it? She needed a friend. Her former colleagues at Everglade Hospital had already trailed off in their communications with her, as she had predicted. Though she missed feeling part of a group, she didn't miss the people themselves. They seemed part of another life already, as if Drake House had swallowed her up into its strange self-contained world.

And it was indeed a strange world, as she learned a few days after tasting Ren's "special cookies."

While on her rounds, Lina ate an English muffin as an afternoon snack. As she passed Mrs. B's open door, the old lady called out to her.

"Come in for a moment!" Mrs. B leaned forward from one of her lavender armchairs. "Do I have a Halloween story for you!"

"About what?" Lina sat down in the opposite armchair, careful not to scatter crumbs on it.

"I had a long talk with Jackie this morning. That woman has some interesting stories, all right."

"Oh, you got something out of her?" Lina took another bite of her muffin.

"I certainly did. It seems in the 1930s, when Jackie was a sorority girl here, there was something of a murder-suicide in this house."

Lina was startled enough to stop chewing. "A murder?"

"Manslaughter-suicide, actually. The first death was accidental."

At the word *manslaughter*, Lina's stomach went into a tail spin. She forced down her bite of muffin, and nodded for Mrs. B to continue.

"You see," said Mrs. B, "Jackie's best friend Julia was seeing one of the houseboys. His name was Sean. The girls had a formal dance coming up, with a fairy-tale theme. It was on campus somewhere. Julia wanted Sean to go with her, but he wasn't comfortable with the idea because in those days the girls weren't supposed to date the houseboys. He was afraid he'd lose his job. But Julia just couldn't live without him taking her to this dance, so she and Jackie cooked up a scheme.

"She got Sean to agree to a private evening at the house while the other girls were at the dance. But what she *really* planned was to slip him some sleeping pills in brandy, and then while he was asleep she was going to call a taxi, have the driver help haul him into the car, and take him to the dance. Then she was going to revive him there—like Sleeping Beauty, you know; only *he* would be Sleeping Beauty and she would be Princess Charming."

"Oh, no," Lina breathed. She winced at the mention of mixing sleeping pills with alcohol. The manslaughter was even medication-related. She felt sick.

"That's right. I guess whatever she and Jackie studied at U-Dub, it wasn't medicine."

"So he died."

"Here at the house. They never did make it to the dance."

"Oh. Oh, gosh." Lina's gaze traveled up to the ceiling as she wondered which of these rooms had been Julia's—and whether she ought to put her head between her knees until the dizziness passed.

"After the funeral," Mrs. B said, "Sean's family brought charges against Julia. She didn't say a word. That night, when everyone was asleep, she went into the garage and started the housemother's car with the garage doors closed, and killed herself with the exhaust."

"So she knew about carbon monoxide." Lina's medical background provided an automatic answer, which was good, since otherwise it would have been hard to answer coherently during her panic attack.

"Isn't it funny, the little gaps in people's knowledge?"

A new thought darted across Lina's mind, and she clutched at it for support, as a diversion. "Then Jackie saw Ren, and thought he was the houseboy?"

"I guess so. She said he looks just like him, but really now, it's been seventy years. I imagine being back in this house made her think so. In any case, it gave her a shock."

A deep breath in and out helped steady Lina's heart rate. She rotated the last bite of English muffin in her fingers. "Why would she want to live here again, after going through something so awful? I wouldn't want to move back into the house where my best friend died." Nor would Lina want to go back to Everglade now, and she hadn't even been friends with Mr. Ambaum.

"She said she had fond memories *after* that—she and the other girls bonded and had some good times. Anyway, it's a lovely house."

"True." Lina tucked the muffin piece into the pocket of her lab coat, and thought about the dark, small garage where Marla and Alan's car now sat. She had been there just the other day, setting out on drugstore errands with Marla. Now she doubted she would ever enter the garage again without remembering what had taken place there. No wonder the basement gave her the creeps. No wonder people said there was a—

She gasped and looked at Mrs. B. "So that's the ghost?"

"Who? The houseboy, or the girl?"

"Either. Maybe both. Do you think it—oh, what am I saying?" Lina wiped her hands on her lab coat. "I don't know if I believe in that stuff. It's just things sometimes...never mind."

"Move around by themselves?"

"Well, yes. Like you said the first day."

"Yes, I said so, but it sounds to me like *you've* seen something."

Lina tried not to picture the ghost of a slain youth turning off the lamp in her bedroom, or slamming the laundry room door. "I can't prove it wasn't a living person. Or me being forgetful. Or faulty wiring, or a draft..."

Mrs. B chuckled. "Always a rational explanation. You're probably right."

Lina's dizziness receded, but her mind remained a muddle. She rose. "I better go. I need to see Gertrude about a prescription. But I'm glad you told me."

"I'll see you at dinner, Lina dear. If you see that ghost, just jump into Ren's arms. He'll protect you!"

Lina smiled weakly, and left the room with Mrs. B's laughter bubbling behind her. Not a half-bad idea, really. Sheltering in Ren's arms sounded lovely. Too bad it would require seeing a ghost.

****

An hour before dinner, Lina encountered Ren in the kitchen mixing dough—cookie dough, to judge from the bag of chocolate chips beside him. Mrs. B's comment returned to her mind and brought a much-needed smile to her face, finally allowing her to set aside thoughts of manslaughter and tormented spirits.

Ren glanced up and smiled back. "Lina Zuendel," he said, with perfect pronunciation. Must have heard her surname from Marla. "How's your day going?"

Lina rested her forearms on the bar. "Not bad. By the way, I think Mrs. B solved the mystery of why Jackie attacked you."

"Oh?" Ren's shiny red spatula worked the dough off the edges of the bowl.

"A houseboy was killed here in the thirties. By one of Jackie's friends."

"Accident, wasn't it?"

"Yes." Lina faltered, a bit deflated. "I guess Marla told you."

"Marla's grandma was the housemother here when it happened. I heard about it a long time ago."

"Everyone knows two kids died here, and no one said anything?"

Ren shrugged. His jaw muscles flexed; apparently he was chewing gum again. "Well, it *was* seventy years ago."

"But what about the...the ghost?" Though the question struck her as absurd, curiosity did nag at her. For one thing, the tale resonated with her own demons; and for another—well, everyone liked a good ghost story.

One side of Ren's mouth quirked, in what could have been amusement or thoughtfulness. He went on working the spatula. "People been telling you stories?"

"Kind of. A couple of the residents said the house was haunted, but I didn't really believe them. Then one night my lamp switched off by itself, and another time the laundry room door slammed shut." She pulled herself upright. "But that doesn't mean anything."

He scraped the spatula on the rim of the bowl.

"Haven't been bitten by one of those spiders, have you? Remember, they can cause hallucinations."

Lina smiled. She watched him seal the lid onto a plastic tub of baking powder. "You've worked here a few years, right?"

"Yes."

"Have you ever seen anything? I feel stupid just for asking. I don't believe in these things. Or at least I didn't before."

He plopped the dough onto a sheet of waxed paper, then set the bowl aside and wiped his hands on his apron. "If you mean, have objects moved by themselves, then—maybe. I swear sometimes I set something down, look the other way, and then turn back to find it flipped over or arranged differently. If you mean, have I seen transparent figures roaming the house, or met any headless horsemen in the alley, then no."

"Hm." Lina dragged a paper napkin around on the countertop with one finger, unsure whether his words were reassuring or disquieting. "Still, don't you think it's odd that you look like this dead houseboy? To someone who knew him?"

"Like I said, it's been seventy years. Memories get fuzzy." He began forming the dough into long rolls.

"A tragedy like that must have been in the newspapers. Maybe I'll look it up at the U-Dub library."

Ren pulled the waxed paper to the edge of the butcher's block and tore it off. He folded it over one of the dough rolls and twisted the ends. "If you think it would help," he said, but he sounded dubious.

Lina took her research idea only as far as a half-hour Internet search that evening. She didn't know enough about the incident to be able to seek specific names—for instance, Julia's or Sean's surnames—and thus had to resort to strings like *Seattle Julia manslaughter suicide Gamma Eta Omicron*. Gamma Eta Omicron had been the letters of the sorority. Lina had spotted them on a dusty set of awards in the file room in the basement. Her web search didn't turn up anything relevant, which was understandable considering how long ago the deaths had taken place.

She then tried the UW library homepage, since Julia and Sean had been university students, and if anyone had carried the story it would have been the school newspaper. But she needed a university log-in and password to access most of the materials, and as she was no longer a student she had no such thing.

She gave up for the night, and blinked at the dark window past her screen to ease her eyestrain. She figured when she had a free afternoon she would walk over to the library and do the research in person. As Ren pointed out, there was no rush. It was difficult to make an urgent case out of the fact that seventy years ago two people had died.

"But now I've got some idea what you're all about," she said to her empty room, "and believe me, I understand." She stretched her arms over her head. "And thanks for giving me an excuse to talk to my own cute houseboy."

She smiled and got up to prepare for her night shift. Tonight was one of the three nights a week when she was on call. In a house with only twelve patients, all of whom were in fair or good health for their age, the graveyard shift was usually quiet, and she could sleep between calls. A pager, handed off to whoever was on duty, would wake her up. Lina had never received more than two calls per night so far, and they were never medical emergencies, just discomforts like leg cramps, insomnia, or gas. Marla covered two of the remaining nights each week; and Consuela, a nursing school student currently working in the kitchen, covered the other two, dozing on the sofa-bed in the Drakes' quarters while waiting for calls.

Lina changed into a long-sleeved T-shirt and a soft pair of yoga pants with a drawstring waist, and set her lab coat and slip-on leather shoes beside her bed. She put the pager in her shoe, and fell asleep within ten minutes.

The beep woke her. She squinted at the clock—half past midnight—knuckled her eyes to clear her vision, and picked up the pager. The electronic display read *Ethel B.* Slipping her feet into her shoes, she reviewed in her mind where Ethel's room was: the second floor, toward the end of the L-shaped house. The back staircase would be the best route.

Lina put on her lab coat and shuffled out into the hall. Only half the corridor lights were on, leaving shadowed patches in between. The back staircase, which only had lights on every other landing, was especially dim. *Cold too*, she thought, folding her arms and shivering as she padded down the carpeted steps. She paused at the window between the third and second floor, but spied only a black, drizzly night and the bare arm of a tree raking at the glass. The window must have been badly insulated, because the cold was pouring into the stairwell at refrigeration strength. In fact—she puffed out a breath to test—she could actually see her breath.

She turned to the stairs again. She didn't know why she felt afraid—only a tree tapping the glass, only an autumn storm making it cold—but as she stepped forward to descend to the second floor, her heart started pounding hard. She took hold of the handrail but couldn't make herself take the next step. She hadn't even been reading Stephen King lately. Why was she scared?

As she stood gripping the rail, the end of an

orange crepe-paper streamer, stuck to the wall as Halloween decoration, untaped itself from the paneling and lifted into the air. It swung and rippled as if someone was standing there playing with it, just as Mrs. B had said about her door. Lina watched, paralyzed. The streamer swung once more and then dropped. Light footsteps thudded on the stairs in front of her, where no one was standing; she felt the floor vibrate.

"Why didn't you get to your patient in time?" she imagined some lawyer asking. "Why did you let poor Ethel Barker die?"

"I'm sorry; I couldn't get down there," she would say. "I thought there was a ghost on the stairs."

She had to go forward. But she could not.

The footsteps approached, faster now, and closer, until with a rush of air they passed her, rustling the streamers. Cold breath blew down the nape of her neck. Lina shrieked and jumped back against the window. She held the pager raised in one fist, ready to strike anyone who appeared.

All went still. *The other residents are playing tricks on me.* Her gaze raced around the stairwell. They cooked up the story about the houseboy and the sorority girl, and then paged her at midnight to catch her here, and then somehow made a streamer dance by itself in the air, and made the stairs shake...

New footsteps padded up from below.

She was not going to stand around and wait for that to happen again, no way. She bolted forward, thundering down the last flight to the second floor landing, and ran smack into someone.

She screamed. The person said something, startled. They untangled their arms and stepped apart.

"You okay?" Ren asked. He still wore his houseboy uniform: white button-up shirt, black trousers, and shiny black shoes. His breath smelled of wintergreen gum.

"Oh. Hello," she said. "Was that you? No, I guess...I don't see how you would have..."

"What happened?"

"Hah. I understand; this is what you do to new people, right? Good job. Had me scared. How did you do the cold air? Got a window open up there?"

He frowned up the stairs. "None of these windows open."

"But it's cold, it's really cold. Isn't it cold?" Her shivers had turned into full-on shakes.

"It's cold." He put his hand on her arm and brought her into the second-floor corridor. "Did something happen?"

"Only, um, footsteps—other than mine—and decorations coming unhinged, and I, I'm supposed to be seeing..."

"Where were you going?"

"Answering a call. Ethel."

"I'll come with you."

"Thank you," she said, grateful he offered without her needing to ask.

Ethel, in a voluminous purple nightgown, blinked at her from her lilac-scented pillow. "I'm so sorry to bother you, honey. My electric blanket isn't working, and it's positively freezing tonight."

"You're right about that." Lina folded up the faulty blanket and found a new one in the closet.

"Was that you thumping down the stairs and shouting?"

"Yes. Just me. I...tripped."

When she had gotten Ethel reheated and tucked in, she said goodnight and closed her door.

Ren leaned on the wall in the corridor. "All okay?"

Lina nodded. "Thanks for coming with me. I'm a little spooked. I don't know what happened." She turned toward the main staircase, avoiding the back stairs for now.

He walked with her, gazing at the light fixtures.

After a few seconds, she added, "I notice you're not saying, 'It was just your imagination.'"

"People don't like to be told that. I could say it anyway. Want me to?"

"I guess not. Hallucinating isn't much better."

"Still, after hearing the old stories today..."

"It could have been my imagination," she finished. "I hope. Kind of."

They climbed to the third floor. "These night shifts are never popular," he said. "Even with Marla. But don't tell her I said that."

"It was the same at the hospital. It got spooky. Only there was always someone around. Someone visible, I mean." She glanced at him. "How come you were up, anyway?"

"I don't sleep much. Just one of those people."

They reached her door. "So next time I have a night shift, if I scream again, you might come running?"

"I will if I hear you."

She opened her door and flicked on her overhead light, bright though it was in the middle of the night. "Well, I doubt I'll sleep any more now."

"You should try. I think it's over."

She looked at him. "What's over?"

He hovered outside the door frame, gazing down, lips pressed together as if he regretted opening them. "Just...these things, they tend not to last. It should be quiet now."

"So you don't even believe it *was* my imagination."

"I'd put it out of your mind. Try to relax and sleep."

"Are you in on this? Really? I won't be mad, just tell me. Is this a trick for the new nurse?"

He sighed and folded his hands behind his back. "No. We like you and want you to stay. It's an unusual house, that's all." He sounded as if he was choosing his words carefully.

"Cold air breathing down your neck, things moving by themselves, that's 'unusual,' for sure."

He smiled at his feet. "Well, call if you need anything. Don't worry about waking me up. My room has an extension; it's on the list on your wall."

"Fine, but—"

"The rest of the night should be quiet. I really think so. Try to sleep." He bowed his head to her like an Edwardian English butler, and walked away.

Chapter Three

On Halloween night, Lina guided a giggling Augusta Beltrayne down to the first floor. Mrs. B, or "Minnie Mouse" as she preferred to be called this evening, had donned a red nose, Disneyland mouse ears with a pink bow, and a polka-dot blouse. Lina wore a brown leaf-patterned bedsheet around her body and a wreath of yellow maple leaves on her head, and picked her way barefoot across the stone floor of the foyer. She planned to say she was a wood nymph if anyone asked.

The large living room dripped with decoration. Fake cobwebs shrouded the corners of the room and the legs of the grand piano, crepe-paper ghosts hung from the ceiling, plastic spiders marched in a winding line along the walls, and an orange and green sign spelled out *Happy Halloween!* above the fireplace. The weather was clear but frosty, and Alan Drake had built a fire against the chill. It cast a glow onto the white carpet; and the lamps in the room were veiled with thin orange scarves, making the room dim enough that Lina could see the stars through the windows. Goofy Halloween oldies played on a boom-box; Marla and Alan, dressed as a nun and a priest, danced a swing for the entertainment of the elderly partygoers.

Lina saw Mrs. B to an armchair and served her a cup of spiced cider. She then joined Marla and Alan in leading the residents in a series of simple party games, like rolling apples across the carpet toward a row of targets, or dressing up un-carved pumpkins with paint and makeup. Whenever children came trick-or-treating to the front door, Lina coaxed them to step into the foyer far enough so the old folks could see them without getting up. There was much cooing, laughter, and "Don't you look darling!" from the seniors, and even the most cynical kids seemed flattered. Lina rewarded them with handfuls of cube-shaped caramels, thanked the parents waiting on the sidewalk, and returned to describe the costumes to the short-sighted Mrs. B, who demanded to hear every detail.

While Lina sat on the carpet, painting eyelashes onto a pumpkin, a dark swirl of motion caught her eye. A cry of delight arose from the seniors. Lina lifted her head to see the Phantom of the Opera set a tray of cookies on the coffee table. He snapped upright with a flourish of cape, smiling under his curved white mask. Lina caught her breath with a surge of unexpected happiness. She applauded along with the other residents.

The phantom pointed to her and crossed the room to flop down on the carpet beside her.

"Ren," she said, "tell me they didn't make you work on Halloween."

"I wanted to. I wouldn't have missed this for the world."

"You're young and hip. You must have better places to be."

"There's nowhere I'm appreciated more than here."

She adjusted the paper towels under the pumpkin, avoiding an answer like, "*I* certainly appreciate you," which leaped all too lightly to her tongue. Instead she answered, "You bring cookies. Naturally you're welcomed."

He tilted his head to take in her outfit. "Let me guess. Yard waste?"

"I'm a wood nymph, thank you very much."

"Just teasing. It's very autumnal. I like it."

Lina cast him another glance. He looked older, more of a man than a houseboy, with his dark eyes shining from the holes of the mask. Or perhaps it was the way he had slicked back his hair. Over the scents of bruised apples and wood smoke and old-lady perfume, Lina smelled styling gel wafting off him. It mingled with his cinnamon gum and with something richer and muskier. Had he put on cologne?

Her stomach seized up in fear as she imagined sidling up to him, inhaling the scent at the curve where his neck became his shoulder, resting her head on the folds of the old-fashioned tuxedo he wore under the cape. *Why fear?* She jerked lint off the pumpkin's stem. *Why am I afraid of everything?*

All she needed to do was say something about his costume. This could be an ordinary conversation if she would just let it.

"Phantom," she said. "Very nice."

"I live in the basement. I thought it would be appropriate."

"Because we have other phantoms down there too?"

"I was thinking because the phantom lived in the basement of the opera house."

"I see. But you don't have an underground lake, do you?"

"Only when we get record rainfall."

Her own laughter caught her by surprise. Ren grinned, and jumped to his feet again. "Alan, should I bring in more firewood?"

Alan Drake, prodding the dwindling fire with a poker, turned around and waved it in the air in agreement.

By the time Ren revived the fire, Lina recovered her composure. Dolly Tidd took a seat at the grand piano and reeled out some old sing-along tunes from memory. While the seniors sang "Swanee River" and

"Marble Halls" and "Oh! Dem Golden Slippers," Lina hummed along, not knowing the words. Ren slipped around the room, collecting used cups and plates and taking them away to the kitchen.

Dolly finished a song, and the seniors clapped. She moved into some experimental chords, and then, finding the right keys, began playing Beethoven's Moonlight Sonata. The serious notes spread like a tranquilizer over the room. Everyone lapsed into rumination. Lina wandered to a window and touched the cold glass. A scattering of stars glittered above, the same ones hundreds of sorority girls on past Halloweens would have seen when they stood right here. With the somber music and the firelight, Lina pictured the final act of Julia and Sean's history more clearly than ever. Poison, collapse, death, screams, tears, silence, funeral, suicide.

You see, she thought, *there are good reasons to be scared.* A girl who once tried a bold romantic tactic in this house ended up killing her lover. You might turn into a grim headline if you didn't keep your wits about you. Only by the grace of Everglade Hospital had Lina avoided being turned into a headline herself.

"For gosh sakes, Dolly, that's depressing!" brayed Marla. Chuckles bubbled up around the room.

"Play something we can dance to," suggested Alan.

Lina did not turn. She gazed at the rhododendron leaves outside the window, some of which wore a filigree of frost.

"Anyone know how to waltz?" Dolly asked, and played a few faltering, looping notes.

"Sure we do!" said Marla.

"I used to, before I grew two left feet!" offered George.

The old ladies murmured that they couldn't

possibly. Lina hugged her bulky leaf-covered bedsheet, her eyes fixed on the stars. She had learned to waltz one semester at UW, when a male friend convinced her to take ballroom dancing with him, but she hadn't done it since. Maybe if she hadn't said no when he asked her to go out dancing socially...maybe if she had suggested to Brent that they do something fun together like dancing, as a hobby...

"I bet you dance. You're a young guy," said one of the ladies.

"A waltz? I learned, once upon a time," said a hesitant, velvety voice. Lina looked over her shoulder. Ren, as Phantom, stood at the entrance to the room, hands folded behind him under his cape.

"Dance with Lina," Mrs. B said. "If she doesn't know how, you can teach her."

Lina felt her mouth drop open, but said nothing.

Ren smiled and ambled forward. "Well, Autumn?" He extended a hand to her. The cautious plinking notes from Dolly's fingers coalesced into a dainty, slow rendition of Chopin's Minute Waltz.

There was no escape. Even tripping over her own feet would not have been as bad as turning him down now, with everyone watching. The background of Lina's vision was a sea of white hair and plastic Halloween masks as she placed her hand in Ren's.

His arm circled her waist and drew her in. "Hand on my shoulder," he reminded her.

She put it there, on the fine-woven wool of his tuxedo jacket.

He held out their joined hands at the side. "Right foot backward to start."

On the downbeat of the next measure, she stepped back and he stepped forward. On beats two and three, they stepped sideways. Then forward for her, back for him, and off to the other side. And repeat. Lina frowned at her bare feet, concerned about going the wrong way and getting them stepped on, but the frown eased away as muscle-memory took over. Simple really, the waltz.

"Well, don't look at your *feet*," called Marla, as she whirled by with Alan.

Lina swallowed, and lifted her face to Ren's. He held the ballroom posture perfectly, as if to keep from intruding on her space. He was about three inches taller than her; a good match for dancing.

"Maybe we should try to move around the room," he said. They had been staying in one square yard of carpet since they started.

Lina nodded, and on the next step Ren swung her around, setting them on a looping path leading past each armchair and sofa. All the seniors laughed and clapped. Lina had to smile at their reactions by the time they completed a full circuit. "You're very good with them," she said.

"Well," he began, then his eyes caught something over her shoulder. He lowered his chin and confided, "I'm not sure they *all* like me."

When he carried her around on the next step, she saw Jackie Clairmont scowling at them from an armchair near the piano. The foot of her cane was planted on the carpet beside her, and she clutched the top of it as if to menace them. Or perhaps she was just having trouble seeing in this dim light. Hard to tell with the elderly.

"But that's not anything *you* did," Lina said, her indignation stirring on his behalf.

"I know. But don't worry about it. It's a holiday; have fun. Dance." At the last word, he sent her outward, spun her, and caught her close again, laughing when she yelped in surprise.

"Sorry." She relaxed. "Haven't done turns in a while."

"Better practice, then. Ready?" As soon as she nodded, he twirled her again.

Soon she got the hang of it. Every spin delighted the old folks watching, so Ren orchestrated several. By the time the song was winding towards its last measure, they had waltzed back around to Mrs. B's chair. As Dolly played the final chord, Ren dipped Lina down to an angle nearly parallel with the floor. Cheers broke out from Mrs. B, George, and Marla. Lina clung to Ren's shoulder, laughing. His mask slipped and tumbled, and Lina yanked her hand out of his to catch it. His free arm ducked under her body to support her.

"Thanks," they both said; and they both grinned. Then Lina lost all words for a second, because she was horizontal in the houseboy's arms, in a firelit room, with his comely face right above hers. His mouth smelled like cinnamon and possibly alcohol—was that mouthwash, or a swig of bourbon? She didn't care. In fact, she wanted a better taste. She wanted to sink onto the carpet and pull him with her; she wanted the phantom cloak wrapped all around her; she wanted to feel his warmth and his weight.

Everyone was watching them. The applause fell quiet. Lina panicked and tried to put his mask back on him, too quickly; it bonked him on the nose, and he grunted and fell to his knees, dropping Lina to her bottom on the carpet. The mask cartwheeled across the floor.

"Oh—I'm sorry!" she said, while the residents laughed.

"It's fine. I'm okay." Ren snagged the mask, took her hand, and helped her up.

"Really, I, I'm such a..."

Smiling, he shook his head, cut her a bow straight out of Jane Austen, swept up the empty cookie tray, and strolled back to the kitchen.

He did not reappear for a quarter of an hour, and by then his mask was back in place and Dolly had stopped playing the piano. The old folks were tired, having been at the party for two hours, and many of them hobbled back to their rooms. George, Dolly, and Betty sat in chairs close to the fire, talking of their parents and of Halloweens past.

Lina led Mrs. B back upstairs, and returned to her own room, still attired in a sheet and a tangle of leaves. She left the light off, and stood at her window in the blue dark. The tip of a downtown skyscraper, five miles away, sparkled between a roof and a tree. It looked out of place and futuristic after such an old-fashioned evening. But out there and all around her lay modern Seattle, with its street-smart men and bold women.

She could have been like that. She didn't have to end up this way. What had gone wrong? She plucked a maple leaf from her head and crumpled it under her nose to breathe in the tea-like scent. How different would life have been if she had spoken to Kenny about the love notes he sent her when they were twelve? What if she hadn't slapped away Troy's hands in high school every time he had tried to touch her breasts; what if she hadn't broken up with him when he said he loved her? Instead of hiding from the world in shame after she had lost her virginity with Scott in college, what if she had returned one of his calls? What if she had moved to Atlanta with Brent like he originally asked her to, instead of deciding it wasn't meant to be and letting him go?

She crushed the leaf in her hand; its dry edges poked her skin. What if, right now, she called Ren's room and asked him out for a drink? It was Halloween, Friday night, and they were in the U District. Festivity awaited, if only she dared enter its realm.

Before timidity could overrule her impulse, she switched on her lamp, grabbed the phone, and dialed the extension listed for "Ren Schultz" on the laminated directory taped to her wall. She let it ring five times before she hung up. He wasn't there. Of course; he was probably still cleaning up the kitchen.

She jogged barefoot along the corridor to the back stairwell, and down to the kitchen. He wasn't there either; the kitchen was deserted. Lina opened the back door, which led from the pantry out into the fenced backyard, and leaned out, keeping her feet on the interior floors but shivering in the icy outdoor air.

"Ren?" she said, but the yard was silent.

She closed the door. As she herself had commented, he was young and hip and must have better places to be. She, meanwhile, was old and pathetic and might as well brew some tea and go to bed. Sullenly, she padded into the kitchen and lit up the gas stove under a kettle of water.

After making her tea she carried the mug out past the living room. George and the two ladies still sat before the fireplace, now singing a round of that spooky folk tune Lina had learned in elementary school:

Have you seen the ghost of Tom?
Long white bones with the flesh all gone,
Ooh-ooh-ooh-ooh, poor old Tom!
Wouldn't it be chilly with no skin on?

A fitting tune for Halloween, but the singers sounded so jolly that it wasn't even spooky anymore. Lina climbed the front stairs slowly, careful not to spill her hot tea. Below, George hollered commands for another song. She paused with her hand on the banister to hear what it would be.

A shove against her shoulder splashed tea onto the carpet. Lina gasped. Her firm grip on the banister only barely kept her from falling over.

"Who's—" she said, but it became clear, as she turned around, that nobody was there.

Imagining things, she thought in a panic. *I'm imagining things.*

Trembling, she knelt and pressed the hem of her sheet-dress against the wet spots on the carpet until the tea was soaked up. Then, mug in hand, she ran across the landing, ready to bolt up to her room and shut herself in with all the lights on, but a wavering voice from the second floor stopped her. Someone was singing in creaky, unsteady tones. Lina peered around the corner. Jackie Clairmont wandered down the hallway to her room, singing the same "Ghost of Tom" the others were singing downstairs.

But instead of "Tom" she was saying "Sean."

"Have you seen the ghost of Sean?"

Lina, though her knees were literally shaking, reminded herself that she was responsible for the well-being of these people, and called out, "Mrs. Clairmont?"

Jackie Clairmont lumbered around to look at her. The doleful tune died away on her lips.

"Can I help you back to your room?" Lina asked.

Mrs. Clairmont put out a hand and touched her door. "No...no, I've made it." She pushed open the door, and squinted at it. "This wasn't my room. I was down the hall. And Julia was upstairs on the third floor, by that rooftop door."

Lina suppressed a shudder. That was her room now, the one near the trapdoor leading to the attic and the roof. Wonderful. Just what she needed to think about during those night shifts.

"Do you need anything?" she asked Jackie Clairmont.

Mrs. Clairmont shook her head as if it weighed quite a lot, and shuffled into her room.

Lina dashed upstairs and shut herself into her room—Julia's former room, if Jackie Clairmont was right. She shucked her wreath and her tea-spotted sheet, wriggled into her nightgown, and sat on the floor with her back against the bed, sipping tea. Everything frightened her now: life, death, love, the idea of calling Ren, the seniors she worked for, and every last room in this house, including her own.

It took another two hours and the reading of some lighthearted Wodehouse stories before exhaustion took the place of fear, and only then was she able to climb into bed and sleep.

****

On Saturday, the first of November, Lina had the afternoon off. Made restless by the autumn sun streaming through the windows, not to mention the strange experiences of the past month, Lina threw on her brown overcoat and a pair of sunglasses and set out for the University of Washington library.

She entered in the wake of two young men who trod heavily under their backpacks. The warm, dehumidified library air swept around her, engulfing her in a smell of books and an echo of vast spaces, making her feel as if she needed to be studying for midterms.

After inquiring at an information desk, she was pointed to the microfiche section. The girl there, with a tiny silver ball pierced through her nostril, perked up when Lina explained what she was looking for.

"Double-death at a sorority? That's wild. Okay, I'll show you how to search on that." She seated Lina at a computer and leaned over her shoulder to direct her.

Limiting the time frame to the 1930s, they turned up the relevant articles in the university newspaper within a minute. HOUSEBOY KILLED AT SORORITY, said the earliest stark headline, dated April 13, 1936. The next day's paper had a follow-up story titled REYNOLDS DEATH RULED ACCIDENTAL.

The day after that: FUNERAL HELD FOR UNIVERSITY MAN KILLED AT SORORITY. The next day: SORORITY WOMAN CHARGED WITH WRONGFUL DEATH. And finally: SUICIDE AT GAMMA ETA OMICRON: TRAGEDY OF REYNOLDS DEATH CONTINUES.

The girl wrote down all the citations and fetched the necessary microfiches. She guided Lina to a microfiche machine, and once Lina had the hang of the dizzying controls, which sent the old-style newsprint flying across the screen at highway speeds, the girl left Lina to her reading.

Lina located and devoured each article, and only after she was done reading all five did she realize that none of them included a photograph of Sean Reynolds, the houseboy. It disappointed her, though the reason was shallow. If he resembled Ren, she wanted to see him.

The last article did have a photo of Julia Grise, accidental killer. Julia shared that title with Lina, perhaps, but not much else. Julia was a pretty girl with a bold smile and a tight, wavy blonde bob parted on the side and dipping over one eyebrow. She seemed glamorous and passionate, whereas Lina was just clumsy. Pushing aside her own guilt and frustrations, Lina examined Julia's grainy photo on the screen, trying to bring it to life, trying to imagine those eyes flashing in flirtation at someone, those lips kissing a houseboy who looked like Ren.

Those bright locks of hair against the concrete floor of the garage.

Lina shivered and went back to re-read the articles. None of them mentioned Jackie by name, but they corroborated and embellished upon Jackie's story. Julia Grise, twenty-one, gave a toxic mixture of sleeping pills and brandy to Sean Reynolds, twenty-two, in what was meant to be a harmless prank to make him fall asleep, at the Gamma Eta Omicron sorority house on Friday night, April 10.

Emergency medics were called, but efforts to revive him failed. Funeral services were to be held Tuesday.

Sean Reynolds, they said, was a fourth-year UW student, living at Gamma Eta Omicron as a houseboy and pursuing a Bachelor of Science degree in Mathematics. Julia was in her third year and was studying Art. Sean's family, from across the Sound in Port Townsend, was coming in for the funeral but had nothing to say to the papers.

The second article rehashed the tragedy, which was ruled an accident. The third covered the funeral and offered a few obituary-like observations about Sean Reynolds. He had played baseball in high school in Port Townsend, he had been a good student, he had talked of becoming a math teacher or bookkeeper. The fourth article turned sinister. The day after the funeral Sean's parents slapped Julia Grise with wrongful death charges. They were reputedly hoping for a manslaughter conviction. The "distraught" Grise was not available for comment. The next day, her midnight suicide was front-page news at the UW.

One article ran a photograph of the house, looking as if it was in a different location due to the small stature of its trees. The maple in front, so grandiose now, barely reached the second story in this picture. Lina located her own window on the third floor. Julia's window, back then.

Was the room empty for the rest of that year? Did the girls drape the doorway in black crepe and place flowers at the threshold, and leave it undisturbed to collect dust and ghosts? Lina hoped not. She hoped, for her own peace of mind, that another girl moved in as soon as possible, someone happy and innocent and fresh, who went on to live a successful life and have delightful children, someone whose essence would erase the stain Julia left on it.

Lina found the girl with the pierced nose again, and arranged for photocopies to be made of the articles. While she waited at the counter for the copies, she wondered yet again how on Earth Ren lived so calmly in that basement.

When she returned it was 4:30 in the afternoon, and getting dark. She went to the kitchen first, rather than up to her room, and found Ren sitting at the breakfast bar, writing in a cloth-bound journal. She had seen him doing this before at quiet moments between meals. She entertained the idea that he was a fledgling poet. But now, as she set her photocopies on the counter and took off her coat, she saw he was writing rather fast and too steadily for poetry. Surely a poet would deliberate over each line, choosing words the way a wine connoisseur would choose the right vintage for a dinner.

She could always ask, of course.

"Do you write poetry?"

He glanced up. "This? No, this is just a journal. Little things; whatever's on my mind." He put the cap on the pen and closed the book.

"Oh." Lina seated herself upon a stool and unfolded the photocopies. "Well. I was just at the library. Look what I found." She pushed the articles toward him.

He dragged them over and read the headline of the first one. "Ah. Did your research." He spread the articles out on the counter.

"Yes. Interesting stuff. Depressing, though."

Ren nodded. He lingered on the photograph of the house. "Look how small the trees were then."

"I noticed that, too."

He swept them into a stack without having done more than skimmed them, and hopped off his stool. "So what will you do now? Hold a ghost vigil in the garage?"

"God, no. I don't actually want to *see* anything."

"I wouldn't either." He collected the journal and pen. "I better put this stuff away. Got a spinach salad to make."

"Hm. Spinach." Lina wrinkled her nose.

He pointed the pen at her, backing toward the stairs. "It'll be good, with the dressing I make."

"Fine. I'll try it."

He lifted his chin in acknowledgement and disappeared down the stairs. Lina picked up her coat and the photocopies, and walked slowly alongside the breakfast bar, re-reading one of them. Ren was back before she got to the end of the paragraph; he bounded up the stairs, ducked into the pantry, and emerged in the kitchen tying his apron around his waist.

Lina called, "See you at dinner," and moved toward the stairwell.

"See you."

She put a foot on the step, then stopped and wheeled toward the basement stairs. She needed another box of tissues, and had been meaning to go down to the storage area and get one.

Trying not to be daunted by the low ceilings and vault-like shadows between shelves, Lina plucked two boxes of tissues from the supplies in one of the storage rooms, and hurried out. When she got to Ren's door, the door to his "tiny little room in the basement," her feet slowed. He was upstairs, involved with spinach. She could have a peek inside. Just out of curiosity.

Sure. Innocent curiosity. His personal effects interested her, to be truthful; most notably that journal. Was she mentioned in it? Did it say, *Last night I danced with Lina, who I find very attractive*? Or possibly, *Got shanghaied into dancing an endless waltz with this weird woman who lives here; I think she's about forty*? Or did she not rate a mention at all?

She took a quick look around, then gripped the doorknob and twisted.

It was locked.

She retreated, chastising herself for the attempt. That was practically stalker behavior right there. How would she feel if he crept into her room and sniffed through her belongings? She'd find it creepy, that's how she would feel.

Look, Lina, she thought. *If you like him, flirt with him, but don't spy on him.* No wonder her relationships didn't work out. Had she always been this weird?

Chapter Four

For the first two weeks of November, Lina kept away from Ren's door and from Ren himself when possible, to avoid being tempted into any further stupid behavior on her own part. He struck up conversations with her sometimes, but they qualified as small talk and tended not to last more than two minutes. Instead, she catered to her elderly patients, took walks in the rain with her black umbrella, and sat at the piano in the living room, where she frowned at sheet music and plinked out notes. If she ended up playing the melody line of a certain Chopin waltz rather often, then it was her one indulgence, and until someone commented on it she would keep doing it whenever she pleased.

The house, too, was quiet. Nothing jumped out of its place; no unseen hands touched her. She almost believed it had been her imagination—the cold breath, the shove on the shoulder. These things had other explanations.

She awakened one morning to deep silence. It was dark outside; her clock read 4:51. She burrowed down against her pillow to go back to sleep, but a sense of small, busy movement caught her eye. Tiny shadows like moths whisked across her window-blinds. She pushed back her blankets, went to the blinds, and parted them with two fingers. A childlike thrill warmed her stomach. It was snowing! The maple drooped under a film of white, the grass and front path had gathered a patchy layer of slush, and the black spikes of the iron fence stood out against the snow-dusted street. The garden lights lining the walk twinkled like elfin mushroom lamps in Christmas Land.

She pulled the cord to raise the blinds. As she stood admiring the view, hugging herself against the chill (the radiators had not yet started up this morning), a figure walked into the yard from around the side of the house, leaving a dotted trail of footprints. Her heart jumped in fear—an intruder?—and then, upon recognizing him, shifted into a different and happier drumming.

In his usual white shirt and black trousers, with snowflakes sticking to his dark hair, Ren stopped at the fence and looked out at the street. He shivered and rocked up and down on his toes—Lina wondered in amusement why he hadn't worn a coat—and tipped his head back to let the flakes fall on his face. They were large and wet, so he looked down, shaking his head like a spritzed cat and dabbing his face with his sleeve. Lina grinned. She considered opening the window and calling to him, but didn't want to wake anyone up.

He turned toward the house. Lina waved at him. He held still for a long moment, the puzzlement on his face barely visible in the snow-light as he stared at her from three floors below. Then a smile broke like dawn over his features, and he waved. Lina attacked the brass clasp on the window and tried to open it. It was stuck, and would not budge. She made him a helpless gesture. He stood grinning, watching her, arms folded tight in the cold. She held up her palm to tell him to wait, and dashed away from the window. She stuffed her bare feet into rubber galoshes and flung a wool blanket over her flannel nightgown.

Something thudded against the windowpane, startling her into a shriek. A round blob of water and ice crystals splattered against the window, leaving gray slush sliding down the glass from the impact mark. She returned to the window to waggle a finger at him. He continued to grin, massaging his snow-chilled hands. Then she flung her door open and darted along the hallway, down the staircase, and out the front door.

She emerged into cold air and a confusion of falling flakes. Her breath made white clouds around her. Ren stood on the walk, illuminated from below by the garden lights. His damp hair curled against his temples, and his white shirt was turning transparent at the shoulders as the snow melted into it. He still shivered and hugged himself, but smiled as if perfectly happy.

"What are you doing out here at 5 A.M., you crazy man?" Lina hurried out to him and flung half her blanket around him before thinking twice.

He clutched the blanket to hold it in place. "I saw it was snowing." He sounded surprised, as if it should have been obvious. "Besides, you're out here too. Who's crazy now?"

"I only came to ask you what you were doing." Lina laughed, giddy that they were sharing a blanket in the snow at five o'clock in the morning, that their shoulders were touching, that he smelled like clean skin and bubble gum and damp cotton.

"You gave me a bit of a scare up there." He nodded to her window.

"Why?" She imagined a pale-clad figure standing up there, and began to see his point. "Oh. I looked ghostly?"

"I thought so, for a second."

"Mrs. Clairmont said that room used to be Julia's. The one who killed herself."

"Yeah. I heard. Probably what gave me the idea." Then he tossed his head to dash a snowflake off his cheek, shaking off the gloomy fancy at the same time. "But you don't look a thing like her," he added playfully.

Lina looked down at herself. His observation was all too true. Not only was she an ordinary brunette rather than a fetching blonde; she also wasn't dressed to flatter at the moment. Her washed-out nightgown, which she'd owned for eight years, hung to her shins, covering the tops of her brown rubber galoshes. She wasn't wearing makeup and hadn't brushed her hair before running downstairs, which clearly indicated a lapse in sanity. "No," she said. "Unfortunately, I don't look like her."

Ren tilted his head in a shrug. "Just as well. She's not my type."

Whether or not it was honest, it lifted Lina's spirits. Despite the icy damp she felt comfortable and warm.

"I came out to shovel the front walk," he added. "This will probably melt soon, but just in case anyone goes out early..."

"Will you let me get you a coat first?"

He smiled down at her, eyes bright from the fairy-lights at their feet. "How about this, nurse lady? I'll get my own coat, and some gloves too, and you put on some proper outdoor clothes and meet me back here."

****

On Thanksgiving night, Lina slipped into the guest room that used to be her bedroom, and shut the door. She leaned her back against it and took a deep breath, savoring the darkness and the quiet. She didn't fear ghosts here, in this 1960s craftsman house in Tacoma, and never had. In fact, she might welcome them. They would have to be an improvement upon the living.

Through the walls drifted the muffled noises of her mother and her mother's boyfriend singing "Blue Christmas" on a karaoke machine. Lina's brother heckled them. Her aunt and uncle hooted with laughter. Lina could practically smell the sherry from here. She'd had some as well, but not enough to feel like making an ass of herself.

Her family still didn't know the real reason she had left Everglade Hospital. She meant to tell them, but couldn't bear the thought of what it would do to their image of her, the nurse in immaculate scrubs, the girl who did her family proud by rising from the depths of Tacoma to the heights of Pill Hill. She gave them the same story she had told Marla and Alan at her interview, and to her dismay it made her family even more impressed with her. They were still impressed now, two months along, and made her the subject of one of their many Thanksgiving toasts.

"But I'm taking a pay cut," she pointed out. Didn't matter. They thought it was great, her working with old people and getting to live in a mansion! And by the way, this cyst on her brother's chin ("Mom, don't grab my face!"), what should he do about that?

The worst, though, had been when her brother had piped up, "Hey, I know this guy who dated this chick who worked at a hospital near your old one, and he said some nurse gave a patient the wrong drug—like, she messed it up and gave him a lethal injection. Same exact stuff they use for the guys on Death Row. Chlorine, or fluorine, something like that."

Lina stared at the stem of her sherry glass. "Potassium chloride."

"That's it! Were you there when that happened?"

She nodded. She hoped she wouldn't vomit.

"God!" said her mom. "Why would they even keep that stuff in a hospital?"

Lina swallowed until her throat felt less dry. "Well...in small doses, it's good for treating low blood potassium, but if you took too much by mistake..." She didn't want to go on. She prayed for a distraction.

She got one, at least. "Good thing you left, then," said her mom's boyfriend, and laughed heartily. "You know what? I'm thinking of quitting my job too."

The others veered into a discussion of whether or not the guy should give up his job managing an apartment building in Tukwila, and Lina had excused herself.

Now, though she no longer felt sick, she wondered if it would be unethical to make up an excuse to leave early and drive back to Seattle. She had agreed to be here until Sunday, a span of time that stretched before her like a ten-year prison sentence. She longed for the calming prattle of Mrs. B, the placid notes of the grand piano, the comforting background sounds of the kitchen staff clinking pans.

Most of all she missed Ren. That day in the snow, it wasn't as if their friendship had bloomed into love. They hadn't kissed or arranged a date or wrestled playfully in the slush or anything. But they had talked about so many things, both the fun and the deep—books, websites, urban legends, bizarre medical conditions—that she considered him one of her best friends now.

So maybe one of these days she'd actually find out his age. That would be useful to know before kissing him.

Before she could change her mind she dove onto the bed and snatched the cordless phone from the night table. Without bothering to switch on a lamp, she punched in the string of numbers on the lighted keypad, and settled onto her back as it rang.

Someone answered. "Hello?" Ren's smooth voice caused Lina's breath to catch. She had dialed the house's main line, not his room, but apparently she struck lucky.

"Hi." Lina ran her palm down her sweater,

smoothing her too-full stomach. "It's Lina. Just calling to say Happy Thanksgiving. You know, check up on everyone."

"Well, hello, nurse lady. Making sure no one got food poisoning from the stuffing?"

She grinned. "Yeah. More or less."

"We're all fine so far." Behind him she heard the murmur of multiple voices, the contented purr of a dinner party. "How about you?" he asked. "How's Thanksgiving going?"

"Well...the food was all right."

"It was better than 'all right' here. We made quite a spread. You can feast on the leftovers when you come back."

"I bet you make a mean cranberry sauce."

"As a matter of fact, I do."

"You know, we have a cook. How come you seem to make half the meals?"

"Because I like to," he said. "I get a little better each year."

"Must be satisfying. Maybe I should have gone to culinary school instead of rushing into nursing."

"Here, wait, let me shut this door." There was a pause, then a drop-off of the background chatter on his side. "There. Now I can hear better."

She pictured him leaning on one of the leather-covered armchairs in the small room near the front stairs, with the television standing quiet behind him. Was he in the dark too? Were the lamps on, or was there only the street-light cut into stripes by the wooden blinds?

"So you rushed into nursing, did you?" he asked.

"I had tunnel vision about it. Let's put it that way." She switched the receiver to her left ear and held her right arm up above her, viewing it in the faint light. "I burned my arm pretty bad when I was twelve. I was in the hospital a couple days. There was this great nurse, an older lady, who really impressed me. I decided that was what I was going to do, and I stuck to it."

"It's a much nobler calling than making food."

"I don't know about that. Especially your food."

He chuckled. "Well, thank you."

"I wish I'd stayed there with you...guys." Lina almost forgot to add the last word.

"Is it that bad?"

"Let's see." She wriggled her shoulder blades deeper into the bedspread. "I get to the house yesterday, and my brother's sitting on the front step and says, 'I have a major hangover; don't talk too loud.'"

"A hangover, on a Wednesday? Must be a college student."

"He's thirty. He just has friends who throw a lot of parties. Then we get here and I meet Mom's newest boyfriend. My parents got divorced when I was eighteen." A part of her mind was scolding her for babbling about her personal issues, but something—his reassuring voice, or the warm darkness, or the sherry—loosened her tongue.

"Complicated modern families," he said.

"I'd never met this guy till tonight. She's had about ten boyfriends since splitting up with my dad. Nobody worth keeping. Now everyone's singing karaoke, after Mom spent most of dinner harassing my brother and me about how we're never going to give her grandchildren at this rate."

"I've never tried karaoke," Ren mused.

"It does not go well with turkey. Trust me."

He laughed. "You're unusually forthcoming with opinions tonight."

"I've had alcohol. Mom's boyfriend mixes a stiff martini. Then there was wine with dinner, and sherry afterward."

"Now who's the hard partier?"

She smirked. Her eyes followed the outlines of

objects in the room, lit up by the blue-green glow of the clock on the headboard. "So Ren, why aren't you with your family this weekend?"

She heard a squeak of leather as if he was settling into an armchair. "Well, my parents have been dead for years..."

"Oh. I'm sorry."

"It's all right. And I'm not really close to my other relatives. We don't see each other anymore."

"No siblings?"

"I have a younger sister, but...she's got good people looking after her." Ren emitted a breath that might have been a panicked laugh. "I don't know why I'm telling you this. It doesn't matter."

"How much younger is your sister?"

Silence for a few seconds. "Ten years."

"So she's...twelve?" Lina guessed.

Even longer silence. "Yeah. Twelve."

Lina closed her eyes. Finally. An age, and an age every bit as young as she had feared. "When I was a senior in high school, you were in second grade," she said, then flinched, for she had clearly betrayed she was calculating his age, not his sister's.

"I have an old soul. As they say."

Her hand fell back onto the pillow. "I wish I'd stayed there," she said again.

"We would have been happy to—" His words broke into a splutter. Lina heard a thump and a ruffle.

"What was that?"

"A magazine just *flew* at me." He sounded more put-upon than disturbed.

Lina sat up. "By itself?"

"Yeah. It was there on the coffee table, then it was knocking me in the chest."

"Which magazine?" Lina didn't realize it was a funny question until Ren laughed.

"*Reader's Digest.* Though I know you were

expecting *The Satanic Monthly*."

"I just meant, if it were a big, heavy magazine it would hurt more."

"It's small," he said. "But solid. Okay, I've had enough of the house behaving like this."

"Yeah." She switched on the nightstand lamp and squinted against the brightness. "That's one thing I don't miss right now. It just *flew* at you? Really? There's no way it could have been knocked toward you by something falling over?"

"It was lying flat, with nothing near it. I was looking straight at it when it happened. But it's nothing new. Forget it."

"Something shoved me on the staircase," Lina said. She hadn't told anyone, but now she wanted to. "On Halloween. Shoved me hard."

"Oh? Sure you want to come back?"

She smiled with one side of her mouth. "Hey, at least there's no karaoke."

"Well, it'll be good to see you. Now I think I want to get out of this room."

"I should get back too. They'll be wondering why it's taking me so long to change my shoes."

"Then I'll see you Sunday?"

"Sunday."

****

On Sunday night, back at the house, she stood on the third-floor fire escape and watched clouds scud past the stars. She pulled her overcoat tighter around herself and breathed the wet air. Traffic and wind blended into a soft background rush. Rooftops and fences and lighted windows formed a mosaic before her; some houses already sported Christmas lights, sparkling in dotted lines along rain gutters.

Lina wasn't on call until the night shift. Mrs. B rested in her room, listening to a book on CD. Marla and Alan were watching a movie in their quarters. And Ren...Ren busied himself cleaning the kitchen.

Or organizing boxes of decorations in the basement. Or polishing the hardwood floor of the dining room. He had been busy all day, only allowing half a minute to smile at her and say a few words over the breakfast bar. Lina shouldn't have been dissatisfied. What did she expect, a hug? He was busy. Everyone was busy this time of year.

She wanted to tell him the horrifying stories of Christmas shopping with her mother and brother, or at least discuss the poltergeist incident further. But when she introduced that topic, as his mop moved between them, he didn't seem interested in pursuing it.

Perhaps the real question was, why did the friendship of this one young man matter so much to her? He was too young, too evasive, and anyway she probably was just trying to get back at Brent—not that she wanted *him* back, and not that he ever would come back anyway. Yet every time she tried to push her thoughts elsewhere, somewhere more responsible and independent, they bounded back to Ren like a helium balloon to a ceiling. Did her method of getting on with life after the disaster with Mr. Ambaum necessarily involve finding a new man and being loved by him despite what she had done— even though Ren didn't know what she had done? Was that it?

As if her thoughts summoned Ren, he appeared below her now: a gleam of white snagging her eye downward through the rungs of the fire escape. He exited through the back door, from the pantry. Lina moved forward and gripped the cold railing. He unlocked the gate in the tall fence and opened it. Lina's lips parted to call his name, but then he stepped out into the alley and...vanished.

A startled, confused sound escaped her mouth. She leaned over the railing, peering at where he should have been. Yes, it was dark down there, but she had a clear view over the fence into the alley, and she should have been able to see his white shirt.

"Ren?" Her voice sounded timorous and lonely in the quiet night. Nobody answered her. She tried again. "Ren!"

If he were walking away, he should have appeared in one of those patches of street-light, either up the alley or down. But he didn't.

She must not have been seeing the whole picture from up here. There had to be an explanation. She dashed into the house and ran down, down, down the stairwell until she hit the ground floor. Out she burst into the night, and tugged open the gate in the fence. She stepped out into the alley and looked up and down. "Ren?" she called again, weaker this time.

A chilly breeze touched her face; nothing more.

She withdrew and went back inside. She walked past the breakfast bar (he wasn't in the kitchen), through the dining room and parlor (not there either), and across the foyer to the living room. She stopped short. He knelt next to the fireplace, lifting a garland of artificial pine boughs out of a cardboard box.

"Were you..." She wasn't sure how to go on.

He looked over his shoulder. "Hi. Was I what?"

"Outside? Just now? Behind the house?" She entered the room. "I was on the fire escape and I saw you come out the back door. Then you kind of disappeared."

"I've been in here. Decorating." He frowned at her. "Sure it wasn't someone else?"

"There's not really anyone else in the house who looks like you," she said, but now she was uncertain. "You weren't out there, about five minutes ago? You didn't go into the alley?"

He shook his head, separating the garland from a string of white lights tangled around it. "I've had no reason to go out in the alley tonight."

She paced a few steps and leaned against the mantelpiece. "But I saw you." Even to herself, her voice sounded frail. Suddenly she had it. She drew a quick breath. "The ghost."

He paused. "Ghost?"

"What if I saw the ghost? The houseboy—you look like him, right? Because it did look like you, and vanished right into thin air." She stopped when she saw the expression on his face. "Okay, I know. It's a stretch."

"You've had a stressful weekend."

"Oh," she groaned, having thought of a new possibility. "Those spiders. Hobo spiders. The hallucinations—oh, no, I probably got bit in my sleep or something."

"Any other symptoms?" He had freed the garland from its companions, and stood to attach it to the mantel.

"I don't think so, but...okay, you know what? I'm going to bed. And then, tomorrow, I'm making an appointment to get my eyes checked."

He chuckled. "Don't worry about it."

"But I don't see things. I'm not that kind of person."

"Then maybe I did go out there, and I forgot about it."

"Yeah, and then you somehow evaporated. Never mind. Goodnight, Ren." She stepped over the box and walked across the room.

In her room, Lina locked her door, undressed, and examined every inch of her skin for spider bites. It took fifteen minutes and the use of a hand mirror. She didn't find anything, but was aware a spider bite might be hard to spot. Frustrated with herself for hallucinating, or with Ren for lying, or with someone else for tricking her eyes, she put on her old flannel nightgown and went to bed.

It took only a few days for her mood to recover, though. The alley illusion was the kind of thing you forgot and shrugged off. The farther she got from the event, the less of an event it seemed. He probably only slipped out for a smoke and didn't want the household nurse to scold him for it.

Anyway, what counted was that he was talking to her again. All their conversations, as December arrived and advanced, were the kind of conversations you had with friends—bantering, teasing, some honest concerns.

One Tuesday evening, after Ren had changed a smoke-alarm battery on the third floor, he showed Lina how to get onto the roof. He climbed the white-painted ladder set into the wall a few yards from her bedroom door and pushed open the trapdoor in the ceiling. Beckoning to her and telling her not to be afraid, he ascended into the darkness. Lina followed, holding her breath against the thick dust she was sure would cloud around her. But the attic crawlspace was fairly clean—or at least the wooden beams were, which she and Ren walked upon.

"This way." Ren had become a voice and a flashlight, five feet ahead of her. He shone the light down onto the beam for her until she got close enough to clutch another ladder, this one rough-hewn. Then he turned the light to the roof, and found a latch. With a twist and a push, a square of wood cracked open. Cold, fresh wind and a splatter of mist washed onto Lina's face. "Up we go," said Ren, and scuttled to the top like a squirrel.

He reached a hand down. Lina clasped it, thinking how she had not held his hand since they danced on Halloween. In a few lumbering heaves, clinging to the dusty rungs on the way, she emerged onto the roof. Once she had gotten her footing, he let her go. She thought of the ghostly staircase shove on Halloween, and wanted to grab his hand again, imagining how deadly such a shove would be up here. But he climbed out of reach, striding to the peak, so she stood and collected her courage, looking around.

Drizzle blew through her hair. She scraped a shoe against the shingles, feeling the reassuring traction. Even after a score of wet days and nights, it was not slippery.

"Huh," she said. "It's not as steep as it looks from the street."

"You walk by that ladder every day and you never came up here till now," he chided.

"Well, I thought it was steep." She smiled.

"Everyone should get on the roof of their house sometime." He beckoned with a tilt of his head. "Come see."

Lina approached him, stepping carefully, not looking toward the ground. She reached the top, and stopped to admire the dark shimmer of Lake Washington, which she hadn't realized was visible from here. Its edge was wreathed with lights, and a sparkling line—the floating bridge—cut straight across it. "Wow," she breathed.

Ren took her shoulders and turned her to face the city. From up here she could see more than just one piece of skyscraper. A handful of others pushed their shining tips into view, and the blue edge of the Space Needle's saucer peeked above a hill. "Someday," Ren said, close to her ear—and for a moment she thought he was being serious—"all this will be yours."

They broke into laughter. His hands squeezed her shoulders and let go.

Chapter Five

On a Sunday night, four days before Christmas, the seniors got a treat in the living room: a choir of schoolchildren paid a visit. The staff had arranged dining-room chairs in rows so the residents could sit and enjoy the songs. Lina, sitting next to Mrs. B, glanced back and saw Ren leaning against the entry arch. He winked at her. With a grin she turned forward again.

The children shouted "Merry Christmas!" in unison at the top of their lungs, and filed out. Lina and Mrs. B stood up. They chatted with Alan and George while Ren whisked away the chairs. He pulled the sofa back into place, and lingered to fix a drooping length of tinsel on the Christmas tree.

As Lina walked Mrs. B toward the stairs, Mrs. B stopped in the foyer and squinted upward. Lina looked up too, and felt her lips twist in a smile.

"Is that mistletoe?" Mrs. B asked.

"Yes, it is," said Ren, strolling up with his hands folded behind him. "Fresh-cut from an oak tree yesterday."

"Well, we're standing under it; isn't there a rule about that?" Mrs. B beamed at him.

Lina tried to slink away, but Mrs. B gripped her arm with the strength of an eagle's talons and yanked her back.

"Why, yes, I believe so," Ren said, and stepped up to Mrs. B. He kissed her on the cheek, and she laughed. Then he swiveled and brushed a kiss onto Lina's cheek. His gum smelled of peppermint, like a candy cane. "Happy Yuletide, ladies."

Lina, dazed with delight, was putting together an answer when George shouted behind them, "Me next!"

And before she had even gotten to know it, the soft imprint of Ren's kiss was wiped out by a bristly, loud smack from George Lambert. While George proceeded to lay a kiss on the squawking Mrs. B, Lina glanced at Ren and found him watching her, eyes alight with mirth.

At his shoulder appeared a tangle of dark red—Marla Drake's hair—and below it, a sardonic smile. "All right, you crazy kids. If I'd known how much fuss you'd make over that mistletoe, I wouldn't have picked it up."

The group dispersed, tittering like children. Lina led Mrs. B up the staircase. She ducked a look through the banister and caught Ren glancing at her over his shoulder. They both smiled and moved along. Lina's heart thumped more quickly than it needed to for the mild exercise of climbing stairs. Life felt glorious, until, with a pang like a whiplash, she remembered she had to go home to Tacoma on Christmas Eve. At least this time she was only staying two nights.

Mrs. B patted her arm at her doorway. "Aren't we lucky?"

"Yes, we are," Lina admitted.

"You're welcome," added Mrs. B.

Lina fell asleep easily that night, unafraid of the dark. She was happy knowing who she shared the house with, knowing the loveliness that warmed the cold basement.

A beep jangled her awake. She started, and looked around the shadowy room in confusion. It was not her alarm clock, nor the smoke detector, nor the doorbell. What was it? It took another electric jingle before she understood it was the pager; she was on call.

Lina flung back her blanket, looked at her clock—it was only midnight—and picked up the pager. *Augusta B*, it said. Mrs. B, right next door. She put on her slippers and rushed over.

What she found there when she snapped on the light was so strange she could only stare for a moment. Mrs. B was in bed, covered with books and magazines. Stacks and heaps of them. Her hand, which had escaped to grab the alert button, flailed in the air. As she tried to shift, a stack of *National Geographics* tilted and slid. Yellow-bordered issues thudded to the floor.

"Mrs. B, what did you do?" Lina started transferring armfuls of magazines from the bed to the carpet.

"Goodness, Lina, I didn't do this. How on Earth could I?"

"Then how did they get here?" Lina examined the bookcase behind her, but it was too far away. If anything had fallen off the shelves, it would have landed on the floor. Besides, most of the magazines had been in stacks on the floor to begin with.

"They just started falling on me. I woke up when the first few landed, and then there were more and more, just piling up." Her voice quavered. For once, the unshakable Mrs. B was shaken.

"So someone was in here?" Lina pulled a heavy hardcover dictionary from Mrs. B's lap, and felt Mrs. B's ribs and hips for fractures.

"I couldn't see anyone," said Mrs. B. "It was dark, and my eyes are bad anyhow."

"I know, I'm sorry. I'm confused. I don't know who would do this. Or why."

"I'll tell you one thing. I'm pretty sure nobody opened that door until you came in just now. If anyone else was in here, then they're still in here."

Lina froze, then turned, rising to her feet. "Did you hear anyone?" she whispered. Her eyes flew to possible hiding places: the closet, the small bathroom, the space beneath the bed.

"No, and I don't think you will find anyone." Mrs. B pushed away the last magazines and sat up.

Lina grabbed a pair of scissors from the bookshelf, and advanced to the dark bathroom. She had seldom been more afraid in her life, but she couldn't let anyone do this to her helpless old friend and get away with it. With a grunt she kicked the door open, sliced the scissors through the air, and flicked on the bathroom light. No one there. She turned and stalked toward the closet.

"Lina, I really don't think you'll find anyone."

"Then how did those books get there?" Lina yanked open the closet. Mrs. B's clothes hung there innocuously, nothing more.

"You know this house does strange things," Mrs. B said.

"But it's never done this before, has it?" Lina dropped to her hands and knees and looked under the bed from a safe distance, still clutching the scissors. Nothing but magazines and dust-bunnies.

"No, but I didn't do it myself, and it's a strange thing for a burglar to do, don't you think?"

Lina sank back on her knees. "Very strange. Mrs. B, forgive me for asking, but have you ever been known to sleepwalk?"

"No; and even if I did, how would I get myself under all those things?"

"I don't know. Listen, I think we should wake up Marla and Alan. Whoever did this could still be in the house."

"Oh, fiddle. If anyone broke in, they'd just steal the silver and the TV set. They wouldn't traipse all the way up to the third floor and start throwing books onto old ladies."

"Maybe someone else was sleepwalking." Lina flourished the scissors to punctuate her new idea.

"One of the other residents."

"Well, then they ran away in an awful hurry, because those magazines kept falling right up to the second you walked in."

"Are you sure?"

"As much as I'm sure of anything these days."

Lina lowered the scissors. She felt queasy. "I'll stay here tonight, in the armchair. I'll keep watch."

Mrs. B swatted at the air. "You don't need to baby-sit me. I'm sure we scared it off."

Lina emitted a shaky laugh. "You think I'm staying here for you? I'm not going back to bed alone, no, ma'am."

"Do what you like, then. Turn off that overhead light, would you? Even to a blind woman it's too bright."

Lina obeyed, though only after switching on a desk lamp instead. "I'm just going to get a blanket from my room."

Mrs. B, already settled down, grunted in answer.

Walking down the quiet midnight corridor, even with the lights on, terrified Lina further. The clicks and clangs of the radiator, echoing through the walls, sounded like Jacob Marley rattling his chains. At every step she feared the lights would go out as they had once done in her room. The ladder leading to the attic trapdoor was veiled in shadow, and she shuddered as she thought of venturing up there now, without Ren's glowing flashlight to guide her.

Upon entering her room she stopped short. Her blankets and pillows were strewn across the floor, which was not how she had left them. She grabbed the nearest blanket, ran back to Mrs. B's room, and huddled in the armchair with the scissors in her hand, even though logic, as far as it went regarding ghosts, told her a weapon was useless. She did not fall asleep until the familiar thumps and clatters of the kitchen staff beginning breakfast preparations started up downstairs at 6:30 A.M.

She woke up a scant hour later when Mrs. B's alarm clock went off. Lina dragged herself to her feet and stumbled downstairs to fetch coffee and tea. She forgot Mrs. B's oatmeal and had to go back for it. On the return trip she ran into Ren.

He frowned when he saw her. "You okay?"

"The house kept us up most of the night."

"The house?"

"Poltergeists. Ghosts. Books, magazines—flying, stacking up under their own power. I know; I'm hallucinating. But then if I am, explain to me how Mrs. B ended up under a stack of books too heavy for her to move by herself." It sounded nonsensical to her now, but he wasn't laughing.

"Is she all right?"

"Just a couple bruises. I think she must have been sleepwalking. Or someone else was. Someone else who also wanted to throw around my blankets, and then disappeared without a trace."

He couldn't have been able to follow her from those disjointed words, but he looked concerned all the same. "I should have come up. I was awake most of the night, and I thought I...heard something once."

The thought of calling him had definitely crossed her mind, but she hadn't wanted to wake him. "Well," she grumbled, "I need to get cleaned up."

"Okay. I'll come up to the third floor and look around; see if I can spot any signs of a break-in. Just to ease your mind."

"Thank you."

Half an hour later, wet-haired and wrapped in her blue terrycloth robe, Lina returned from her shower, and stopped in her doorway. Ren stood at her bookshelves, bending to read the titles.

He straightened up. "Sorry. Got distracted by your books. I haven't found any signs of a burglar, though."

"That's good, I guess." She came in and picked up a comb from her vanity counter, then paused. Combing her hair while standing here in nothing but a bathrobe seemed too intimate a thing to do while talking with Ren. She picked specks of lint off the comb's teeth. "What about the door to the fire escape?"

"Tight as a drum." He strolled toward the corridor. "Doesn't look like anyone got in or out."

"So that leaves ghosts. Great."

He turned as if to leave, then stopped, leaned on the door frame, and folded his arms. "You think they're real, then?"

"I don't know what to think. It's that, or someone's toying with us. Would anyone be toying with us?"

"I'm not doing it." His tongue transferred his chewing gum from one side of his mouth to the other; Lina caught a glimpse of pale blue. "And I don't think it's the Drakes or the old folks either."

She set down the comb and raked her wet hair back with her fingers. "I didn't mean to accuse you," she mumbled. "I've never lived with ghosts before. What are we supposed to do?"

"Just live with them, I guess." His words were quiet. When she looked over, she found his gaze lingering halfway up her body.

She looked down. Her robe was gaping at the chest, tugged open by the motion of her arms. She seized the folds together in one hand, though by now he must have caught a glimpse of her breast. His gaze flitted to the far wall. He unfolded his arms, his hands swinging clumsily, with nothing like their usual steadiness and skill. Her skin tingled beneath the terrycloth, from the unexpected draft of air and the even more unexpected image of what those hands might feel like upon her flesh. Her lungs felt tight, as if she could not take a deep enough breath to fill them. She was mortified, but at the same time thrilled. He had checked her out. He was curious.

Footsteps approached on the hall carpet. Ren looked over his shoulder.

"What you doing all the way up here, Ren?" shouted Marla from down the corridor.

"Just checking for intruders." He backed out of Lina's room.

"You know you're not going to find them." Marla arrived in the doorway, examined Lina's state of undress, and shot a glance back at Ren.

Lina's lips tightened, and she grabbed the comb and started detangling her hair.

"I better go check on the bread," Ren said. Over Marla's shoulder, he nodded farewell to Lina.

"Thank you for coming up," Lina called back. She kept combing as she spoke, and half hoped she had flashed him another peep of skin.

Ren slipped away, and Marla took his place at the door. "Heard our ghosts were bothering you and Mrs. B."

"Something sure was."

"I never warned you about that stuff. Maybe I should have."

"I probably wouldn't have believed you."

"Yeah? What about now?"

"I can't see how else to explain it. *Are* there ghosts?"

Marla planted a hand on her hip and gazed past Lina at the window. "Wish I had a better explanation. But I don't."

Lina set down the comb and picked up a bottle of hand lotion. "I'd rather not go through another night like last night, that's all."

"Nobody likes those. But they're rare, and you

get used to it." Marla moved into a brighter tone of voice. "Say, you're not seeing anyone, are you?"

"No." Lina squeezed lotion onto her hand and rubbed it into both palms. "Why?"

"My nephew Gary's starting grad school at U-Dub in the spring. He's moving to town in January to get a place to live. I think you two might get along. You should come to dinner, double-date with me and Alan."

Lina smiled dryly. "I'd have to think about it. What's he going to study?"

"Business. Going for his MBA. Real smart kid."

"Well, I'll consider it. I can't think straight right now, after last night."

"That's okay; I'll ask you later." Marla barked a laugh. "Thought it'd be a good idea, 'cause trust me, you don't want to date anyone you work with."

Lina's hands slowed as they spread the lotion onto her knuckles. In the mirror she saw her chest rise, and her face turn pink with rage. But when she spoke, she knew she sounded apologetic. "That's true. There can be problems."

"Well, especially a houseboy. That's all I'm saying."

Lina replaced the cap on the lotion and set the bottle aside. "Right." But she had no idea what Marla meant. Why "especially a houseboy"? Was it still the 1930s around here? Anyhow, advice against dating coworkers was rich coming from a woman who ran a business with her husband.

"I'll find you a picture of Gary," Marla said. "He's a real sweetheart."

"Since you mention it..." Lina took an emery board from the vanity and fiddled with it. "Is there something I should know about Ren?" She kept her eyes down. She felt the heat blazing in her face.

"Oh—no, it's just, he's not the type for dating."

"Not the type?"

"Well, you're not dating him anyway, so it doesn't matter. Just my unwanted advice!" Marla laughed again.

Lina put down the emery board and turned away. "I need to get dressed."

"I'll get going. Say, don't worry about those ghosts. It's been going on for decades and we all still love living here."

"I'll try to get used to it." Lina opened a bureau drawer and selected a pair of socks.

"All righty. I'll close your door."

When Lina heard the latch click shut, she waited five seconds, trembling, then spun around and pitched her balled-up pair of socks at the door. It bounced off the painted wood, right where Marla's head had been a moment ago, and tumbled under her desk.

"None of your business," she whispered. "None. Of. Your. Business."

She flung off her bathrobe, yanked open a drawer, and grabbed a stick of deodorant. While she applied it, arm over head, she stared at her naked torso in the vanity mirror. Well, why shouldn't he look? She had nicer breasts than some of the actresses she'd seen in movies. Her shoulders were attractive, too. Straight, with lean-muscled upper arms. He would have been able to see that on Halloween—her sheet-dress had left her arms bare. And with her hair getting longer, she was showing a fair amount of feminine charm lately.

"That's right." She tossed aside the deodorant and raked through a drawer for her hair dryer. "Think we'll even wear lipstick today. Deal with *that*."

After getting dressed, she retired to a living room sofa with her comfortably worn copy of *Pride and Prejudice*. Nibbling one corner of her lipstick-tinted mouth, unaccustomed to the cosmetic taste, she flipped to the confrontation between Elizabeth Bennett and Lady Catherine de Bourgh. It had occurred to her that her conversation with Marla had been similar—or would have been, if Lina were as brave as Elizabeth. As she read she heard the lines in Marla's voice and her own, instead of the characters'.

"Do you not consider that a connection with you must disgrace him in the eyes of everybody?...You are then resolved to have him?"

"I have said no such thing. I am only resolved to act in that manner, which will, in my own opinion, constitute my happiness, without reference to you, or to any person so wholly unconnected with me."

Lina yawned behind her hand. Well, at least one aspect of her case was the same as Elizabeth's; all it had taken was someone telling her she should stay away from Ren, and now she liked him more than ever. Maybe she had a rebellious streak after all.

She closed the book and folded her hands over it. Lady Catherine, of course, was Mr. Darcy's aunt and was worried about the family's social standing; that was why she opposed Elizabeth. But why would Marla oppose Lina? Marla was no relation to Ren, and anyway, this wasn't nineteenth-century England. Few modern Americans took objection to honest young women whose finances were only starting to rebound from paying off medical school.

Maybe Marla was trying to divert Lina's mind from the idea of ghosts, give her something new to fix her emotions on. If that was the case, then it had worked. Or...maybe Marla wanted Ren for herself.

Lina squirmed in repulsion. Marla was married, yes, but these things did happen, and Ren was undeniably charming. Perhaps they had already indulged in an affair. Perhaps they were having one right *now*. Lina cringed and shifted on the sofa cushions, shutting her eyes against the pale sunlight.

No; no way. Marla was a decent-looking woman, but not the sort of beauty a fifty-something woman would have to be to attract a handsome twenty-two-year-old. Or was it true that men weren't choosy, and would take anyone who was willing?

No, still impossible. Marla loved Alan; everyone knew that. She wouldn't cheat on him. Besides, Marla and Ren never sparkled with chemistry around each other, the way lovers would. In fact, the only people Ren had shown affection to, in Lina's memory, were herself and the old ladies—and with the old ladies it was just a grandchild variety of affection.

Which left herself. Lina smiled and wriggled down against the cushions. Marla must have seen it too, and for some reason didn't like it. Maybe she feared they would engage in tactless displays of passion if they started dating—shocking the elders by making out in the kitchen or pinching each other in the parlor. (As if Mrs. B would be shocked. She would only laugh. And George Lambert would yell encouragements.)

Lina stifled a snort of laughter in her shoulder. The idea was absurd. Marla ought to have known they would behave themselves. Just imagine Ren settling down on top of her now, on this elegant living room sofa—planting a knee on either side of her hips, twining his fingers into hers and pushing them into the cushions, bending to press warm lips to her mouth and taste her tongue—no, she and Ren would never do such things.

Unfortunately, she drifted into a dream in which they were doing exactly such things. His hands coasted along her breasts, caressing them through her sweater; his hips sank heavy against hers; his mouth tasted of roses, odd but alluring. She murmured and sighed to him, inviting and pleading for more.

He pushed himself up then, his weight lifting from her body. "Why did you stop?" she protested.

She opened her eyes. Her heart failed her for a moment.

Ren himself leaned over her. He stood behind the sofa, resting his elbows on the back of it and leafing through *Pride and Prejudice*, which he must have picked up from her chest. Her face felt hot. Lord, she hadn't moaned in her sleep, had she?

Ren smiled. "Sorry. Didn't want to wake you up, but George was looking for you."

"How long have I been asleep?"

"I wouldn't know, but it's 11:30 now." He turned a page, smile still pressing a dimple into his cheek. "Sounded like a vivid dream."

Kill me now, she begged the powers above. She cleared her throat, sat up, and patted her hair. "Hm. Weird. Don't really remember. Um, what does George want?"

He handed the book back to her. "Something about a prescription refill. He said your beauty is making his heart go nuts. Exact quote."

Lina chuckled. "Then I better hurry before anyone else's beauty becomes a problem."

Ren offered her his hand. She took it and he helped her off the sofa.

As they crossed the room, Jackie Clairmont shuffled in with her cane, clutching a magazine. She stopped and stared up at them, her head wobbling on her neck like a newborn kitten's.

"Hi, Mrs. Clairmont," Lina said.

Ren nodded to the old woman and moved forward.

But Mrs. Clairmont reached out with the magazine and touched his arm, stopping him. "It wasn't your fault." Despite her croaking voice, she sounded kind. "I'm sorry for what happened to you."

Lina was too embarrassed on Ren's behalf to look at him.

"Oh. It's all right," he said, sounding tentative and surprised.

Lina laid a hand on Mrs. Clairmont's arm, deflecting the magazine. "Well, you get the living room to yourself. We were just on our way out. Is there anything I can get you?"

"No, thank you." Jackie Clairmont tottered past them.

Lina watched her go, then turned and joined Ren, who was drifting into the foyer, his chin tipped down. Lina thought she understood. Nobody wanted to be reminded of an unpleasant experience, even by apology. Still, the apology hadn't been *that* unsettling, had it?

"So I'll see you at dinner?" she said.

He glanced at her, as if surprised to find her there. "Yeah. See you." He veered off to the dining room.

Lina stood at the foot of the stairs, clinging to the newel post. She wanted to run after him, seize him by the shoulders, and...and either demand he tell her what was going on, or twine herself around him and pry his sealed mouth open with kisses.

As if either approach would work. Dreams— such unfair hopes they put in your head. Lina turned and trudged up the stairs.

****

Christmas came and went with little fanfare and no ghostly activity. Lina saw her mother and brother again, and found them no more palatable than she had at Thanksgiving. The day after Christmas, still at her mom's house in Tacoma, she treated herself to another phone call to Ren.

This time she dialed his direct line. It was nine o'clock at night and she didn't really expect him to answer. But he did.

"Hello?"

"Ren? It's Lina Zuendel."

"Oh, Lina *Zuendel*. Not one of the other Linas I know." He sounded like he was smiling.

She lay back on her bed in the guest room. "I, uh, just remembered that you helped me stay sane over Thanksgiving, so I thought I might try the same medication again."

"Medication now, am I? Always the nurse. How can I help you?"

"I...I don't know." Though she had planned to launch into all kinds of recent annoying remarks made by her family, she became shy now at hearing his voice. "Ever seem to you that Christmas gets less fun as you grow up?"

"Of course. You have to start spending money."

"And visiting family. Or not visiting them if they're far away."

He apparently understood. "Who are you not visiting this year?"

"My dad. He lives in Philadelphia. Haven't seen him since last summer." She wanted to add more. How she felt like her dad had written off the rest of them as embarrassments, even herself, the respectable nurse; how she always remembered it was her dad, not her mom, she wanted to please by doing so well in school...

"I know what you mean," Ren said. "I miss my folks this time of year."

"God, I shouldn't complain to you, when you're actually an orphan."

"Oh, I don't know. The living are usually more trouble than the dead."

"True. The dead can't tell you how much you disappoint them."

"I hope no one's actually said you're a disappointment." He sounded offended for her.

"Well..." She closed her eyes. "I broke up with

91

this guy Brent, a doctor, back in spring. Mom, she doesn't care; she goes through guys fast enough herself. But Dad really liked Brent. They got along so well when Dad came out to visit; went golfing together and everything. So when I told Dad we broke up, he said, 'You let him go? You're not going to get many chances at men like him. You got to hang onto a good thing when you've got it.' "

"Ouch."

"Which actually is true. But..."

"Bad time to say so."

"Yeah. So why do I miss my dad?" she said.

"I think we get attached to people who challenge us. Whether it's wise or not."

"That's a deep observation. I will have to think about it."

"I doubt he's actually disappointed in you," Ren said. "I doubt anyone is."

Lina's eyelids drifted open. She smiled. "I knew it was a good idea to call you."

"Lina?"

Her heart started thumping. "Yes?"

"I like you."

"I like you, too."

"And I will probably disappoint you someday."

Her smile shifted to a frown. "What do you mean?"

"I always do. Believe me. Something comes up, and..." He sighed. "I just wanted you to know, when that time comes, I really did like you."

"Did?"

"Do. Still. Just remember it, all right?"

She blinked at the ceiling. "What brought this on?"

"I seem to have trouble keeping friends. And I suppose I'd like to change that, but I'm not sure I can."

"Oh. Well, I understand. I'm the same way."

"Okay." They were both quiet for a moment. "Ah, I just remembered," he added, "I said I'd run the tablecloths through the wash tonight."

"All right. I'll let you go."

"I'm looking forward to seeing you. If I haven't already disappointed you." Sounded like the smile was back.

Confused, she smiled anyway. "No, I look forward to seeing you too."

"Bye, then."

"Bye." She hung up, and kept her fingertips on the warmed phone receiver for a few minutes, as if touching him that way. "Friend." At least she was that.

When she returned to the old haunted mansion in Seattle the next day, and paused to gaze at the tinsel-wrapped Christmas tree, she was surprised to feel the type of holiday thrill she thought she had outgrown. She wanted to scoot underneath the tree on her back and look up the trunk, and imagine she had wandered into a glittering fairy-forest that was miraculously warm even in winter.

Or, she wondered as she touched the white lights and garlands, was she just feeling the effects of her crush? Was this simply how it felt to enter the house where *he* lived, to look at the decorations *he* put up?

She couldn't resist. She went to the kitchen first.

Ren in his apron instantly filled her field of vision like the star on a stage. He appeared to be sealing leftover dough into plastic freezer bags, but her heart leaped as if he were singing a serenade below her bedroom window. She thumped her soft suitcase onto the floor. "Hi!"

He looked up, beamed, and dusted his hands on his apron. "Hi! Hey, check this out." He moved toward the pantry, beckoning her along.

Lina followed, turned the corner, and exclaimed

in admiration. On the counter stood an elaborate gingerbread house, two feet tall, complete with chimneys, front steps, windows drawn with icing, and dark candy wafers lined up as shingles on the steep roof.

Lina gasped. "It's *this* house! Ren, did you make this?"

"You recognized it. I'm flattered."

"It's perfect; of course I recognized it! How did you do it?" Lina bent to examine the licorice-trim rain gutters.

"It's a Christmas tradition of mine."

"You could get into any culinary school in the world with this, Ren." Lina bent down to look closer. He had even sketched in the tops of the basement windows in icing. "This is amazing."

"But you can't eat it," said Marla, who had appeared behind them.

Lina straightened up, chastened at the mockery in Marla's voice. Was that a veiled 'hands-off' message again? If so, Marla apparently intended it for Ren as well; she was looking right at him.

Ren's gaze dropped to the floor. "No. But you can eat those." He nodded toward another table. Lina glanced there and saw a tray of gingerbread men.

"That'll be fine," Lina said. "I wouldn't want to break this into pieces anyway."

Marla grunted a laugh without opening her lips, and sauntered away.

****

On the morning of December 31 Lina reclined on a living room sofa with a book, looking out the window every few minutes to see if the rain had turned to snow yet, as the forecast predicted.

Marla walked in. "There you are. Looking all over this house for you!"

"What's up?"

Marla held out a photograph. "Found a picture

94

of Gary for you. My nephew."

Lina took the picture and examined the man, about her own age, standing between two older women. His warm, good-humored smile and tousled sandy hair gleamed in the flash. He wore wire-rimmed glasses and a maroon sweater vest over his white shirt. "Looks nice. How old is he?" she asked, though it didn't matter anymore.

"Thirty-two or thirty-three, I forget. He's in town now. We could all do dinner next week."

She handed the photo back to Marla. "He's a good-looking guy, but I can't promise..."

"Oh, no—no pressure! Just thought you should meet each other."

"Okay. I guess so." Lina looked out the window.

Marla looked too. "Miserable day." She tapped Lina on the shoulder with the photo and walked off.

Lina stayed a few minutes more, watching the rain but not seeing it. Resolve spread through her system like a drug. That woman's interference had gone far enough. Marla was about to see what her little words of wisdom actually inspired.

Lina closed the book and got up. Near the foyer a mirror hung on the living room wall. She looked into it and smoothed her hair, and licked her lips to bring color into them. With a deep breath she went to the kitchen.

She found Ren in the pantry, twisting the handle of a can opener around giant cans of tomatoes. He was alone. The day cook and Consuela were working together at the ovens. They wouldn't overhear.

"Hi," Lina said.

Ren sent her a sidelong smile. "Hi. Need some tomatoes, by any chance?"

"Uh, actually I was wondering...do you want to go see a movie this weekend?"

He wiped tomato juice off the can-opener blade

and moved to the next can. "Rent one, you mean?"

"Go out for one, I was thinking. Might be nice to get out of the house once in a while."

Ren's head was still bent over the tomato cans. "What, just meeting me up on the roof isn't enough?"

"I like the roof. But the thing is..." Lina looked at her foot in its dark blue wool sock, as she pushed a cereal flake around with her toe. "Marla's trying to set me up with her nephew. I'm sure he's nice, but...I don't think I can say yes or no without asking you, because..."

The can opener barely moved. Ren thumbed a loose scrap of label under the blade, tense, waiting.

"Because," Lina said, "if I was going to get set up with anyone, I would want it to be you."

Ren released his breath. His eyebrows moved in surprise, but he still didn't look at her.

"I know it's sudden," Lina rushed on. "You don't have to decide this second." *Though it would be nice.*

He gestured with the can opener. "I...I'm flattered, I really am, but..."

"It's okay. Never mind. I just thought I'd ask."

He pushed away the opened can and pulled over a new one. "It isn't that I don't want to. It's that..."

"He can't. He's under house arrest."

The words came from behind her. Lina whirled around. Marla stood with one hand on her hip, fixing a level gaze at Ren.

Lina did not speak. She turned again and looked to Ren. He hadn't spoken either, but his face confirmed everything. A flush suffused his cheeks; his gaze burned into Marla with frustration. Then he closed his eyes and turned his head aside, as if ducking an invisible blow. He moved past, side-winding between them. "Sorry," he murmured. He jogged down to the basement and slipped out of sight.

Lina sucked in her breath; her gaze staggered to

Marla. "He is?"

"Sorry, kiddo. Tried to warn you."

Chapter Six

"What did he do?" Lina sat in a squishy armchair in the small room adjoining the Drakes' bedroom. She hadn't been in here since her interview. It added to the strangeness of the situation, being called into a part of the house she rarely saw, to discuss something she never imagined possible.

But at least now she understood what Ren had meant by disappointing her.

Marla dropped into a matching chair across from her. "Same old story. Got mixed up with the wrong kids."

"Did they steal cars? Run drugs?"

"He's not dangerous. He won't hurt you, or the residents, or anyone. You don't have to worry."

"But what did he do?"

Marla's glance slid to a bookcase against the wall. "It had to do with drugs."

Lina, sickened, let her gaze fall to the carpet. Was she ever going to escape from chemical complications? "Did he take them, or just carry them, or..."

"He did enough to get in trouble."

"I never even guessed." Lina chose her words to reproach Marla, albeit obliquely, for not telling her.

"Well, he's not dangerous, like I said. And as you can imagine, he doesn't really want people to know."

"Do the seniors know?"

"Nope."

"How long ago was all this?" Lina asked.

"Oh, years. It's been a while."

"Then how long is his sentence? When can he leave?"

"It's kind of indefinite."

"That doesn't make any sense. They give you a sentence when you're tried. You get to know how long you're in for. Don't you?"

Marla got up from her chair and paced between Lina and the bookcase. "His case is weird. I don't know the details, or why it ended up the way it did."

"Aren't there lawyers he can talk to?"

"Lina." Marla stopped in front of her. "He doesn't want us meddling. He wants to suffer it out and pretend he's got a normal life. All right?"

"Does he know we're having this conversation?"

"Sure, yeah. Whenever anyone gets too close, I've had to tell them."

Lina squeezed her fingers between her knees. She hated it, the idea that Ren showed her such favor only because he couldn't go outside the house for normal girls his own age. She also hated thinking of the others, probably more attractive, before her. And of course it disturbed her that he was a criminal. Granted, so was she, in a sense, but she didn't appreciate the reminder. "How many have you had to tell?"

"Not many," Marla said. "He usually keeps to himself. He decided to be stupid and make friends with you, I guess." When Lina looked up in disbelief, Marla's mouth fell open and she thrust a hand toward Lina. "I didn't mean it like that! Gosh, I can't keep my foot out of my mouth some days."

Lina forgave it with a limp lift of her fingers, and slumped back in the chair. "I assume I shouldn't tell anyone."

"If you care about him, you won't."

"I don't really know him," Lina said, feeling with despair the truth of that statement, "but I'll respect his wishes."

"Good. You're a good kid."

"Can I ask how he ended up here?"

"We knew him through the family. He asked if he could stay here when the trouble all came down. We said yes. It's a big house and we could use the help. And we figured he'd be more comfortable here than..." Marla looked out the window. Pale winter light fell across her coarse features. "Somewhere out there."

Lina got up and walked toward the door. Then she looked back, in a flash of insight. "Did Mrs. Clairmont really recognize him, then?"

Marla shot her a glance, eyes sharp. "What?"

"Maybe she lived in the neighborhood where he and his 'bad crowd' used to hang out, and saw him doing, I don't know, illegal things."

"Oh. I don't remember where she lived, so..."

"And then she got the memories mixed up," Lina said. "Being in this house. She saw a guy she associated with some sort of trouble, and mixed him up with the murdered houseboy—Sean Reynolds, right?—because she was back in the sorority where it happened." Lina stopped, seeing the way Marla was staring across the floor and chewing on her lip. "It's just a theory. It doesn't matter."

Marla released her lip from her teeth. "Guess it's as good a theory as any."

"I won't bother Mrs. Clairmont about it. I won't tell anyone. I just thought...well, I hoped something finally made sense."

"Honey, very little in this world makes sense. And even less in this house."

All day Lina kneaded the new development in her mind, pinching it like a fretful child poking at a bruise. So many things he had said sounded different now, took on whole new shades of meaning. It was finally clear why his sister was under the care of other people, instead of his own. She now understood why he had crawled into every corner of this house, right to the very crest of the roof. He had nowhere else to go.

Things she had said to him also returned to torment her. If she had known, she would have been more tactful. *"You're young and hip; you must have places to be."* And, of course, she would not have grilled him on whether or not he had stepped out into the alley one December night.

From what she knew of house arrest, he wore some sort of device—an ankle band, most likely—that would set off an alarm if he stepped outside the perimeter of the property. But maybe if he ducked into the alley and stayed right up against the fence, he would not set it off. He would have learned, over the years, the exact boundaries of his prison. The Drakes probably wouldn't like him doing it, nor would his parole officer, so if he did slip out for a taste of freedom, he would dive straight into the shadows the second he escaped. Therefore it had looked, from her vantage point, like he disappeared. After that, he must have heard her calling him, and dashed back inside while she was running down the stairs, and then pretended he had never been out at all.

And he let her think it was the ghost.

The ghost! Poor Ren! All this time Lina had wondered how he could stand to live in the basement of a haunted house, when the truth was he had no options. When he asked to stay with Marla and Alan, had he known about the manslaughter-suicide and the subsequent poltergeist? Would it have stopped him? Possibly not. It wouldn't have stopped her, because she wouldn't have believed it. You had to live with these things and see them with your own eyes before you really began to believe that ghosts and poltergeists existed.

A sudden sick feeling washed through her. She

might have fallen to her knees, if she hadn't been on her knees already, writing down numbers on Gertrude Brown's medical chart during a routine checkup.

What if there wasn't a poltergeist? What if Ren had been doing it all along? It was irrational behavior, yes, but he had reason to be frustrated and bored. He could have rearranged her blankets. He could have dumped magazines on Mrs. B's bed and escaped into the hallway before Lina got there. True, Mrs. B didn't think anyone opened the door, but her eyesight couldn't be trusted.

He wouldn't do those things, though. Would he? Risk hurting an innocent old lady just to make Lina and the others believe in the ghost? Was he that strapped for excitement? Besides, Lina's lamp had gone out by itself with no one else in the room. The laundry room door had slammed shut, and the laundry basket flipped over, while he was all the way up in the kitchen. She had felt that shove and that cold breath on the stairs. Ren himself said a magazine had flown at him.

So what.

She told Mrs. Brown that everything looked normal, and began packing up her supplies.

Maybe he had lied. Maybe she imagined the assaults on the stairs. Her lamp and the laundry room incident proved nothing; old houses had drafts and electricity fizzles. There was always a better explanation than the supernatural. What if Ren devised some of the pranks? Would he admit to it if she asked him, as a friend? Maybe if she admitted to her own horrible mistake?

She put away the last supplies and creaked to her feet. Her knees ached from the cramped position. "Well, you're my last patient today, Mrs. Brown. Think I'll go rest a while before dinner."

"Thank you, Lina. Don't forget our party

tonight."

Oh, yes. It was New Year's Eve. "I won't forget," Lina said.

Before dinner she knocked on Ren's door in the basement. Her heart hammered. *I just want to talk,* she would say when he opened it. *I want you to know I understand. It's okay. I still want to be friends with you.*

He didn't answer. Lacking the nerve to call out to him through the door, she slunk back upstairs.

At dinner he did not come out to serve. He stayed in the kitchen and left the table-waiting to the two girls. She decided he needed time before facing her. All right. She could wait.

The "party" Mrs. Brown referred to consisted of sipping sparkling cider and watching the Space Needle fireworks on TV. Lina sat with the four sleepy seniors staying up till midnight, and considered going up to the roof to see those fireworks directly, but didn't, because Ren might be up there.

Lina felt sorry for him, for his humiliation, but she also still felt uneasy, unsure what to say to him next. To think, she had imagined being next to him at this moment, as the calendar year turned, giving them another excuse to kiss. She twisted in her seat, sipped her cider, forced a smile at the confetti Mrs. B flung, and wished the world were different.

****

On Tuesday, January 6, Lina woke up to falling snow. Seattle's temperature had been in the twenties for days, and the snowflakes were feathery and dry like the snow in the Canadian Rockies, not wet and slushy like Puget Sound usually got. Lina watched from her bedroom window, smiling at the beauty of the flakes accumulating on the frozen ground and parked cars.

Ren trudged out with a wheelbarrow full of sand to scatter on the front walk. Remembering a different snowy morning not so long ago, Lina felt her smile wilt. She watched him a while, but he failed to turn and look up at her like last time. He had dodged her like a venereal disease for the past week, in fact. Saddened, she turned away.

She performed her morning rounds of checkups and visits, and spent her free afternoon in the living room with a sandwich and a crossword puzzle, frequently glancing out to admire the wintry landscape. Toward the dinner hour, the doorbell rang. Sensing no one else nearby, Lina dusted crumbs off her hands and got up to answer it.

The man on the doorstep smiled and waved a glove-clad hand at her. He was about Lina's age and had a broad, symmetrical face, with glasses and dark-blonde hair that flopped onto his forehead. "Hi, Drake House! Are Marla and Alan around?"

"I think Marla might be. Can I tell her who..."

"Tell her it's her long-lost nephew Gary."

"Oh!" Lina stepped back, opening the door further. "I've—yes, of course. I've heard of you. Come in."

"Thanks." He stepped inside and stomped his hiking boots against the mat. Chunks of snow fell off the soles. "I picked a stupid day to drive across town and visit, but I needed to turn in some forms at the U, so I was in the neighborhood." He unzipped his ski coat.

"Right." Flustered at being confronted with her blind date, Lina turned and flagged down Consuela, the serving girl, who had come out to see if the door had been answered. "Consuela? Um, could you get Marla, please? Tell her Gary's here."

"She's in the kitchen," said Consuela. "I'll tell her." She turned and bustled off.

"Come, sit down," Lina said.

They went into the living room, where Lina hastily knelt and folded up her scattered newspaper.

"So. You seem a little young to live here," said Gary.

Lina looked up. He sat in an armchair, flipping the end of his striped scarf back and forth, grinning. She touched her forehead, remembering she hadn't introduced herself yet. "Sorry—yes. I'm Lina. The nurse."

"I thought so. Marla's mentioned you. She's been talking about having us all go to dinner."

"Right." Lina sat on the sofa and arranged the newspaper on the coffee table, avoiding his gaze.

"Hope my girlfriend's in town by then. She'd get a kick out of Marla."

"Oh. Your...girlfriend's moving to Seattle too?"

"Yep. Just had to wrap up her job over in Pullman."

"I see. Good." Lina leaned back on the sofa cushions, relieved. He already had a girlfriend. Thank God. Gary was attractive, but she was still stinging from the whole Ren catastrophe, and dating someone else simply wasn't a possibility right now. "Does, um, Marla know you're seeing someone?"

"I told her, but I bet she didn't believe me. Probably thought it was an excuse so I wouldn't get set up with her latest employee." He winked at Lina.

Lina smiled. "Does she try to set you up a lot?"

"Only every chance she gets. It actually worked one year, when I had a summer job in Seattle. Nice girl. She was helping out in the kitchen."

"The kitchen?" Lina studied her nails. "How long ago was that?"

"About ten years. Yeah, it was '94. Just after I'd graduated from Wazzu." Pullman's WSU, like UW, had its own special pronunciation among the initiated.

Ten years ago, Ren would have been twelve. Probably hadn't started working at the house yet. Perhaps hadn't even started on his criminal career yet. No possible connection there. "Nice house to work in," she said. "By the way, did she—the girl you dated—ever think it might be haunted? I hear stories, is all."

"Oh, yeah." Gary laughed. "This place scared her half to death."

A chill invaded Lina's limbs. "What happened?"

He shrugged. "She said stuff moved around by itself. Like maybe someone was playing tricks on her, but she couldn't figure out how. One night she woke up because the blanket was being pulled off her. Said she watched it haul itself right out into the middle of the room and fall to the floor."

Lina tried to smile. "Wow. Strange."

"Oh, and actually, there was one thing I saw too. We were moving her desk across the room, and we had put the phone on the floor. Well, it began to ring. We were carrying drawers, so we couldn't get to it right away. It rang a few times. When she finally picked it up, no one was there; must have hung up. No big deal, right? Then we remembered. *We unplugged the phone.*"

Lina's breath stopped for a moment.

"She held up the end of the cord and showed me," he said. "Definitely unplugged. To this day I'm not sure how that happened. Of course, I never did understand electronics."

Lina managed to laugh. "Scary."

"Yeah. So, has anything like that happened to you?" He looked at her with cheerful expectation, as if they were telling each other jokes.

She looked out the window. "No. Not really."

Marla strolled into the living room, hugged her nephew, and started lecturing him about how he shouldn't drive in this weather. She herded them into the dining room, where dinner was being served. Gary met Mrs. B, who immediately started flirting with him. The Drakes, Mrs. B, Gary, and

Lina all sat at a table together, where Marla was finally made to understand that Gary did in fact have a real, live girlfriend.

"Oh!" she said in dismay. "And here I was trying to hook you up with Lina!"

Lina shook her head, enduring the torture. Gary grinned at her.

Ren came out, a pale, sculpted Narcissus in comparison to the warm, wool-vested Gary. "Coffee? Tea?" he offered, as always.

Lina scooted her cup forward for coffee, and glanced up at him. He didn't look at her, just filled her cup.

"Tea, please, Ren dear," Mrs. B said. He leaned over to comply.

"I hope you're still coming out to dinner with us," Gary said to Lina.

"I will," Lina said.

"Good!" said Alan. "We'll have fun."

Ren snapped upright as if his spine had been smacked with a ruler. He shot a final glance around the table. No one else wanted tea or coffee, so he stalked away. Lina's stomach knotted up. Was Ren actually jealous over her? Battling pity and fondness, she pulled apart a dinner roll and listened to her tablemates' conversation.

"Still have a houseboy, huh?" Gary said to Marla.

"Yep. Can always use the help around here."

"Wasn't Annette seeing a houseboy of yours?" He turned to Lina and added, "Annette's the girl I told you about, who used to work here."

"I don't remember," said Marla, tugging at a lock of her hair.

"I'm sure she was. That's why you set me up with her, remember?" Gary laughed. "You thought he was bad for her or something. In fact, wasn't he under house arrest?"

Lina's fingers fumbled. A piece of dinner roll went flying and disappeared under Mrs. Brown's chair across the aisle.

"Aw, water under the bridge," Alan said.

"Let's not go there," Marla told her nephew in a stage whisper, and scrunched her nose with a smile. Her gaze then moved to Lina. Marla patted the air in a gesture she presumably meant to be reassuring, while she mouthed something like, "We'll talk later."

Lina shut her own mouth, which had fallen open. What in God's name was going on here?

She didn't get to confront Marla until after dinner, once Gary had driven away on the packed snow. Then Lina stopped Marla at the dining room entrance and asked, "Has Ren lived in this house for ten years? Or was Gary talking about someone else who was also under house arrest?"

"Huh. Guess maybe it has been ten years." Marla's gaze strayed across the room, as if she was thinking it over.

"Then he's not twenty-two. Unless he was under arrest and dating some college girl here when he was twelve."

"I'm not sure how old he is." Marla frowned, continuing to study the far wall. "Did he say he was twenty-two?"

"He let me believe he was."

"Doesn't quite add up, does it?" Marla laughed, as if it were funny.

"So, he's twenty-six? Twenty-eight?"

"I told you, kid, I'm not sure, and I'm not sure it matters."

Lina slid her left hand up her right arm, fingering the scar tissue under her sleeve. "I'm confused. I don't know what to believe. That's all."

"Honey, it's a sticky situation. No one wants to hurt you or upset you. Look, I didn't know he claimed to be twenty-two. If I'd known, maybe I would've straightened you out."

"All right." Lina sighed. "I've been stressed out, I guess."

"No problem. You get some rest." Marla squeezed her shoulder, then turned her attention to Consuela, who was balancing a stack of plates. "Consuela! Heaven's sake, let me help you." She hustled away.

****

But even after a good night's sleep the situation still did not look normal—far from it. Lina no longer thought it useful to press Marla for information. Marla was acting as suspicious as Ren. Alan probably wouldn't be any better. And even if she managed to corner Ren and threaten him with a kitchen knife, she figured he still wouldn't tell her the truth.

She didn't wish to pull Mrs. B or the other seniors into it, and promised not to tell them anyway. That left her more or less on her own.

But something here was definitely off. Ren had been under arrest for over ten years, an absurdly long time for juvenile drug possession. She looked for the ankle band, but had never seen it. Were criminals allowed to keep them hidden? Also, she never saw a parole officer come to meet with him, though possibly they kept those meetings secret to avoid alarming the seniors.

But why had he lied about his age? Maybe his name wasn't real either. Then who was he? Did he and the Drakes have some kind of conspiracy cooked up? Maybe they were *all* criminals.

Trouble was, none of them seemed like it. Sure, she hadn't known many criminals, but those three had never acted violently, cruelly, or unscrupulously, as far as she had seen. They were all *nice*.

She returned to her room after a blood-draw visit to George Lambert, and thumped her supply kit onto her desk next to the phone. Seeing the phone reminded her of Gary's story, of the girl Annette who had suffered the same miseries as Lina; attachment to the unattainable Ren, and torment by a malicious poltergeist. That assumed the ghost existed, which she had to admit seemed likelier after hearing Gary's memories.

"I don't know," she murmured, running her fingers over the phone's buttons. "Are you real after all, ghosties?"

She didn't expect an answer, and in any case, it was time to go down for lunch. But as she turned to the door, she caught something yellow quivering in the corner of her vision. She looked over her shoulder and blinked in astonishment. The Seattle phone book, the volume with the yellow pages, hovered in the air above her desk, turning as if suspended on invisible strings. Lina's heart rate took off at a flying gallop. Her skin went cold—or was the room itself cold?

The book fell to the desk with a clap, knocking a notepad and two pens onto the floor. Hand flying to her chest, Lina skittered backward, staring at the phone book like it was a rabid animal. After a moment she dove forward and grabbed it, poring over the cover for bits of tape or string or anything else that would have held it up. Nothing. She looked up at the ceiling for the same thing, and palmed the nearest wall. Again, nothing.

With a whimper, she dropped the phone book onto the desk, wheeled around, and ran out of her room.

She picked at her lunch, jumping whenever someone moved behind her. She didn't want to tell anyone what had happened, because she didn't want to be made fun of, or to hear there were some things you simply had to live with, such as ghosts in your room.

After lunch she crept back into her room, peering around the door, half expecting to see writing in blood on the walls. But everything was as she had left it. Phone book on the desk, notepad and pens on the floor. She put everything back on the desk and settled in for a web search on what to do if your house is haunted.

Two hours later, after frightening herself further by reading tales of what other people claimed to have seen, including but not limited to a tall man flying around a chandelier, a bone-white figure sitting in an armchair and watching television, and children with eerie black eyes, Lina shut off her computer and turned on the radio for music. All she learned in the way of combating her problem was what folk wisdom had already taught her: talk to your ghosts. Ask them to go away. It usually worked.

Lina positioned herself in the center of the room and looked at the ceiling. "Please go away." Her voice sounded thin and high. "Please stop bothering us. You're scaring us. I know you've been here a long time, but please, please move on now."

Nothing happened, of course. The radio went on playing, the lights stayed on, the afternoon winter sun did not duck behind a cloud. But the silence felt like disdainful indifference. The ghost was there, Lina was sure. It just didn't want to move.

Chapter Seven

Sometimes when Lina lay in bed at night, the thought of the ghost was too much to bear. Her heart pounded, her lungs constricted, and her gaze darted around the room from shadow to shadow; or, conversely, she shut her eyes so she wouldn't see anything. She made herself think of sunny spring days (woefully far ahead from this vantage point in mid-January) and loyal watchdogs sitting beside the bed to guard her (would Marla let her get one?). She bought a nightlight in the shape of a seashell, and felt better for its warm yellow glow, but even that innocent seashell caused her dread. What if it got switched off by invisible hands? Wouldn't that be twice as bad as not having a nightlight in the first place?

But nothing new had happened since the phone book incident, and the nightlight always did stay on, so Lina managed to sleep even on the worst nights.

Once in a while in her dreams, she found herself kissing Ren, at which point the dream went one of two ways. Half the time he turned into something worse, like a skeleton or a werewolf or the Green River Killer, and chased her through the house with all the lights off, and she woke up in a sweat. The other half of the time, he crushed his lips against hers, hoisted her onto a kitchen counter, and wrapped her close around himself. She awoke in a different kind of sweat on those days.

She had to speak to him again.

On a morning in the middle of January, two weeks after learning of his house arrest, she sat at the breakfast bar with her coffee, pretending to read the paper. The cook, a large and scowling woman who hardly spoke to anyone but Marla, rolled out a pastry sheet on the butcher's block while Ren stacked clean dishes in the cupboards. When the cook sent him down to the basement to get some canned apricots, Lina slipped off her stool and quietly followed.

At the bottom of the stairs, with the concrete ceiling low enough for her to reach up and touch, she took a breath of the dank air, and stepped forward into the doorway of the storage room. She slid her left hand up her right sweater cuff, and stroked her scars, praying for courage.

Ren looked over at her. His hands froze on the shelves.

"I guess we've been avoiding each other," she said. She tried out a smile.

He pushed some cans aside to look at the ones behind them. "I guess that's best."

"Maybe not. I...I've known people with drug problems, you know. I'm a nurse. I was just surprised, because you didn't seem the type—and I don't mean that like it sounds, but..." She was already going about this all wrong, insulting him without intending to. Great.

He didn't look at her. "I really don't want to talk about this."

"I'm sorry. I only want to help. Can't we talk like we used to, at least?"

He tugged out a huge can bearing a dusty white label painted with yellow apricots, and thumped it onto the concrete floor at his feet. Crouching there, he glanced at her, then looked away. "Marla interfered because I asked her to."

Oh, Lord. Lina's throat swelled and her eyes stung. "You..." She swallowed to steady her voice. "You couldn't just tell me yourself that you weren't interested?"

He traced circles in the dust on top of the can. "I don't want to get close to anyone. I told her to stop me if she saw it happening."

"Why? What's so awful about..." Lina stopped, wiped her nose, and stared aside at the faded red curtain covering the tiny basement window in the stairwell. She decided she didn't actually want to hear his explanation on why getting close to her would be awful. He wasn't attracted, period. "All right." Her voice creaked. "Sorry to bother you." She turned and set her foot on the bottom stair.

"You didn't bother me." His answer was almost a whisper. "You just need to forget me."

She glanced over her shoulder.

He stood now, leaning the side of his head on the metal shelves, watching her. Dust floated in the faint beams of light from the window.

She forced a smile on top of her misery. "Fat chance." Then she turned and fled up the stairs before giving him the satisfaction of seeing her cry.

****

Out of pride and humiliation, Lina respected Ren's request, and didn't try to speak to him for the rest of January. Mealtimes became a minor circle of hell for her. She discovered depths of acting she didn't know she possessed, smiling and conversing with her tablemates as if unaware of the silent young man filling her water glass. She made a special point of paying attention to Gary when he came to dinner again, laughing at his remarks, telling herself she wasn't being petty, was merely trying to enjoy life.

But it was no use. She couldn't live like this, with ghosts on one hand and heartbreak on the other. One late January day she decided enough was enough. She would find a new situation. She had done it before. She logged onto the Internet and started browsing ads, anything in the Seattle area along the lines of *Wanted: Live-in Nurse*. Though it made her queasy, she copied and pasted a few promising listings into a document file. If she felt brave after lunch, she thought, she would call and investigate them.

She roused Mrs. B from her books-on-tape to give her the mid-day calcium she always took. "Is it that time? Goodness," said Mrs. B. After swallowing the calcium, she squeezed Lina's arm in both hands. "I don't know how I ever did without you, Lina dear. I feel so much better having you around."

And with a twist of the heart, Lina doubted very much she would make those calls.

But she had one last test to see if fate would drive her out.

She knocked on the door to Marla and Alan's quarters.

"Come in," Marla yelled.

Lina entered. Instead of her lab coat for this visit, she wore old jeans and a zip-up sweatshirt, with her ponytail held by a pink band. Today she wanted to look like the plain Tacoma girl she was; no illusions of prestige.

Marla was in the middle of bills, from the look of the paperwork on her desk and the spreadsheet on her computer screen. She took off her bifocals and blinked at Lina. "Hey, kiddo. What's up?"

Lina sat down in the same armchair where she had learned Ren's criminal history. "There's something I want to tell you."

Marla swiveled her desk chair to face Lina. "Okay. Shoot."

"I wasn't fully honest when I interviewed here." Lina spread her palms on her knees and stared at the backs of her hands. "The reason I left Everglade was...I accidentally gave a patient the wrong medication. He died."

Marla said nothing, so Lina added, "His family didn't press charges. The hospital was willing to keep me on. But I couldn't get over what I did. So I left."

"God almighty! That's terrible!"

Lina nodded. Her pulse pounded in her temples. "Now that you know, I'll understand if...well, whatever you think is best."

"Lina, you nut." Lina looked up. Marla was staring at her with a mix of concern and exasperation. "I *meant,* it's terrible what you must have gone through. *You* aren't terrible. It was an accident, right?"

"Of course, but..."

"So that's all? That's what you came to say?"

"Yes, but shouldn't you..."

Marla put her glasses back on and cocked an eyebrow. "Kiddo, if you want out of this place, you're going to have to up and leave on your own. I'm not going to fire you, and certainly not over a thing like that. You're a hell of a good nurse."

Lina hadn't realized it, but Marla's simple statement of confidence in her was all she had wanted to hear. Tears filled her eyes. She gripped her knees to keep from crying. "You sure?"

"Sure, I'm sure. The way they run you poor souls ragged at those big hospitals, I'm surprised these things don't happen every minute. Don't beat yourself up."

"Thank you." Lina swallowed. "I thought you should know."

"Things'll get easier, kiddo." Marla regarded her over the top of her bifocals. "Hey. Can I trust you with a new duty?"

Lina blinked to keep the tears from spilling. "Okay."

Marla opened a polished black box on her desk, counted out a small stack of dollar bills, and handed them to Lina. "The first drawer on the right, inside the kitchen, under the breakfast bar. That's the candy drawer. You keep it stocked, you hear?"

Lina laughed, wiping her eyes. She folded the money and put it in her pocket. "All right."

"Good stuff only, now. Chocolate. Come in for petty cash when it gets low." Marla winked.

****

Lina's mood improved slowly as the days lengthened, but winter still reigned both outside and in. The ghost activity stayed quiet, so at least she relaxed for a while on that front. On the other— speaking to Ren—she planned to try again, just a few polite words to test the waters. Despite his brush-off, her curiosity and tenderness built up day by day, because hadn't he thrown her a tiny crumb of hope? Wasn't there at least a "Please save me" under all the "Leave me alone"? The more she thought about their past conversations, the more convinced of it she became.

She watched him on a February morning at the breakfast bar as he refilled her coffee without asking. He had taken to doing that lately, perhaps to show he did still like her, as he once promised over the phone.

"Ren," she said.

He paused. "Yes?"

"I just wondered..." She slipped her finger into the mug's handle. "Do we have any half-and-half?" Definitely not what she wondered, but it would do for now.

He nodded. "I'll bring it."

"Thank you."

He brought it, she thanked him again, and that was the end, but it was the first conversation they'd shared since she had confronted him in the basement, and she breathed much easier for it.

Her improved mood lasted only a few hours. An

email that evening from Brent brought it crashing right back down.

Again the message was sent to his entire address book.

Hello friends and folks!

Well, some of you already heard and some are going to be really mad at me, but Joanne and I couldn't wait. We got married on Saturday at the courthouse. That's right, the deed is done! We're busy house-hunting now, and then we're going to take a week-long honeymoon in the Bahamas, but we're hoping to have a little party to celebrate after that. I know it's a long way but if anyone wants to fly out we'd love to see you! Also, no gifts are required, but since her family insisted we did register at a couple places. I put the links below. Hope you're all as happy as we are!

Best,

Brent and Joanne

Lina hadn't expected it to hurt. She couldn't figure out why it should hurt. But, oh, it did hurt. She turned off the computer, grabbed her overcoat and purse, and stumbled out into the night.

Or was it rage? She walked the bustling, chilly sidewalks near the University, past neon signs, rumbling cars, loud music, and trendy shops. It felt like rage in a way—a tightness in the chest, a desire to scream, yell, and hit someone. But grief often felt like that too, didn't it?

She wanted to get herself a treat, a consolation. Expensive chocolate? Cosmetics? A new outfit? All too clichéd. A book? Too boring. She lifted her head and found she was outside a liquor store. She smiled sardonically and went in. Might as well pour herself into the Zuendel family mold.

It was starting to rain when she got back to the

house with her paper bag. Dinner had been over for an hour—she missed it—and the kitchen and dining room were deserted. Lina wriggled out of her coat near the breakfast bar, set her bottle of ruby port on the counter, and went into the kitchen to fetch a tumbler.

She poured herself some port, and carried the drink to the steel-doored refrigerator in the pantry to scrounge some leftovers. "Least I'm not stupid enough to drink without food," she muttered between sips. "Even if I am drinking alone." She spotted a foil-covered tray on the fridge's top shelf—probably the remainder of the pasta casserole that had been on tonight's dinner menu. She tried to reach it on tiptoe, realized it would be a two-handed operation, and set her drink on the counter to tug down the tray. It slid forward, heavier than she expected, and she cursed, stumbling backward, ducking her head in expectation of casserole raining down upon her.

But the tray stopped before tipping over. Someone else caught it, someone with warm arms right above her ears, a white-shirted someone who smelled masculine and familiar.

"Careful," Ren grunted, heaving the tray onto the counter. "Jeez."

"Oh. Hi." She felt like an idiot, then decided it didn't matter. Ren already knew she was an idiot. Most people did, really. She sighed and peeled back the casserole's foil. "Thank you." She shoveled some of the pasta-and-vegetable mixture into a bowl, and pushed the bowl into the microwave. As the food heated, she swigged her port. "Some days call for pasta and alcohol. You know?"

"Sure."

She tapped her forehead. "Where are my manners? You want some port? I know you're old enough." She said the last sentence with irony, now that she knew he was probably closer to thirty than twenty. Still looked younger than her, though. Lucky so-and-so.

He shook his head and leaned on the door frame. "No thanks."

"Suit yourself." The microwave beeped. Lina took her food to the breakfast bar and sat down. "So, we're talking again, I take it."

"Looked like you could use a listener."

"You'll listen to me, but you won't talk about yourself?"

"Something like that."

She shrugged, loading pasta onto her fork. "There are worse guys in the world, I guess."

A smile flickered on his lips. "Bad day?"

Lina swallowed a bite of casserole and washed it down with port. "Oh, not really. I'm just wondering whether I should buy a wedding present for a guy who, less than a year ago, was my boyfriend."

Ren winced. He walked over, opened the candy drawer, took out a handful of chocolates wrapped in Valentine-colored foil, and placed them on the counter in front of her.

She laughed, then put her face in her hands. "I'm pathetic."

"No, you're not. We've all had days like this."

"People have left you and gotten married to someone else?" Her skepticism came through in her voice.

"Yes." He sounded calm.

She let her hands drop, and took up her fork again. "Oh, I suppose it could be. You're..." Not twenty-two. She didn't say it, though. She no longer felt like pointing out his mistakes and half-truths. She didn't know his whole story, and anyway, she missed him. His presence and kindness comforted her. In addition, he was really adorable. She pushed aside that last thought and said, "Please, won't you have some port? Or food, or something? I don't want to feel like you're the bartender and I'm the complaining drunk on the barstool."

He shrugged, walked around the counter, and hopped onto the stool beside her. He unwrapped a miniature Mr. Goodbar and took a bite. "Mm. This is better. I agree."

"Thank you." Lina ate another forkful of creamy pasta.

"So. The doctor's getting married."

She nodded. "Brent."

"And you want him back?" Ren folded up the red foil wrapper.

Lina slurped her port and thumped the tumbler down. "No. That's the stupid part. I don't want him back. But I'm mad, I'm upset, I'm...I'm a loser."

"Why are you a loser?"

"Because...he won. I lost."

Ren glanced aside at her, smiling. "It wasn't a race. And you aren't a loser."

"He dropped me, went to Atlanta, got true love and a Bahama honeymoon and an obscene pay raise, and instead of going with him I stayed here and got nothing." Lina shoved her empty pasta bowl away and grabbed a mini Hershey bar.

"Wouldn't say nothing." Ren peeled off the wrapper from another chocolate. "Gary seems like a nice guy."

She didn't understand for a moment, then laughed. "I'm sure his girlfriend agrees."

"Oh. You're not..."

"I'm not with Gary." Her port glass was empty. She poured more. "Didn't even get a chance." She sipped the drink. "See? Loser."

He shook his head, swallowing a bite of chocolate. "Got to stop saying that."

"Why? I am a loser. I screw things up. I'm clumsy. There's nobody I'm really close to. I'm not witty or clever or funny." She thought of the laughing hospital staff watching her collision with Sara, and added, "Except unintentionally."

Ren chuckled. "That remark was funny."

"See? I didn't mean it to be."

"That one was too."

Lina groaned, folded her arms on the counter, and rested her forehead on them.

Ren's fingers stroked her ear, smoothing her hair away from her face. Her eardrums began to ring in pleasant shock, but she still caught his every word. "I shouldn't say this or do this. But if it makes you feel better, I like you." His voice was low, and it accelerated the delicious dizziness in her veins that the alcohol had ignited. "And I know I'm not the only one. You'll be happy again someday, much happier than your brainless doctor."

Lina raised her head. He was close to her, watching her, leaning on the counter while his hand slid down her neck, along the collar of her old gray long-sleeved T-shirt, fixing the tags maybe.

Oh! No, not fixing tags—he was caressing her. Maybe *seducing* her. She realized it in a flash, and also realized that it was exactly what she wanted. With courage that could only have come from the port, she snared his neck in one arm, hauled him toward her, and dove in for a kiss.

Their lips tangled; he was kissing her right back—and within two seconds, of course, she fell off her stool. But that didn't matter. Ren caught her, tugged her up against him, and went on kissing her. His mouth teased her lips apart; she tasted peanuts and chocolate on his tongue; his arms wound tight around her, his long hands squeezing and stroking. Without meaning to she emitted a whimper of surprise and happiness, and he echoed it, injecting what sounded like desire.

As suddenly as they had started, they stopped.

Or rather, Ren stopped. He slid away and hopped onto the floor, holding her at arm's length. She stared at him, dazed. He stared back, breathing fast, cheeks and mouth flushed.

"Bad idea," he said. "Tempting, so tempting—but bad."

Her head spun. "Bad? Why?"

"I can't. You—you need to be with someone other than me."

"I don't want anyone else."

"You need to be with someone who can leave the house."

"That doesn't matter. I'm happy staying here if you're here. Besides, you'll be able to leave someday, right?"

"I don't know. I—" He paced away. "Please, let's just forget it."

"Can't you tell me..."

"There are things you don't know. Things I can't tell you. I'm sorry, Lina, I'm really sorry, but—"

"There are things you don't know about me too. At Everglade, I—"

"I know about the man who died. Marla told me. It doesn't matter; no one should hold that against you." He glanced at her as he paced. "Don't be mad. I asked her about you; I wanted to know. I—" He put both hands on his head and swiveled away. "I like you, I wish I could help you, but this isn't the way."

"Talk to me. Please."

He looked at the ceiling with what appeared to be misery, then turned away. "I need to go out."

"Where? Where can you go?"

"Just...outside." He was nearly to the pantry door already. His eyes widened when he looked back. "You should go out, too."

Puzzled, she frowned. "Why? What do you—"

"Look out!"

Even as he spoke, the port bottle flew across the

kitchen and shattered. Lina leaped off the stool. "What in the..."

"Don't stop." His voice throbbed with urgency. "Don't even go clean it up. Go. Go *out*."

Lina stared at him. He waved her away with a flap of his hand, and rushed out. She heard the back door open and close. Stung, frightened, half-drunk, and not wishing to be left alone with the poltergeist, Lina seized her coat and ran the opposite way, out the front door and into the winter night.

He doesn't like me as much as I thought he did, was the juvenile, pointless sentence that repeated itself in her head as she walked around the neighborhood, holding her coat's hood up against the drizzle and wind. He would kiss her—once—but he wouldn't stay with her. Nobody would stay with her. Oh, he was a special case, probably a criminal; she shouldn't be so depressed and bewildered over him. But, of course, she was. On top of that, she lived in a nerve-wracking old house where objects liked to throw themselves around at inopportune moments— not that any moment was a great time for a ghost to throw things around. And in the basement of this eerie house lurked Ren, beautiful, mysterious Ren, who seemed to know *something* about the ghost activity but wouldn't say what, along with a thousand other things he wouldn't say.

If only she knew what exactly had happened to him, maybe she would feel better, or at least understand. Maybe. And she needed something to make her feel better because, dear heavens, it wasn't fair to be torn away from such a good kisser after just a few seconds.

****

It would be idiotic to stop talking to each other again, she thought; and when she went downstairs at 7:30 the next morning, she was determined to say hello to him despite the pounding in her eye sockets.

He and the cook were there already, preparing the day's meals. Lina's stomach flip-flopped at the sight of him, but she pressed forward. She had Mrs. B's oatmeal to prepare, if nothing else.

"Morning," he said.

Some of her muscles relaxed. Good, he was speaking to her. "Hi." She cleared her throat and took down the box of oats. "Any glass left to clean up?"

"Nope. I got it."

"Thank you."

The cook thwacked a head of lettuce in half with a knife. Lina cringed at the sound. Ren smiled at her, very briefly, and Lina felt better. He continued assembling salad. She took the oatmeal upstairs.

Still, an occasional smile and civil conversation didn't quite constitute the blissful relationship a woman dreamed of having. The puzzle of who Ren was, and why he acted the way he did, nagged at her every waking moment, and in dreams too. Every few nights now, as February progressed and spring approached, Ren kissed her in her dreams, touched her, tore clothes off her, and tumbled with her onto all manner of luxurious surfaces. Lina was, in short, losing her mind with frustration and longing.

When she happened to bump into him on the front staircase one afternoon, she halted him and said, "Um, I was thinking."

"Yes?"

"I'd just like to talk to you, and try to understand."

He spread his palm on the wall and bowed his head. "Talking is more than I should do. I'm sorry." He tried to move past.

She stepped into his path. "Please. I just want to know what's wrong. Last chance."

"Last chance before what?"

"Before I stop asking you."

"I'm afraid you're best off not asking, then." He glanced at her with what looked like regret, and slipped past.

Fine. I only said I'd stop asking you, she thought. *I didn't say I'd stop trying to find out.*

She spent all her free time the next week on the Internet, scouring for any mention of his name or any arrest record that sounded like his. Google and its peers turned up nothing. She considered hiring a private investigator, but couldn't bring herself to call one; she recoiled from the idea as she would from picking up a worm with her bare hands.

Not until Valentine's Day, as she saw him writing at the breakfast bar, did the obvious solution strike her: that journal. What he wrote in there must give some clue about his secrets. Surely it wasn't all grocery lists and poetry—and even if it was poetry, that would provide clues too. The question was, how did she get hold of the journal? It wouldn't be ethical of her to read it without his permission. Would she look into it anyway if she had the chance?

Damn right she would. Curiosity and confusion tormented her; and anyway, by kissing and fondling her instead of pushing her directly away, he had given her some kind of right to know about him. Or such was the excuse she invented to ease her mind.

So how would she get a look into the journal? She mulled over the problem in the laundry room as she hauled wet clothes into the dryer and started up the washer for a new load. He locked his room, and she didn't want to break in—not that she would know how. Those hairpin and credit-card tricks never worked in real life. Then how...?

A thump from the wall startled her. She turned, but didn't see anything unusual. The laundry detergent was not dancing in the air by itself, as she rather feared it might be. Anyway, the sound had come from the other side of the wall, and it hadn't been particularly ghostly. It had sounded more like something falling over.

She shut the lids of the washer and dryer, and ventured out into the basement corridor. On the other side of the wall was a large storage area, dim, grimy, and musty-smelling, with crowded plywood shelves sagging under old boxes and crates. Heaven only knew how long some of this stuff had been down here, Lina thought, noticing the accumulation of dust. Though the light was feeble, trickling in from one tiny dirt-smeared window, she discovered what had made the sound. A large cardboard box lay on the floor on its side.

This needn't be supernatural, she reasoned, and approached it. Things fell off shelves sometimes. Contents shifted; the house's inhabitants and machinery made the shelves vibrate; and, after years of living together, a box and its shelf parted company. Lina pushed away images of long-hidden human bones, and knelt beside the box.

The top flaps had once been held shut with clear packing tape, but the decades had yellowed it and robbed it of its glue, and it had given way; the flaps now fell open. Lina spotted the corner of a picture frame inside, with balled-up newspaper used as padding. Dreading the spiders and mice that might have moved into the box, she nudged a wad of newspaper out of the way, and when no spiders went skittering forth, she took hold of the picture frame and pulled it out.

The picture was so large it took up one whole side of the box. Almost two feet wide and a foot tall, it was what the sororities called a composite: a frame containing the head-and-shoulders portrait of every girl in the house in a given year. The year in this case was the school year 1934-1935. It was written in fancy calligraphy beneath the words

"Gamma Eta Omicron" in the center.

It didn't take her long to find Julia Grise. It was the same photo used in the newspaper articles, but much clearer here. Now Lina detected the shine in Julia's eyes, the twinkle of a necklace beneath the collar of her blouse. She practically felt on her own head the weight of those thick blonde tresses gathered around the ears and brow. A survey of the two dozen other faces brought Lina to the conclusion that Julia had indeed been the most beautiful girl in the house.

A row above, Lina found the other name and face she would have heard of. Jacqueline Jackson, now Jackie Clairmont. Jackie was not Julia's equal in beauty. Her eyes and cheeks were a bit puffy, her face a bit jowly, her hair a bit dry. Still, her smile was frank and amiable, and softened Lina toward old Jackie. She even considered bringing the composite upstairs with her to show Mrs. Clairmont, but then decided it might not be a good idea. She didn't want to stir up unpleasant memories.

Lina propped the composite against a shelf and looked deeper into the box. She found old university-theater playbills, programs for commencement ceremonies, and several envelopes of photos. She opened one. The envelope was falling apart, but the photos inside were clean and glossy, black and white with wavy cut edges. She flipped through them, stopping now and then to gaze at a familiar room or part of the garden. Most of the photos had writing on the back, in that spindly hand everyone seemed to have had in the early twentieth century, spelling out vague descriptions like *Spring Fling* or *Dressing for the Valentine Play*. She found one taken in the dining room—*Monday Night Dinner*—and stared at it. She brought it closer to her eyes and tilted it toward the light.

Five girls sat at the table, smiling, hands in

their laps—no one she recognized; no Julia or Jackie. All of them appeared to be wearing white. China and crystal gleamed on the tabletop. The wallpaper was different than it was now. But none of those things interested her at the moment. She studied the houseboy with the silver water pitcher in his hand. He stood behind the table in profile, as if turning to leave. She knew that stance, that figure, that clipped dark hair, those shoulders in a button-down white shirt. She would have recognized them anywhere.

So this was Sean Reynolds. It had to be. No wonder Jackie Clairmont flipped her lid upon seeing Ren for the first time; Ren was a dead ringer for the late Sean. Of course, Sean's face in this photo was smaller than her thumbnail; Lina's imagination could have been filling in the details. Still, she set the photo aside, deciding to keep it for now. It was interesting, if nothing else.

Her knees hurt from crouching on the floor, and she heard someone coming down the stairs from the kitchen. She put the composite and the other items back into the box, heaved it onto its shelf, and walked back into the corridor, carrying the photo.

Ren's door was open. Light spilled from his room onto the concrete floor. He must have been the one whose footsteps she had just heard. She moved quietly, curious to get a look inside those sacred quarters. The room slid into view as she approached. A tiny chamber, six feet square, with walls painted pale green, and unpainted wooden beams as a ceiling. In the second she had to look at it, she also saw a tidily made bed against one wall, a desk with a laptop computer, old dark-red curtains concealing a window near the ceiling, and a surprising number of bookshelves. Ren placed the journal onto one of these shelves, next to scores of books similar to it.

Lina prepared to speak up, show him the photo, use it as an icebreaker. But he sensed her standing there and his glance snapped toward her with the closest thing to hostility she had ever seen on his face. His meaning could not have been clearer if he'd said, "Stay out." So she muttered "Hey," and slipped away, back to her laundry. *Guess that kiss hadn't guaranteed any soft feelings after all,* she thought, wounded.

But she barely had time to think it. She opened the laundry room door, and shrieked, raising her hand to cover her mouth. Her wet clothes, torn out of washer and dryer both, were flung all over the room. Crumpled in corners, snagged on the tops and sides of the machines, dangling from the shelves and the doorknob. She had not heard it happen; there had been no footsteps until Ren's just a minute ago. He hadn't had time to do it, despite that hostile look.

And her shriek brought him running; evidently dropping the unfriendliness in the face of alarm, he appeared beside her and sucked in a breath when he saw the clothes everywhere.

"I'm going to assume you didn't do this," he said.

"And I'm going to assume *you* didn't."

"You assume correctly." He stepped into the room. "Do you need help, or..."

"No." Even in the wake of the scare, she foresaw the embarrassment of him helping pick up her soggy underwear.

"Are you sure? I—"

He was stopped by the sound of a crash and a howl from upstairs.

"Someone fell," Lina gasped, rushing for the stairs. Ren followed at her heels.

They ran up past the breakfast bar and into the dining room. Jackie Clairmont lay on her side on the hardwood floor, struggling to get up. Marla and Alan held her arms and told her not to move. The serving girls fluttered around looking frightened, and two dazed seniors watched from the nearest table.

"Someone pushed me!" Mrs. Clairmont insisted. "I was pushed!"

"No one was near her," said Consuela.

Lina looked at Ren, the only person she had told about the shove on the stairs. He looked back at her, uneasily.

"I know, honey," Marla assured Consuela. "Now, Jackie, you just hold still, all right? We don't want you to hurt yourself getting up too fast." She turned. "Ren, call nine-one-one, will you?"

He nodded and dashed away.

"I was pushed!" Mrs. Clairmont said. "She pushed me! I told her I was sorry!"

Goosebumps rose on Lina's limbs. She knelt near Marla, and did her best to help soothe Mrs. Clairmont and discover where it hurt. Soon the medics arrived, a familiar flashback to Lina's hospital days with their strong, efficient voices and their smell of sterilized sheets and latex gloves. They decided to take Mrs. Clairmont away to X-ray her hip; naturally one did not want to take chances with the elderly. They lifted Mrs. Clairmont onto a stretcher; Marla held her hand and walked beside her, talking to her.

At the curb Marla peered out the back doors of the ambulance at Lina. "Make sure Mrs. B doesn't get the gossip all wrong, you hear?" She winked. Lina nodded. A medic shut the doors, and the ambulance pulled away.

Lina looked up at the gray sky, down at the perpetually wet sidewalk, shivered, and walked back inside to take care of her scattered laundry.

The line of light falling on the basement's concrete floor stopped her. Ren had not closed his door. In all the commotion, he had probably forgotten.

A wicked idea jumped to mind. She looked around, then crept down the hall and slipped inside the small room. It smelled like Ren in here, though she didn't know she would recognize his smell. It was a scent made up of cooking ingredients (butter, flour, spices, sauces), mint gum, fruity gum, bubble gum, books, papers, cotton sheets, and the cologne he had worn on Halloween. She took a deep breath, dizzy with the memory of dancing with him, kissing him.

But she had no time to stand and daydream. She was here without permission; and to judge from his defensive glance earlier, he wouldn't give his permission if she asked. So she stepped up to those shelves of journals—for that was what they all looked like, now that she examined them; journals and other blank books, all marked on their spines with the white ink used in college libraries. The markings were numbers, like 030197 100597. After looking along the three rows of books, she saw the pattern. They were dates. The last two digits were the year ('97, for instance), and the first four were the month and day. The earliest volume, highest up, covered March 9, 1986 (030986) to April 12, 1987 (041287). The latest, at the far end on the bottom shelf, had just one date (082003), because, of course, it hadn't been finished yet.

She swallowed, looked out in the hallway again, then grabbed the most recent one. When she opened it she experienced a strange moment of thinking she had forgotten how to read. Then she thought it might be a language they made up for *Star Trek*.

QRDII KL PGDK CTPT. RCTVPT QGVDKB RCDQ QZJJTP CGQ HTTK ZKZQZGIIV SPV. D OGK HTIDTYT DR. D GJ GORZGIIV XDQCDKB DR XLZIS PGDK GBGDK. TYTPV XDKRTP D BTR RDPTS LA RCT PGDK, GKS TYTPV QZJJTP D JDQQ DR. BZTQQ D'J G CGPS LKT RT MITGQT. VTQRTPSGV TYTKDKB XGQ QILX CTPT, QG

RCTV ITR JT BL LZR ALP RCT KDBCR. D
OGZBCR G HZQ GOPLQQ RLXK RL OGPFTTF
MGPF, GKS QGR RCTPT XGROCDKB RCT QZK
QTR. RCTPT XTPT GORZGIIV FDSQ QXDJJDKB
DK MZBTR QLZKS. D'J KLR QZPT DR XGQ
NZDRT XGPJ TKLZBC RL OLKYDKOT JT RL SL
RCGR, TYTK DA D OLZIS.

It went on like that for the whole book.

Not a foreign language. A code. Lina flipped to
the front inside cover, and then to the back, but
found no tidy alphabet lining up traditional letters
with code letters. Even with such a guide, she
wouldn't have had time to decode it while standing
there.

Frustrated, she put it back, but couldn't bring
herself to give up and leave. She wanted to take one
of the books and try her hand at cracking the code,
even though that would mean stealing.
Unfortunately, the one she really wanted was the
latest one, because he might mention her in it; but if
she took that one he would certainly notice.

Time for a decision. Footsteps came and went
over her head, in the dining room. He was bound to
come down again any minute. She hedged and
fidgeted and finally pulled down an older book
(2/21/94 - 5/10/95), rearranged the surrounding
volumes so he might not notice the gap on the shelf,
and hurried out into the corridor, hugging the
journal to her chest. Gary did say summer of '94 was
when Annette had worked here, didn't he? Yes, she
was almost sure of it. Maybe, then, if she couldn't
read about herself, she might at least learn
something about Ren and Annette.

In the laundry room she dropped the book and
the old photo into her basket, and pulled all her wet
clothes from their scattered locations. She threw
them back into the washing machine, started it up

again, and took her laundry basket and the journal up the stairs, jogging fast and not stopping on any of the landings. She rounded the corner in the third floor hallway and almost ran into Alan.

"Whoa, careful there!" He smiled.

"Sorry." She tried to catch her breath.

"You look worried. You okay?"

"Yeah—just, you know, concerned for Mrs. Clairmont."

"Sounds like she'll be okay. Marla went with her; she'll let us know."

"Thanks, Alan." She moved past him toward her door.

"Sure you're all right?"

"Yes. Thank you. Really."

He smiled again, waved at her, and went away.

She shut her door and opened the journal.

ATH RXTKRV LKT. GKLRCTP YTPV OLIS SGV CTPT. D RCDKF TYTPVLKT'Q QRGPRDKB RL BTR XCGR RCT MGMTPQ CGYT HTTK OGIIDKB QTGQLKGI GAATORDYT SDQLPSTP. XT OLZIS ZQT QLJT QZKQCDKT GKS XGPJRC. TYTK ALP JR DR'Q HTTK STMPTQQDKB. G QRTM LZRQDST RCT IDKTQ LKIV PTYDYTQ JT ALP GHLZR GK CLZP.

Right.

But Lina Zuendel, enthusiast of the *New York Times* crossword puzzle, was no stranger to cryptograms, assuming she had a cryptogram here. She knew a thing or two about solving them. She had just never solved one so *big* before.

Much as she wanted to get started on it, she had to photocopy it first. She needed to be able to pencil in possible letters above the script, and erase them and try new ones when those didn't pan out, and she couldn't do that on the original without making a mess.

And now, of course, it was dinnertime.

Reluctantly she slipped the journal into a desk drawer, hiding it under a box of stationery, as if anyone would be going through her drawers looking for it.

Of course, in this house, you never knew.

Chapter Eight

"Jackie is okay," Marla told Lina and the rest of their table at dinner. "Her hip's not broken. But she'll be staying at the hospital for a couple days, and she told me she wants to move out after that."

"Oh, what a shame!" Ethel said.

Marla shook her head and ate a forkful of green beans. "Crazy. We got a waiting list for this place a mile long. Doesn't she know that?"

"She had a personal history with the house," Mrs. B said. "It must have all been too much in the end."

"Yeah," Marla said. "This house doesn't happily let go of its past. I'll grant you that."

"She said someone pushed her," Lina said, gaze fixed on her turkey meatloaf. "A 'she.'"

"Really!" said Betty Carter.

"Probably her imagination," Marla said.

Lina only shrugged, and flicked bits of meatloaf apart with her fork.

"I bet it was the ghost," Mrs. B said to Lina as they returned upstairs. "I bet it was her old friend Julia. Remember, it was partly Jackie's fault, what happened to that houseboy. She said she helped Julia come up with the sleeping pill idea."

"I'm sure they didn't mean to kill him. At least, I hope not."

"Oh, I'm sure you're right. But it could lead to a ghost being rather resentful, all the same."

"I guess."

"I wish that ghost would quit throwing things and pushing people, and just tell us what it wants," said Mrs. B.

Lina agreed. She most definitely agreed.

When she returned to her own room, she walked to the desk, switched on the lamp, and leaned over to examine the old photo from the basement. There sat girls in puffy white dresses and outdated hair, with Sean Reynolds turning away behind them—Sean, the slain boy, who had never even lived long enough to see World War II.

Sad now rather than scared, she slumped down into the chair. She rested her cheek on her hand, gazing upon the lost youth. "Did you want me to find this? Is that what you wanted, for some reason?"

As usual, nobody answered.

****

The next day she took the journal to a copy shop and stood at a photocopier for half an hour, turning each page and pressing the open journal down against the glass, looking around furtively as if Ren would walk in and see what she was doing. Silly thing to worry about, considering he was not allowed to leave the house, but she still felt guilty. After paying for the copies and getting them tucked into a paper bag, she hurried home and put the original journal back into the desk drawer.

She sharpened a pencil, spread out a sheet of scratch paper, and stared at the first page. The groupings of code letters—the words, if such they were—seemed of ordinary length and variance for English. They ranged from one letter to ten or twelve long, suggesting he simply transcribed regular words into their exact counterparts in a jumbled-up alphabet, and didn't regroup them to encode them further.

English only has two common one-letter words: *I* and *a*. In Ren's coded pages, she found two characters that repeatedly showed up as single-letter words: G and D. This suggested that either

G=I and D=A, or vice-versa (G=A, D=I); she would have to try both options.

Lina rolled her shoulders, flexed her knuckles, and started hunting out Gs on the first page.

By dinnertime, two hours later, she was pretty sure that G=A, D=I, and furthermore that Q=S and T=E. One of the other tricks for solving cryptograms was to count frequency of characters. These pages sported a lot of Ts, and since E is the most frequently occurring letter in written English, T=E seemed a good bet. Her assumption that Q=S came from the apostrophe rule: Ren's Q sometimes appeared after an apostrophe, at the end of a word, as the letter S in regular English often does.

With her guesses penciled in above the original text, the first few lines of the photocopy now read as an odd assortment of the letters E, A, I, and S.

```
_E_ _E___ _E. A___E_ _E__ ____A_ _E_E.
   I __I__ E_E___E'S S_A_I__ __ _E_ __A_ __E
_A_E_S
   _A_E _EE_ _A_I__ SEAS_A_ A_E__I_E
_IS__E_.
```

Still not what you would call legible. She stuffed the papers into a drawer and went down to eat. At dinner, while listening to the others talk about Jackie Clairmont's accident, Lina kept an eye on Ren, the walking enigma. Was he a criminal who had done horrible things? Was he a victim of circumstance, wrongly accused? Was he hiding here for his own safety? Was he merely a kid who enjoyed writing in code and lying? And what the hell was his actual age, anyway?

He slipped her a glance from two tables away as he set down a basket of bread. Though the glance lasted less than a second, she felt a shock through all her limbs. She gulped some water and stared at the crochet-work of the tablecloth. She hoped he hadn't noticed the missing volume, hoped his glance hadn't carried suspicion or accusation. Now it was she who was hiding things from him. Did this make them even?

After dinner, Lina sat down with a bag of Valentine candies and sharpened the pencil again. She took a yellow heart from the bag and read the message on it: U R SWEET.

HOW OLD R U?, she thought, smiling, and popped it into her mouth. She spread her makeshift alphabet legend beside the photocopy, and gazed at Ren's handwriting again, waiting for inspiration to strike.

That word *CTPT*, for which she had replaced E for T and gotten *_E_E*, snagged her eye. Words ending in that pattern often had an R between the E's—here, were, mere. Worth a try. On her alphabet legend, she penciled in *P* beside *R*, and tried it out in the first paragraph.

   _E_ __E___ __E. A___ER _ER_ ____A_ _ERE.
   I __I__ E_ER___E'S S_AR_I__ __ _E_ __A_ __E
_A_ERS
   _A_E _EE_ _A_I__ SEAS_A_ A_E__I_E
_IS_R_ER.

So far, so good. The substitution hadn't created any impossible clusters of letters. She then tried H for C, to turn *CTPT* into *here*. Again, nothing impossible. C=H could stay. She zeroed in on the word *RCT*, which she had turned into *_he*. She had already assigned S to another letter, so this word couldn't be *she*. That left *the* as the likeliest contender. To the legend she added the formula R=T, and added T's above all the R's on the first paragraph.

Excited, she grabbed another candy heart and

crunched it between her molars. This was definitely starting to resemble English. Speaking of starting, that was a good bet for the word in the middle of the second line. She filled in phrases here and there: *I think, starting to get what the, have been.* F=K, L=O, X=W, Y=V, H=B.

    EB TWENT ONE. ANOTHER VER_ _O__ _A_ HERE.
    I THINK EVER_ONE'S STARTING TO GET WHAT THE _A_ERS
    HAVE BEEN _A__ING SEAS_NA_ A__E_TIVE _ISOR_ER.

She stared at the last three words of the paragraph, then got it: *seasonal affective disorder.* She penciled those in, filled in the same letters elsewhere, made a few more educated guesses, and soon had the whole paragraph decoded. Heart beating in triumph and excitement, she sat back and read:

Feb twenty-one. Another very cold day here. I think everyone's starting to get what the papers have been calling Seasonal Affective Disorder.

"Oh, Ren, I have you now," she whispered.
After working through the first three pages she had the entire alphabet decoded. She focused on the text as it emerged, and therefore didn't notice right away what the key itself had spelled. But in the middle of a sentence, Lina glanced aside at the alphabet key on her scratch paper, and experienced a shock at seeing a hidden word there. The code began:

A=G
B=H

C=O
D=S
E=T

The left-hand column represented ordinary English, and the right-hand column represented Ren's code. When Ren wrote the journal, every time he needed an A he substituted a G, and and so on. However, only now did Lina see that the first five letters of the right-hand column spelled *GHOST*.

Why had it frightened her? In a house like this, *ghost* was a logical word to build a code around. (It looked as if he had just used the rest of the alphabet in its normal order after that, reversing the last six letters so they wouldn't correspond to their twins.) After a few seconds she returned to the decoding. No use letting one word disturb her.

But her gaze kept drifting to the photo pushed to the corner of her desk, the shot of the Depression-era houseboy who still looked like Ren no matter how often she studied it in search of a difference. Was Sean Reynolds the ghost in this house? And did Ren feel an affinity with him? Were they in some kind of communion? Now that would be creepy.

Well, if such was the case, then he probably mentioned it somewhere in the 150 pages of this journal. She had best keep decoding.

****

Ren in late winter and early spring of 1994 shared many qualities with Ren in 2004, she decided the next morning, having deciphered the first ten pages of the journal. When she had stolen it, she had considered the idea that maybe Ren didn't write it; maybe some of the journals were written by other people. She couldn't imagine who, but the older ones from the 1980s, at least, had to be someone else's work. Houseboy chronicles through the ages?

But this particular journal sure *sounded* like

Ren. For instance, she found occasional references to going "outside the lines," slipping out of the bounds of his house arrest for a breath of freedom. He hadn't called it house arrest, though, nor had he referred to any particular crime. When writing for oneself, of course, there was no need to be specific about major events of the past. You already knew what you'd done.

The strange thing was that he did seem to go outside the boundaries of the house, miles beyond the alley. In one entry he wrote of walking around downtown; in another he mentioned exploring Discovery Park in the Magnolia neighborhood. All right, people on parole did get permission to go out now and then. So why did Marla and Ren make it sound like he couldn't leave the house at all? Had he done something worse since 1994 to confine him more strictly?

She put away the cryptogram and went to the window, pressing her hands to her lower back to stretch her spine. Below, in the cool winter sun, Ren knelt in the garden, clearing fallen twigs and leaves from the flowerbeds to let the crocuses and daffodils come up.

Tending to crocus sprouts—not really the activity you'd expect to find a drug-runner doing. But considering he was in the front garden in full view of passers-by, it wasn't really the kind of behavior you'd expect in someone who was hiding from the law, either. Puzzling guy, truly puzzling.

A clatter made her spin around. Her cup of pens and pencils had fallen over on the desk. She looked around, muscles tensed, though of course no one was there. No one was ever there.

****

The mystery did not become any clearer, the farther she went into her decoding. He still wrote of leaving the house, even going so far as to catch a ferry to Bainbridge Island once. He always seemed to be alone on these expeditions, and there was no explanation as to how he got permission to leave.

Not until an entry from June 27, 1994, did she get the first mention of Annette. *We have a live-in summer temp from the U helping us out in the kitchen, name of Annette,* he wrote. *Nice-looking, with an abundance of natural curls and, it seems, already an interest in getting to know me. Sometimes I wonder what the hell Marla is thinking.*

He changed the topic then, leaving Lina curious. Most likely he referred to the bad idea of bringing attractive single girls into his vicinity when he was under house arrest and forbidden to date them. However, it also revived the chance of a romantic involvement between Marla and Ren. Lina sharpened her attention to look for clues along those lines, much as she dreaded finding any.

In the next entry, written a few days later (he was not very regular in his updates), he turned melancholy over an obituary he had read for an elderly man from Port Townsend. He described him as *my old buddy Dan*, and went on to write, *A beautiful wife, three kids, eight grandchildren, travel to Europe every couple years, a big old house on the peninsula. The life I should have had. Well, I suppose I have a big old house, but no one ever asked me if I might like a different big old house, one that wasn't a thing of total and complete evil.*

That was the closest he had come so far to mentioning the hauntings, and it chilled Lina. Maybe he wrote the phrase facetiously, but it didn't strike her that way.

She hadn't wanted to think of the house or its ghosts as evil. She had wanted to believe any existing spirits here were benign, even if they were unsettling. It disturbed her to hear a darker take on it from someone who had lived here longer.

On an afternoon when night fell early due to the heavy clouds and lashing rain, Lina finally decrypted and unraveled the full tale of Ren and Annette. To hear him tell it, he underwent two weeks of interest, conversation, probing, and teasing from the fetching Annette while working alongside her in the kitchen, and fended her off only half-heartedly, since, in his words, *I'm enjoying the attention, though I know I shouldn't. Let's not kid ourselves; these little crushes are what keep me going.*

One July night, Ren was lounging on the roof, and saw Annette walking back to the house. She looked up and asked how he had gotten up there. He told her he'd meet her on the third floor and show her. Long story short, they ended up kissing under the stars, up on the shingles.

The pang of jealousy this delivered to Lina was brutal. Even her bitterness over Brent hadn't felt so agonizing. She took a few minutes away from the journal, doing yoga stretches on the floor with her breath blowing hot against her legs, before she felt calm enough to return to his account.

His description of the rendezvous was, at least, sensible and not dreamy:

She kissed me. Quite a few times actually. It was nice and I think I can say we'll do it again. I've told her Marla will have my hide if I'm found to be romancing a coworker, and therefore we should not be too public about it. She seems content with this. It won't last, of course. How long before she wants to leave the house with me? How to handle it this time? It's never a good idea. I always know it.

Okay, so he *couldn't* leave the house? How did that work, when he was constantly writing about leaving the house?

In any case, the way he dealt with Annette was,

as he put it, "the route of cowardice." When she came to the inevitable point of trying to lure him out for a walk, he made excuses and finally balked. When she asked him to explain, he said she should ask Marla for details.

The old house arrest tale. Isn't it great? Nothing like being labeled a criminal for my own good. Annette is a rather prim thing when it comes to the law and drugs, so naturally she pretty much stopped speaking to me, though of course there was the usual mumble of "You could have told me." No, my girl, I couldn't have. Believe me.

Lina re-read this section, squashing the pencil eraser against her lower lip. The "house arrest tale"? Being "labeled" a criminal? So he *wasn't* under house arrest? Then why was he collaborating with the Drakes to make people think he was? Why wouldn't he leave the house with anyone else, when apparently he could and wanted to?

She pushed away the pages and picked up the photo of Sean Reynolds without knowing why, except that he looked like Ren. She cast back in her memory for any time she had actually seen Ren leave the property. All she recalled was the night he had gone out into the alley and vanished like a...

She gasped. Her gaze flew from Sean's photograph to the word "ghost" embedded in the code alphabet. She dropped the photo onto the desk as if it were contaminated, and stared at it. The idea was ridiculous. She had heard too many ghost stories. They had warped her brain.

But then it was also ridiculous that a phone book would dance in the air, or her clothes would throw themselves around the laundry room, or invisible hands would shove her on the stairs, or magazines would pile themselves upon a sleeping old woman.

Did they tell you about the ghost?

I have an old soul, as they say.

You! What are you doing here? What did you do with Julia?

Reynolds; Ren. Sean; Schultz. Even the names were similar; he just transposed the order. For the first time in her life, Lina Zuendel hoped she was crazy, hoped none of this was true, because if it *was* true, it would be reason enough to go insane.

****

How could she approach him with such a question? How could she ask "What are you?" when all she had originally wanted to know was "Who are you?" Would he even tell the truth if she did ask?

In the unusually mild weather during the last weekend of February, Lina took the photocopied pages onto the third-floor fire escape, where she sat wrapped in her coat, and continued decoding on her lap. She stayed alert for any movement below, hoping Ren would come out and step beyond the fence in broad daylight. The journal suggested there was something forbidding and important about leaving the property.

As she translated further, she became convinced of it. On one occasion in August, he wrote of the nuisance when the bakery truck arrived in the alley for delivery, and the driver wanted Ren to help unload the bread. *But of course I couldn't go past the gate*, he wrote. To get out of it, he invented a malady for himself (a hurt back) and sent Alan out instead. He added, *Not as bad as when that paper boy saw me disappear last October, though*, and changed the subject.

As she re-read that passage she heard a door open below her, and looked down. Ren walked out, rolling his shoulders up and backward as if they ached. He reached the fence, glanced back at the house (though he didn't look upward), and, apparently satisfied that no one was watching,

146

unlatched the gate and stepped out into the alley.

This time she possessed a clear view. This time the sun shone upon his white shirt as it flashed past the fence and winked out of existence. Trap door? Secret passageway? Illusion? Maybe. But for whose benefit, if he thought he was alone?

She stayed where she was, not daring to move, merely waiting for him to return. A few seconds later he rematerialized in the space between gate and fence, pushed through the gate, and closed it. As he walked to the house, he swung his arms freely as if they no longer pained him. He went back inside, and she was left alone.

Lina sat for a long while on the fire escape, not trying to decode the journal anymore. She listened to its pages flutter in the breeze; gazed at the evergreens, roofs, and bell towers of the U District; and wondered how long this miracle had been going on right under everyone's noses.

At dinner she looked up at him when he filled her coffee mug. An entreaty pulsed in her throat, something begging to be said and answered.

He looked at her. "Anything else for you?"

She lowered her face and stared at the pepper grinder. She shook her head.

Chapter Nine

The next morning, the first of March, when she woke up fifteen minutes ahead of her alarm clock and got out of bed because she couldn't sleep any more, she decided today was the day.

Not before Mrs. B's breakfast, which she fetched with only a murmured "Morning" to Ren. Not before her own breakfast, which consisted of drinking a cup of mint tea and licking a spoon dipped in yogurt. Not before her shower, which almost made her feel calm and collected. But then it was time.

She combed back her damp hair, applied a little lipstick and mascara for confidence, put on her favorite green wool cardigan for comfort, and picked up two items: the journal and the photo of Sean Reynolds. She descended the back staircase and approached the breakfast bar. In the mid-morning lull, Ren unrolled plastic wrap over a huge bowl of fruit salad. Behind him, the cook pulled out the pans she would need for lunch.

Ren glanced at Lina. "Hello."

"Hi." Lina sat down, placed the journal and photo on the bar, and folded her hands over them. "Could you come over here when you have a second, please?"

A wary expression touched his face. "Sure. Let me just put this in the fridge." He slipped his arms around the bowl and carried it to the steel-doored refrigerator in the pantry. Lina watched his feet as he went and returned, noting the details: a film of flour near the soles of his shoes, a scuff of dust on the ankle of his trousers. So real.

He came up to the bar, opposite her, and leaned his elbows on it. "Yes?"

She uncovered the journal and set it up to display its spine. "You could have made this code harder to break."

His face changed; flickers of surprise, anger, and confusion raced across it.

"Yes," he said after a few seconds, "but then it would have been harder to write in. It works if you're trying to discourage casual readers. Not cryptographers." On the last word he snatched it away and looked at the spine, then at her. He clearly awaited an explanation. But then, she could say the same.

"Cryptanalyst, actually," she said. "You're the cryptographer—the creator of the code."

"Where did you get this?"

She looked at her hands, spread on the counter over the photo. "From your room. You left the door open once. I apologize; I had no right."

"And you say you translated it?"

"Yes. I cracked your 'ghost' code." She looked at his eyes when she said the word, and thought she saw fear glimmer in them.

"This is from years ago; why would you care?" He sounded distressed now. He flipped through the pages, glancing at the encoded words.

"I want to know who you are and how long you've been here, and why."

"Oh?" He closed the book and smacked it against the edge of the counter. "And did this tell you anything?"

"I think so." Time for Exhibit B. Lina uncovered the photo and turned it around.

He went still as he gazed at it. Then he asked softly, "Where did that come from?"

"A box, in the basement."

He blinked a few times. "Wow. Thought those

were all buried deep."

"Is this you?"

He picked up the photo to study it, dark lashes moving as he took in the details. "This, I'd say...is Sean Reynolds."

"Then that's a yes?"

He let the journal and the photo sink to the countertop. When he looked up at her, the hostility in his eyes was gone, and the wry weariness in its place shot a thrill through her. He was older than twenty-two, no question; far older. How had she missed it until now?

"Marla isn't going to come save me this time, is she?" Ren remarked.

"It's you. Right? Just say it: this is you."

He glanced back to make sure the cook wasn't paying attention, then answered Lina with a nod.

Never had such a small gesture sent the world spinning for her like it did now.

"How?" she asked.

He studied her for a few seconds in silence, then came around the counter, took her hand, and dragged her away. He led her through the back door into the garden, to a faded picnic table with an umbrella.

It was a cool, dry day; the neighbor's plum tree pushed a flowering pink branch over the fence. Birds chirped in the bushes. Daffodils sprouted in the planting beds. Lina was not immune to spring's charms as Ren dusted off the bench with his apron and gestured for her to sit, but she felt out of place. Surely, for what he was about to tell her, a candlelit musty library in a ruined castle would be more appropriate, on a night with a thunderstorm raging outside.

Nevertheless, here under the hazy high clouds on the first of March, with the breeze ruffling his hair, and sprigs of ivy swaying beside their table,

Ren seated himself across from her and examined the photo again. "It's strange," he mused. "Every day I think about how I would explain it to someone. I'm always wishing I could. But now that somebody actually wants to know, I'm not sure what to say. There's no way to phrase it that doesn't sound ludicrous."

"You're Sean Reynolds, who died here in 1936." Lina nodded and squinted up at the plum blossoms, feeling confused in a dreamlike sense, as if her head and body had disconnected. "Okay. It sounds ludicrous."

"People expect certain things from their ghosts." He traced the photo's wavy edge with his thumbnail. "They expect you to be transparent or scary-looking or floating a foot above the ground. They don't expect you to walk up, shake their hand, and say, 'Hello, I'm a ghost; I've been in the house for the last seventy years and haven't aged a day, but I have gotten pretty good at cooking. Would you like some pie?' "

Lina chuckled without any humor, staring at his rolled-up shirt sleeves and the brown hairs on his arms. Ghost. He had finally said it, but now it struck her as impossible.

"Obviously, I don't usually tell people," he said. "Either they freak out or they don't believe it. Since you're not freaking out, I guess you don't believe it."

She glanced at the house. "Things happen here I can't explain. And, yes, I decided you had to be Sean after I read the journal and saw you vanish into thin air. But..." In the clinical manner she used with patients, she took his wrist and placed her fingertips upon it. "You have a heartbeat. You appear to breathe." She folded her hands on the table. "In my medical opinion, you're not dead. So I guess you're right; I don't quite believe it."

"I'm only 'not dead' when I'm here. I step off this

property, and—" He snapped his fingers. "I cease to exist, at least as far as anyone else can see."

"Why? Is there some reason you're supposed to stay here? Unfinished business?"

His lips flattened and his eyes cut aside, squinting in the wind. "I don't know. No one has ever bothered to tell me."

She felt a pang, not wishing to have hurt him, thinking of the young man who died before getting to fight in World War II and end up with eight grandchildren. But her mind wouldn't let him be that person, not if such a person was dead. A Fountain of Youth theory seemed more plausible to her at the moment than a ghost theory. "It can't be," she said. "You're healthy, you're strong, you can make cookies and dance a waltz and—and save women from spiders."

His smile looked sad. He set aside the photo and got up from the table. "Then I guess I have to make you freak out. Come here."

She rose and followed him.

"You'll notice I usually wear the same clothes," he said. "This shirt and pants, these shoes and socks."

She glanced at his outfit, the usual white-and-black, plus a green apron today. "I guess I just figured it was for your job."

"Right. It was—is—my uniform, but that's not all. These are the clothes I died in, and these are the clothes I always reappear in. If I bring anything else with me when I leave, it falls away at the border, and I come back in this same shirt, same pants, same shoes. So it's easier just to wear them most of the time."

She blinked, feeling the way she felt when someone tried to explain tax returns to her.

He unlatched the gate. "I'll show you." He lifted the sash of the apron and placed it in her hand, and closed his fingers around hers. He stepped backward across the threshold...and disappeared. His cloth-wrapped hand collapsed to nothing; the apron fell away loose in her grip. She gasped and gathered it up. She stared blankly at it, then at the space in front of her where he should have been. Of course she had seen this trick before, from high above, but up close and in the palm of her hand it packed a much stronger wallop. She lunged out into the alley and looked all around, up and down. He was gone.

"Ren?" The tremor in her voice betrayed the terror she had stonewalled until now. "Ren!"

Suddenly he was there, crowding the space in the gateway with her. She shrieked.

He caught her arms. "It's all right, I'm here; it's all right." She leaned against the gate and recovered her breath while he spoke. "Ah, there, see? I knew it was unnatural, you being so calm."

His attempt at levity did not make her smile this time. She dropped the apron back into his hand. "Where were you?"

"Right in front of you. You just couldn't see. It's okay; I know it's hard to get used to." He re-tied the apron around his waist, and took her elbow. "Let's sit down."

She let him lead her back to the table.

"Can I bring you some tea? Food? Anything?" he asked, as she slumped onto the bench.

She shook her head. "I'm all right."

He sat across from her, looking concerned.

"All this time," she said, "seventy years..."

"Not quite seventy."

"You've been here, being a houseboy?"

"That's right."

"You can't leave? There's not an afterlife?"

"I suspect there is. But I'm locked out."

She put her head in her hands, trying to think only about breathing. He waited quietly. Suddenly

153

she laughed.

"What?" he asked.

"For the longest time I thought you were too *young* for me."

He smiled, looking for all the world like a bashfully pleased college boy.

"So," she added, still woozy with adrenaline. "Now I know the big secret."

"I told you you didn't want to know."

"When's the last time anyone else found out?"

"Well, I suspect Jackie knows." He lifted his eyebrows and puffed his cheeks in an exhalation. "Boy, it was a shock to see her again. Guess the feeling was mutual."

"Did she ever say anything about it?"

"Not exactly. But when she said, 'I'm sorry for what happened,' I'm pretty sure she meant the poisoning in 1936, not just the assault and battery recently."

"No wonder she moved out. I wouldn't be able to face you every day with that on my conscience."

He shrugged. "I've never known for sure how much of a hand she had in it. From what I hear, she did give my dear girlfriend the idea." He pronounced Julia's nickname with the appropriate measure of sarcasm. "But neither of them knew better, so it's hard to assign blame. I don't think my parents should have pressed charges either, but...ancient history."

"Who else knows? I guess Marla and Alan."

He nodded. "They run interference when people start asking questions."

"The old house arrest story."

"Yep."

"Then you're not a criminal?"

Ren—should she think of him as Sean?—broke into a surprised smile. "No. Of course not. Disappointed?"

"Relieved. You never did seem the type. That's why I had to know." In a rush of remorse, she took up the journal and pressed her palms to the front and back covers. "I'm so sorry I took this. I didn't know any other way. I tried to ask, but you weren't talking, and neither was Marla."

"It's all right. Relax." He slid the journal out from between her hands. "You're a clever one, you know that? No one's ever swiped one of my journals before. Let alone decoded it."

"It still didn't tell me much. You never wrote about...1936." Saying "your death" seemed too personal. She spared a moment to recognize how bizarre a question of etiquette this was.

"That's because this was 1994. Back in the forties I did plenty of writing about it. I think I've exhausted all the ways to express angst known to man."

"I only saw journals back to the eighties, in your room."

"I ran out of space. The earlier ones are in storage, in the basement." He smiled. "Padlocked. You wouldn't have gotten in so easily."

"Must be a fascinating record. You, here all this time..." She turned the photo around toward herself. "It's horrible. And wonderful."

"I mostly consider it a curse, but it has its benefits."

She nodded. "The telekinesis is rather amazing, though I admit it scares me. How much control do you have over it?"

He gazed at her in confusion before comprehension lit up his eyes. "Oh. Oh, that isn't me. That's...*her*."

When Lina finally understood, the floor of her stomach dropped. "Julia."

Ren shifted in his seat, and looked over his shoulder at the house. "It's better not to say her name. She often seems to hear it, and acts up."

Lina felt cold, and hoped it was due to fear rather than an imminent performance by the poltergeist. "Have you seen her? Does she appear, like you?"

"I haven't *seen* her since she died. But I sense her. I feel it like the weather changing when she's in a bad mood."

"Can you stop her?"

"No. I can only warn people. And I usually don't even do that, because they'd wonder how I know. Marla and Alan don't want to be warned, not unless it's looking like a really bad storm."

Lina nodded. "I suppose I wouldn't want to know either. I'd be jumping at shadows all day."

"Yeah. Like me."

"So the two of you are stuck here. Linked."

"Seems that way."

"And, your family..." She let the question trail off, guessing it trod on sensitive territory.

"They don't know." He bowed his head and scraped dust off the journal. "Parents died in the sixties. My little sister is turning eighty this year, and lives in Coeur d'Alene in a facility like this one. She's a widow with two kids and five grandkids. Once in a while I've gone out there to see them, but it's not easy to go that far."

"The house pulls you back?"

"No. It's just tedious. For one thing, it feels weird when I'm out there, like I'm dreaming or watching a movie of someone else. For another thing, I can only go as fast as a normal person. I can walk, or hop buses and trains, even though I can't touch anything. It's very strange and I don't understand it. But essentially, I ride a bus or train for several hours without being able to bring anything to read, all to see some people who don't know I'm there."

"I see. At least here you can have conversations."

He nodded, balancing the journal on its bending pages. "If Marla's grandma hadn't agreed to take me in, I don't know what I would have done. Gone nuts like my old friend, I guess."

"Does...your old friend...get jealous when you talk to other people? Is that it?"

"Probably. I figure she resents both sides. Them, for getting close to me, and me, for being able to feel alive when she can't."

"What does she want?"

He let out a long breath. "I've asked, in every way I know how. But she's never answered. She's never said a single thing. My guess is she wants this to be over."

Lina shivered. The finality of the statement shouldn't have seemed ominous, considering the participants were already dead. But death, she guessed now, was only the first chapter in the world's possible torments. "I suppose you've thought of exorcism."

He swung the journal between his palms. "Didn't work. For either of us."

She huddled her cold feet together in their loafers, under the bench. Her stomach felt hollow and the chill of the March air had penetrated her sweater. "Well. I'm glad it didn't, in your case, at least."

Ren laid the journal flat, aligned it with the edge of the table, and sat up. "I consider it a success that you haven't run off screaming. People have, in the past. And then generally I never see them again."

"I believe it. But I'm not going anywhere." She tilted her head from one side to the other. She was so tense it felt like cement had been poured into her neck muscles. "So, what now?"

"Now? I should get back to work. As for you, I only ask that you don't tell anyone."

"Is it all right if I talk to Marla?"

He nodded. "One of us will have to." The corner of his mouth curled upward. "She's going to be annoyed with me."

"After all her efforts to shield you."

"Yep." Ren stood and offered her his hand. She took it, and although in every respect his limbs and clothing felt normal, she wondered if she could ever touch him now and not remember he was dead.

She followed him to the back door of the house, which he opened for her. She paused before entering. "If your name's really Sean, what do I call you?"

"Oh." His arm slid higher on the door, and his eyebrows flickered up, as if he was grateful to get an easy question for once. "Ren is fine. My buddies in high school used to call me that, short for Reynolds. Besides, wouldn't people wonder if you started calling me Sean?"

She shrugged. "Just thought, if you had a preference..."

"Come on." He gestured her inside. "We're letting in all the cold air."

He entered the kitchen, apologized to the cook for dallying, and started slicing French rolls for sandwiches. Lina toasted an English muffin, peeled slices of cold cuts and cheese from the tray of sandwich makings, and poured herself a cup of coffee. "I better get to work," she said to Ren, balancing her plate and mug.

"Okay. Talk to you later."

Ascending the stairs took a huge effort. Her legs felt weak. She was breathing like someone in a fever when she reached the third floor, and had to pause to sip her coffee before continuing along the corridor.

"There you are," said Mrs. B when Lina came into her room a few minutes later for a checkup. "I'd been wondering what became of you."

"Sorry. I was outside. Having a look at the flowers."

"Oh, bring me some when you get a chance, won't you? Something that smells nice. And we'll hope that ghost doesn't go scattering them around." Mrs. B laughed.

To Lina the words felt like a swallow of poison. Her stomach clenched. The ghosts were real, the last hour wasn't just a dream, and there were many, many things that felt terribly wrong about the situation and would never feel right.

She set down her clipboard and medical bag, afraid she would drop them. "Okay. I'll bring in a...few hyacinths, or something."

"Thank you, dear. Now let's see if my vision has gotten any worse this week."

Although Lina doubted her capability of staying here another minute without (as Ren predicted) running out the door screaming, she sat down, produced the eye chart, and began testing Mrs. B's vision, because that was what she had come to this house to do.

When she had some time alone in the quiet hour before dinner, she found she did not want to rush down and see Ren yet. Her stomach had not entirely settled, though it felt better after accepting the English muffin sandwich, and the thought of facing him (a ghost! a real ghost!) only roiled it up again.

As Lina looked out her window, she saw Marla drive up. Lina darted downstairs and popped through the door to the garage. "Can I help with the bags?"

"Thanks, kid." Marla nudged the car door shut with her hip.

Lina took a heavy paper bag of office supplies from her. "I talked to Ren. Or should I say 'Sean.' "

Marla clamped her mouth shut into a flat line,

and glared at the wall. "That turkey," she said, but her next look at Lina was kind. "So he told you?"

"Yes. The summary, at least."

"All right. Grab that other bag. Let's get out of this garage."

They settled again into the armchairs in Marla and Alan's sitting room. "My grandma was the housemother here, you know, when those two kids died," said Marla. "Shook her up pretty bad. Still, nothing else happened for a while—no ghosts or anything. Then one night a year later, she walked out into the kitchen to get a glass of water, and there's her dead houseboy Sean, standing right in front of her.

"She about fainted, of course. But he didn't look dead. He told her not to worry, said he wasn't sure how he got here but he just wanted to talk. Turned out he'd been wandering around the world as a ghost that whole year, and finally got up the nerve to come back and visit the house. Soon as he stepped onto the property, he realized he could feel stuff, smell stuff, be visible again, all that. But he couldn't do it anywhere else; just here.

"Pretty soon he's crying his heart out at the kitchen table, because he can't go back to his family, and everyone thinks he's dead. Well, he *is* dead, of course, but he's stuck here. My grandma was a softie; she took pity on him and told him to come talk to her if he got lonely, even though he scared the daylights out of her. He just had to stay out of sight of the sorority girls, see, because a lot of them would recognize him. It was five or six years before he could come work here and not run into anyone who knew him from before."

Lina's chest ached at the thought of the austere, quiet Ren crying his heart out. But who wouldn't have wept in his situation? "Those were the stories your grandma told you, growing up?" she said. "You must have lost a lot of sleep as a child."

Marla laughed and slapped the arm of the chair. "Nah, I was twenty-five. Me and Alan, couple of newlyweds with a big idea, went to talk to my ma about moving into this house with Grandma, and starting up an old folks' home. Figured we'd get a great place to live and a business to run, and take care of Grandma in the bargain, since she was getting old and someone had to. Well, my ma, she knew the story about this place; she just hadn't told us kids. All I knew was the house always gave her the creeps. She hated visiting here. So she said, 'All right, but you get your grandmother to tell you about that houseboy first. You want to live there, you ought to know about the ghosts.' I thought: the houseboy, the ghosts? What do they have to do with each other? Went to talk to Grandma, and I found out."

Lina attempted a smile. "Were you as freaked out as I am?"

"You kidding? I thought it was the neatest thing I'd ever seen. She took us outside and had him step over the property line so I could see for myself. Did he do that for you?"

Lina nodded, dropping her gaze to her lap.

"I made him do it about ten more times," Marla said. "Thought it was just great. Me and Ren, we were buddies from that day on. Alan, now, he took a couple years to get used to Ren. Wasn't sure what to make of him. But now, you've seen 'em; they get along fine."

"Then it is possible to get used to it."

"Ren's the easy part to get used to. It's the other one who's spooky."

Just that phrase, "the other one," lifted the hairs on Lina's arms. "When did she first act up?" she asked, remembering not to name Julia aloud.

"Couple weeks after Ren showed up. It was like

he woke her up, coming back here. He was the first one she went after. Then she started bothering other people too."

"People who made friends with him," Lina guessed.

"Mostly, yeah. She hasn't given me and Alan much trouble, probably 'cause I don't have designs on Ren. But girls who get cozy with him..." Marla shook her head. "They've never stuck around long. Man, I feel sorry for that kid. The girls, too, but mostly him."

"Have there been a lot of girls?"

"Every couple years, seems like. Most times, it's just a flirtation, and then we tell them the house arrest story or some other excuse, and they take off. Sometimes we haven't even had to tell them. They just get mad at how shifty he is, and leave." Marla stretched out her legs and kicked one foot on top of the other. "But a few stick around anyway, even when they learn the truth. Still, they always leave too. How can you build a future on that, you know?"

"Right." Lina's voice was soft.

"Some people who find out, they just run out of here in a panic. Last time someone did that, back in the eighties, screaming bloody murder, we decided not to risk it anymore. That's when we came up with the house arrest story. 'Don't let me do this ever again,' Ren said to me. 'Stop them before they get close.' Well, he changes his mind every time a pretty lady walks in, of course." Marla glanced at Lina. "I think at heart he's never stopped being twenty-two."

Lina breathed in small puffs, her gaze tottering across the ceiling. "I don't know what to do."

"If he told you, he must like you. Couldn't hurt to be his friend, if you think you can stand it."

"But what if—she—acts up even more? She's already targeted me and Mrs. B."

"Well, remember this." Marla sat forward.

"You're alive. She's dead. You're the stronger one."

"Ren's dead too. That's a lot to absorb."

"He's not really dead, not when he's here. He's a living, breathing, real boy. Except he doesn't eat or sleep. Other than that, he's every bit as alive as you and me."

"Doesn't eat? But he did. He had chocolate with me." Lina closed her mouth before disclosing what happened after the chocolate.

"Did he? Then he must *really* like you." Marla chuckled. "See, food's like anything else—he can't carry it across the property line with him, even if he's swallowed it. So..."

Lina thought about it for a moment. "So partially digested food just...falls to the ground?"

"Uh-huh. Well, chewed. Not digested exactly. The fluids and stuff go away too. Still, kind of off-putting. He'd rather not deal with it."

Even to a nurse, this was a new one. Lina nodded. "Huh. Weird."

"That's why he goes through so much gum. Gets some new tastes without having to swallow anything. And sleeping, he says, is just a waste of time. He can step off the property and come back all recharged, no matter what's wrong with him."

"So if he gets tired or hungry..."

"He ducks outside the lines for a second. Gets more done than most of us that way."

Lina sat up. Fascination started to push aside fear. "Does his hair grow? Does he shave?"

"Same deal. If he stayed here for days, without leaving, it would grow. But for a clean shave and the haircut he died in, he just hops outside and comes back."

"Incredible. Amazing."

"Yeah. You can see why he doesn't want people to know. Tabloids, scientists, paranormal junkies—everyone and their dog would be beating down this door to get a look."

Lina nodded. "I'll try to be respectful. I won't make him do tricks."

"He doesn't mind a few people knowing. In fact, he likes it. It's not often he gets to tell someone." Marla shook her head again. "God, it must get lonely."

Lina strengthened herself with another deep breath. "Then I'll stay."

"Good!" Marla beamed. "You'll get used to it. Honest, you will."

"I'll try." It was all Lina could promise.

Alone in her room, she got out the articles from the library, sat cross-legged on the floor, and re-read each one. Now when she looked at that headline, HOUSEBOY KILLED AT SORORITY, she felt the cold horror of knowing the victim. It was the same way she had felt in high school one summer when a classmate was killed in a car crash, and she had only found out about it by picking up the newspaper on her mother's front porch. It also brought back tremors of how she felt when signing her statement regarding Mr. Ambaum's death at the hospital.

Sean Reynolds had been studying math at the University. He thought maybe he would be a teacher. He had played high school baseball and was a good student. His funeral was held Tuesday, April 14, 1936, in Port Townsend, the town where he had grown up. He left behind his parents, and a sister who was twelve years old when her big brother died.

The words of the newsprint swam in her vision. She threw the articles aside, letting them scatter over the carpet, and pressed the heel of her hand to her eyes.

The boy I love is dead, she thought. The sentence carried the kind of pathos that could only make her cry on a day when she felt particularly weak. For it was stupid, so stupid, to mourn his death when he was downstairs right this minute setting tables for dinner.

She hardly looked at him when he was near her dinner table that evening. But when he was across the room she couldn't stop staring at him. It had become quite ridiculous by the end of the meal, and she felt she owed him an apology.

As he took away their dessert plates she turned to face him. The other people at her table were talking and weren't likely to hear her. "Would you like to walk in the garden tonight?" she asked.

His chest lifted as if he had drawn a long-awaited breath. He responded in his usual polite tones, "That sounds nice."

"Seven o'clock?"

"Seven o'clock." He inclined his head to her and whisked away the dishes.

She walked Mrs. B back upstairs, and at her door the old lady asked, "Do I get to know what's happening at seven o'clock?"

Lina smiled and dealt Mrs. B a light punch on the arm. "Didn't know you were listening. Shame on you."

"I'm going blind, Lina, not deaf."

****

Ren's shirt glowed with the ultraviolet tint that attaches itself to white items in the dusk hour. They walked the concrete path side by side.

"So, what's new?" Lina asked.

"Oh, nothing much. Told a nice girl about me today. She took it pretty well. I'm keeping my fingers crossed."

Lina smiled at an azalea bush. "For what?"

"Mostly I'm hoping she won't be scared off."

"Well, I hear she called you out here for a stroll. Imagine that's a good sign."

"Wonder if she wanted to say anything in particular?"

Although it was tempting out there in the fragrant twilight, Lina did not say, "I think I love you." She was too shy; too terrified of the implications; and anyway, such a statement needed to be slept on before being spoken.

So she watched her brown shoes as she walked, and shrugged one shoulder. "I talked to Marla."

"Oh?"

"She gave me some of the history. I'd like to learn more."

"Okay. Such as?"

"Tell me about the house in the old days."

"Sorority life?" he said. "Ah, that was a challenge."

"I can imagine. Pretty girls everywhere."

"Relentless, curious girls, who weren't supposed to 'fraternize' with the houseboys but did anyway."

They reached the wooden table with the umbrella. Lina swiveled to sit upon it. "So you were forbidden fruit."

"Mm-hm."

"You were afraid of losing your job," she added, remembering Mrs. Clairmont's story, "when you were seeing Ju—her."

"Would have been grounds for dismissal. Made it romantic at the time, sneaking around and breaking rules. Now it just seems stupid."

"You weren't stupid. The rules were." She didn't dare add that Julia was a little stupid as well—drugging her date, for God's sake.

He looked at the high wall of the house with its bright windows. "The irony is, I met girls later who I *would* have died for."

"But not that one?"

He stooped and picked up a pebble. "Not that one." He enunciated the words clearly. He pitched the stone against the house; it bounced off the bricks and rustled in a bush.

"Well. I'm glad there were better ones eventually." Not that she *was* glad, exactly. She was in fact wildly jealous.

"In a way," Ren said, "I was happiest when Marla and Alan arrived to turn it into a retirement home. I thought, finally, I'd get to be around people my own age. My real age, I mean."

"Ninety..."

"Ninety-one in November."

Lina supposed he'd heard all the jokes about how great he looked. She kept her mouth shut, imagining they were in poor taste anyway.

"But as it turned out," Ren went on, "I couldn't really talk to those folks about growing up in the twenties, or living through the Depression. I could let *them* talk about it, but I couldn't say, 'Yeah, I remember that.' I've always had to pretend to be twenty-two, whatever that meant for the time I was living in."

"So during Vietnam you had to pretend you were dodging the draft?"

He crouched and picked peeling paint off a container of roses. "Invented a heart condition for myself. Same one I used during World War II."

"But nobody actually has any paperwork on you, do they?"

"You mean, would I really have been drafted? No. 'Ren Schultz' is unregistered with Social Security, doesn't have a driver's license or a birth certificate, and doesn't pay a dime in taxes." He paused. "Come to think of it, maybe I am a criminal."

Lina smiled and slid back farther on the table. "So how many girls lived here in the sorority days?"

"Capacity was thirty." He abandoned the rose container and sat beside her. "And the house was at capacity most years, till the mid-sixties."

"Thirty? Wow." To Lina, the house felt crowded

enough at sixteen residents.

"That wasn't even all the members. They had sixty, seventy, eighty girls some years. They just couldn't all live here. The live-outs had dorm rooms or apartments. It's still that way in the Greek houses."

"Do the houseboys still live on the property? That seems kind of..." Lina wasn't sure of the best word, but Ren understood.

"Risky? Yeah. These days, they usually don't. Some girl would constantly be down there; or he'd be sleeping upstairs with her, even though guys usually aren't allowed on the upper floors."

"You couldn't go upstairs?"

"Oh, God, no. Strictly forbidden. Rules were tight. The girls weren't even allowed to wear jeans on campus till sometime in the sixties. Would've gotten called up in front of the Standards Committee for it."

Lina laughed, not just at the quaintness of the old rules, but at the fact that he knew so much about the internal runnings of sororities. Then she remembered why he knew about it, and stopped laughing. "So...how did you avoid all the inquisitive girls, if this was before the house arrest story?"

"I used the rules when I could. Said I was going to get in trouble. Rose, Marla's grandma, backed me up if I needed it. But sometimes..." He chuckled. "Sometimes I let them get me."

Lina echoed the chuckle, turning it rueful. She envied those girls so much it ached. Though the thought scared her, she yearned to know what it was like to be a ghost's lover—this ghost's, anyway. She couldn't tell yet which side of the teetering scales would win. The side determined to find out, or the side that had learned from past hurts and wanted to run away.

Above all, she felt sorry for him; and also for

those girls, now grown up, who must have had some extremely strange memories of a particular college romance. "I don't blame any of you," she said. "I understand the temptation, on both sides."

He smiled, aware of the compliment. "Better to have loved and lost, and all that."

"I hope it's true. I've lost often enough."

"Oh, back to this, are we?" He turned to her with a grin. "Listen, this Brent guy's an idiot if he was willing to give you up. So don't you dare call yourself a loser over it one more time, or I—well, I've been told I'm absolutely wicked when it comes to tickling people. You've been warned."

She laughed, looking down at her feet, swinging them under the table. "Well, thank you." She risked another glance at him. He too had his head bowed, and his gaze fixed on his shoes. Sliding over and kissing him would be the daring, romantic thing to do right now; letting him know she didn't mind embracing a ghost, if he was interested—which he probably was, to judge from that remark.

But she did mind, didn't she? Her natural aversion to death still held her at bay; she needed to know more first, needed time to accept it. She cleared her throat and tried out a new topic. "What happened in the sixties to make the sorority close?"

He started telling the tale, which, to her relief, had nothing to do with ghosts. Rather, the Greek system in general experienced a plummet in popularity in the latter half of the sixties, and many sororities nationwide had to close chapters. Some houses, like this one, never recovered.

This led Ren and Lina into a discussion of Rose Helman, Marla's grandmother. It was nine o'clock when they finally went back inside so Lina could take up the night watch, and Ren could give the kitchen a scrub-down.

They stood at the foot of the back staircase, their

point of separation.

"So, Miss Lina. Now that you've called me out, what do you think? Willing to stick around?"

Lina rested her hand on the railing and eased up onto the first step, balancing there at his height. "Yes. I'm willing."

"Good." He leaned his arm on the wall, watching her. She thought he was going to say more, but he only smiled.

"Well..." She went up another step, backward, and parted her lips to say goodnight. Then, for some reason, the scales tipped. She stepped back down, put her arms around his neck, and drew him into a hug.

He caught her close and held her. She felt his sigh against the nape of her neck.

"Thank you for trusting me," she said.

"Thank you for believing me."

She squeezed him tighter. "Goodnight."

"Goodnight."

She turned and dashed up the stairs, two at a time, her feet feeling light as air.

Mrs. B looked up with an open-mouthed smile of expectation when Lina entered to help her into bed. "How did it go?" she asked.

"It went fine. Ready for bed?" Lina slipped a hand beneath Mrs. B's arm.

"Yes, I'm ready, thank you. Did you get a kiss, at least?"

"No, I did not get a kiss. Nothing happened."

"Spring is young yet," said Mrs. B. "And so are the two of you."

Lina helped Mrs. B out of her sweater. "Oh, we aren't that young."

Chapter Ten

Over the next week, Lina and Ren spent their free hours together in quiet corners of the house and garden. They engaged in no further physical affection except a nudge once in a while during a moment of laughter. But now her heart jolted every time his thick lashes lifted to dart a glance in her direction. What they talked about was usually related to his ghostly existence, but with each passing day she minded less and less that he was a ghost.

Julia noticed, of course. Almost every day—or, worse, every night—she acted up. Lina awoke one morning to find all her CDs taken off the shelves and placed in a single towering stack on the carpet. Two different nights she woke up shivering, for the room was ice-cold and her blankets were six feet away on the floor. Once, in the afternoon, while typing email, she watched in wonder as the cord for the window-blinds bobbed and jerked, though the window was closed and there was no breeze.

But none of this actually harmed her. Lina, though never the possessor of anything resembling a sixth sense, did not feel endangered by Julia's random pranks. It was simply that Julia was *there*. Testing her, maybe. Watching.

Lina spoke to her once in a while, told her she understood Julia's frustration, and hoped to help both ghosts by being Ren's friend and learning more about their past. Julia made no sign of hearing her.

Lina did not tell Ren about any of Julia's antics. Why worry him? He had already dwelled too much upon Julia over the past seventy years. Someday Lina would ask for his theories, but not yet.

One night, two weeks into March, Lina paused in a dark patch of lawn under the maple tree and rested her hand on its trunk. "Will you answer one question?"

Ren put his hand on the trunk too, above hers. "I'll try."

"If I were to ask you out again, even knowing what you are, what would you say?"

He looked up through the branches at the purple dusk sky. "I would say roughly the same as I've already said."

"Well...I understood you were saying no, but I didn't know then..."

"I said no because it wouldn't have been fair to you. I *wanted*..." His index finger trailed down the trunk and poked her on the back of the hand. "To say yes. But I still think it's not fair to you."

"Don't worry what's fair for me. Let me be stupid. Because, if you want it, well, I still do too."

He bowed his head, and puffed out a sigh. Without looking, he found and covered her hand with his own, on the trunk. "You can't know what you'd be getting into."

"We've spent the last two weeks talking about what I'd be getting into." Lina emitted a short laugh. "Julia? I can deal with it. Being stuck in the house with you? I hardly go out anyway. You're older than I thought? I like older guys. It'll end in tears, maybe? 'Better to have loved and lost,' you said."

He lifted his head, his fingers curling around hers. "Crazy woman. I've told you I'm interested. What I can't figure out is why *you* would be interested in *me*."

In the night air, among the bushes and shadows, he was a glow of white with dark hollows for features, two sparks of reflected street-light for eyes.

He looked as if he could blow away on a strong gust of wind and dissolve into shreds. But he didn't frighten her, not anymore.

"You're fascinating," she said. "The things you've seen, the things you can do..."

"So it's a freak-show?"

"No! I *like* you, stupid."

"All right. I'm sorry." Was that a laugh in his voice? He drew her closer, and ran his fingers down her ear. "Anyone ever tell you you've got the cutest ears? I'm a sucker for cute ears. Bet you didn't know that."

"No." She laughed in surprise. "How would I?"

"Maybe if I wrote about it in my *journal*." He took advantage of her indignant gasp by hooking an arm around her waist. Next thing she knew, his lips were up beside her head, making her think he was going to whisper something. But instead they captured the outer ridge of her ear, and traveled down, leaving slow kisses along the way.

Delicious shivers shot down her spine to her heels. She let her forehead touch his neck, and breathed in the warm scent of him.

"Well," he sighed, "so much for keeping my distance."

Cold water and warm lips touched her mouth at the same time. As she closed her eyes she heard rain start to tap on the bushes and the street. She and Ren went on kissing. She feared nothing, not poltergeists, lightning, death, being seen, nor being in love. It seemed the safest thing in the world to nestle here in his arms as the spring sky shook droplets down upon them.

When the shower crescendoed in a rush, sending water dripping off the branches and down their faces, Ren broke his mouth away. Lina felt him laugh. She opened her eyes and saw the gleam of his teeth.

"Seems to be raining," she commented.

"In Seattle. Imagine that."

She leaned her cheek to his chest. "Ren?"

He held her and rocked her back and forth. "Mm?"

"What did you write about me in your journal?"

She felt his low laugh as a rumble against her ear. "First day? 'Another new nurse. Sweet smile. Great skin. God give me strength.'"

"You did not."

"Did so. Next few entries: 'So far have saved Lina from a spider and a poltergeist attack. She's analytical, not just scared. She thinks things over. She likes crosswords and books and toast. Have to stop imagining how compatible we'd be.'"

Lina snuggled closer. "And on Halloween?"

"That was, 'Watch it, old boy. You almost kissed her in front of the entire house.' Then Thanksgiving, when you called me..." He bowed his head to nuzzle her temple. "That was the first time I wrote a certain four-letter L-word in regards to you."

Raindrops seeped through Lina's shirt, but she closed her eyes in pure happiness. "What did you write?"

"Something like, 'I almost told her everything. I'm crazy. I'm probably in love again. In a word, I'm screwed.'"

Lina smiled, lifted her head, and demonstrated her appreciation with another kiss.

The front door opened. "Ren?" called Alan. "That you?"

Ren turned. "Yeah, it's me and Lina."

"What are you doing in the rain?"

"It just started," said Ren, laughter bubbling through his voice.

"Well, can you come help me move the tables?" They were transferring some dining room tables to the living room tonight for an arts-and-crafts activity.

"I'll be right there."

"Thanks!" Alan's silhouette left the door frame.

"We better go in," Ren said.

"You go. I promised Mrs. B I'd bring her some hyacinths. I'll get them and then come in."

"Okay." Holding her shoulders, Ren pressed another rain-dampened kiss onto her mouth, and jogged to the house. The door shut behind him.

Lina, who had been laughing every few seconds, now jumped into the air with a squeal. She tilted back her head and opened her arms, thanking the very sky. Half running and half dancing, she darted off into the darkness of the side yard where the hyacinths grew. So *that* was what kissing a ghost was like: unbelievably exciting. You'd think your lover being dead would put a damper on the thrill, but Lina was here to tell you she pitied everyone who never knew the blessed experience of snogging a ghost in the rain.

She was snapping off wet hyacinths, barely able to see them, when something shattered on the paving stones beside her. She tumbled over in shock. The item sounded heavy, and after peering at it a moment she identified it as one of the rectangular pottery flower-boxes that were attached to the windowsills.

But...Lina stood and looked at the house. The bed of hyacinths was clear over by the fence, thirty feet from the house. The wind tonight was mild, pushing rain in small gusts, nothing like the hurricane force it would take to hurl a heavy clay box full of wet soil and plants all the way over here. It really must have been...thrown.

The fear she had been so cavalier about overcoming flooded back over her. She was alone in the dark, and Julia was jealous.

With her handful of hyacinths, Lina bolted for

the back door of the house. Her wet fingers twisted and tugged, but the handle was locked. She beat her fist on the door. "Hello? Ren? Anyone? Please, let me in!"

Everyone must have been away from the back kitchen and pantry, moving tables in the front of the house. No one answered.

Crash! Another flower-box shattered, two inches from her feet. She jumped away with a shriek. As she retreated she looked up at the windows. A few of them were lit, but all of them were shut. Nobody among the living was up there pushing things down.

Even as she watched, a metal pail sitting beside the door, filled with gardening trowels and spades, swung itself up into the air and zoomed toward her. Lina dodged. She felt the pail strike her on the spine as it flew past, and heard the tools smack and scatter against the fence.

She unlocked the back gate, darted out, and sprinted down the alley. Gravel crunched and slid under her shoes; rain pelted her eyes. Her heart pounded so hard she could barely breathe.

She got around the corner and onto the front sidewalk. The two porch lights flanking the front door, and the row of fairy-lights along the path, beckoned her with their homey warmth. She opened the iron gate and stumbled up the walk, panting.

Something small hit her on the shoulder. She spun around. A pebble clattered to the ground. As she stared at it, another hit her in the ribs. She whimpered and flew up the steps to the porch. This door was locked too, and she nearly burst into tears. She rang the bell and began knocking. "It's Lina! Let me in!"

Beside her, one of the porch lights went out in a shatter of glass, as if someone had thrown a rock at it.

"Let me in!" she screamed.

The door opened. Alan, her savior, looked stunned.

Lina shot inside and slammed the door shut, even though the poltergeist lived in here, too, and not just in the garden. It didn't matter. She needed to be around other people; she needed to get out of the dark.

"What's the matter?" asked Alan.

"The..." Lina tried to catch her breath. She saw George and a couple of the elderly ladies hovering near the stairs, staring at her. "The back door was locked, and, um...some flowerpots fell off the walls, and out here just now, the porch light broke and went out." Her eyes met Alan's.

His features turned grim, and he nodded. "Come on." He guided her toward the stairs. "We'll fix all that tomorrow when it stops raining." He moved his hand back and forth on her shoulders, like her father used to do when she was a teenager and was upset about something. "Want to change into something dry and come down and help us?"

Lina nodded.

"Bring Mrs. B, if she's bored," Alan added.

Lina remembered Mrs. B's flowers, and looked at the purple hyacinths in her hand. They had been reduced to four specimens, all with bruised or broken stems. She emitted a tiny laugh. "Oh, well. They still smell nice."

"Our ghost chasing you?" boomed George, as Lina put her foot on the first step.

Ren's figure emerged in the corner of Lina's eye. She turned. He had darted out of the living room and now lingered beside the polished table in the entry. Uncertainty and worry clouded his eyes.

"Must be," Lina answered to George. She gave Ren a measured nod, to tell him to stay there; she was not a baby, she would be all right.

"He always goes after the pretty ones!" George

added.

Lina sent him a startled glance, then realized George was referring not to Ren but to "the ghost;" and that the two, in George's understanding, were separate people.

What a mess. She smiled weakly at George, and jogged up the stairs.

After collecting herself and combing her hair, she came back downstairs to help set up the room. She was distracted, swinging from blushes and secret smiles with Ren, to panic at the thought of their future. The existence of a mad spirit attempting to maim her also complicated things.

Okay, so now she had snogged a ghost in the rain, and she wouldn't mind doing it a few more times. But what was she supposed to do after that? Settle down and live with him in this haunted house for the rest of her days? Raise a couple of half-ghost kids?

It was laughable. She was overthinking it. Life dealt people a strange hand once in a while; couldn't she just appreciate it and move on? Relationships didn't have to last forever, nor did they have to involve marriage and childbearing. But that would be preferable. That was what she had always assumed 'the right man' would bring; it was a natural, traditional thing to want. And she already cared too much about Ren to ensnare him into an attachment she intended to leave if it became inconvenient. She wanted him more than anyone, and couldn't envision a happy life that didn't include seeing him daily. But Ren's situation—Ren's existence, really—introduced a whole new set of fears no rational woman ever expected to face.

He knew about her fears and doubts, too. She saw it in the way he watched her. He looked as if he was trying not to get his hopes up. Women had loved him before, then left him when they decided they couldn't live with this. She didn't want him to worry, so she smiled and tried to look reassuring. But she didn't think she fooled him.

Lina found him by chance in the kitchen at nearly ten o'clock that night, when she went down to return a coffee mug.

One light was on, the lamp above the sink. Ren stood beneath it rinsing a tray. A striped dish towel hung over his shoulder. Upon hearing her step he turned and lifted his chin. "Hi."

"Hi."

He turned off the water. Silence loomed.

She advanced, holding out the mug.

He dried his hands on the towel and took the mug from her.

"Thanks," she said. "Exciting day."

"Quite."

"Kind of exhausting."

He nodded.

"So I'll..." She pointed across herself, toward the stairwell. "Get Mrs. B to bed, then turn in."

Ren took her hands and looked down at them. "Is this the first time she's done anything lately?"

Lina knew he wasn't referring to Mrs. B. "They've only been little things," Lina hedged.

He lifted his head to look at her, dismayed. "I don't want..."

She waited, but he didn't finish the sentence; he turned silent instead, in frustration. "I know," she said. "I'll be fine."

"She..." Ren cleared his throat, and went on in a steadier tone, "She probably won't do anything else tonight. She has limited energy. When she acts up, it wears her out, and nothing happens for a day or two."

"Oh. Good."

"I'm sorry I bring..." Again he stopped, words seemingly of no use. He shook his head.

Lina ran her thumbs over his knuckles. "Stop worrying."

He smiled sadly, and leaned down to kiss her. It was a chaste kiss compared to the one in the garden, but it was what the situation called for. She appreciated that her boyfriend was a gentleman.

All right. So he was her boyfriend.

****

As Ren predicted, the poltergeist was dormant that night. But Lina still did not sleep well, and the next day the conflicting emotions and insomnia rendered her scatter-brained.

"You're all in a dither," Mrs. B said, summing it up nicely.

Lina paused in her fourth attempt to get Mrs. B's braid right, a task that normally took one pass. She met Mrs. B's squinting eyes in the mirror. "Sorry. I'm a little sleepy."

"You've been in a dither for days. If anything's bothering you, I do hope you know you can tell me." The lined face in the mirror now looked kindly, not impish. "I like to think of you as my granddaughter, not my servant. I want to help you if anything's wrong, even if it's just to listen."

As Lina's last living grandmother had died seven years ago, Mrs. B's words almost moved her to tears. "Thank you." She rebrushed Mrs. B's wispy white hair, and smiled. "I don't feel like a servant. Far from it."

"Good. Then is anything wrong?"

"I've just been..." Lina waved the hairbrush. "Thinking about relationships. Whether I should get into one; whether I really like being alone. I thought I did, but—maybe it's worth rearranging my life for someone. If they're the right person. How do you know? How many complications are too many?" She set down the brush and started braiding. "And so on."

"First of all," said Mrs. B, "we must dispense with this 'someone' nonsense. You're talking about our Ren, so we might as well call him that."

Lina spluttered a few sounds of protest.

"Well, aren't you?" said Mrs. B.

"I only meant, in theory, these issues..."

"Theories don't work with relationships. Particulars do. And this particular is named Ren."

Lina sighed and tucked a bobby pin into Mrs. B's hair. "It's that obvious, huh?"

"I practically need to take off my sweater every time you two are around it gets so warm in the room."

Lina burst into giggles and nudged Mrs. B's shoulder. "You do have a way with words."

"I think you're perfect for each other. I'm delighted for you. I can't imagine what's giving you cold feet."

"Well, there's...the age difference."

"Fiddle. What, six years?"

Lina hesitated. "A little more than that."

"It won't matter as you get older. I was eight years younger than Robert." Robert was Mrs. B's late husband, a former city councilman of Seattle. He died in 1991.

Since it would only matter *more* as they got older, Lina skirted that and moved to the next problem. "Also, he has to stay here. It's complicated and I can't really explain it, but basically, we couldn't live anywhere else."

"I thought you liked Seattle."

"I love Seattle."

"Then what's the problem?"

"It would be nice to be *able* to go someplace else."

"Circumstances change," Mrs. B said. "I'm sure someday he'll be able to leave. You're thinking too far ahead anyway. Make it work now, and you'll go right on making it work in the future."

Lina smoothed Mrs. B's hair, and secured a loose strand with another bobby pin. "The trouble with right now is even stranger."

"Why? Is he seeing someone?"

"No...it's actually about someone he *can't* see."

"What does that mean?"

She put the finishing touches on Mrs. B's hair and rested her fingers on the chair's back. "Would you believe the ghost is jealous?"

Mrs. B looked bewildered. "The ghost? In this house I suppose it's foolhardy to say I don't. But— the *ghost*? What in the world are you talking about?"

"We're guessing it's Jackie's friend who died here. She was in love with a houseboy. Remember?"

"Yes, I remember."

"Now she's attached herself to Ren. And she targets anyone who gets close to him. Which means me. And even you, by extension."

Mrs. B's features shifted toward exasperation. "Oh, for heaven's sake. Just because I believe there's a ghost, and just because I've convinced you, doesn't mean you can use it as a reason to shy away from that boy. Don't make me slap some sense into you."

"I know it's ridiculous. I tell myself that every day. But I keep seeing signs that it's true, and it's only going to get worse." Lina turned away. "I can't really talk about this. Some of it involves...his private life, and I'm not at liberty..."

"Now, Lina, I trust you to make good decisions. If there's something more serious than ghosts behind all this, then I know you'll do what's right. But if that's really your only reason, then I can't imagine what's come over you!"

"Me neither."

"So your future might be difficult. So a ghost might throw some magazines around. Are you going to give him up over that?"

"I don't know."

Mrs. B stared sternly in Lina's general direction in the mirror. "I would give up a whole year of what's left of my life for one more day with Robert. Life is really too short to be making up reasons why you shouldn't go down there and throw your arms around that boy like you want to."

The room sparkled in the sheen of the tears that rose to Lina's eyes. She leaned over Mrs. B's chair and kissed the old lady on the cheek. "Thank you."

"You're welcome; now shoo!" Mrs. B fluttered a hand to send her out.

Downstairs, Lina found Ren alone at a dining room table in a slant of afternoon sunlight, leafing through a binder. Cookbooks were stacked beside him, and a pen seesawed between his fingers.

She slid an arm over his shoulders, and fell into his lap, capturing him in a hug.

"Hey," he greeted in surprise. He set the pen down and embraced her.

"Hello." She slipped aside to the nearest chair.

"To what do I owe the pleasure?"

"Mrs. B commanded me to go throw my arms around you."

"Ah. She knows of our little dalliance?"

Lina lowered her eyes to his thumb, which she slid between her fingers. "She guessed a long time ago."

"Her matchmaking attempts *were* kind of obvious." He smiled. "Not that I minded. So. How are you, today?" He asked it quietly, and she understood it wasn't small talk.

"Fine. I mean, I'm 'all in a dither,' like Mrs. B said, but there hasn't been any new activity since last night."

"Good."

She squared her shoulders. "I want to ask you some things, all the same."

"Okay." He set his free hand on the table, and rolled his fingers across the cover of a cookbook. "How about I finish organizing these recipes, then meet you at the picnic table?"

A spatter of rain against the window overruled his suggestion.

"Or, the living room," Ren said, after turning and looking outside.

"I'll be at the piano."

She was plinking out a Scott Joplin piece when Ren came in.

He slid onto the piano bench beside her, straddling it, and looked at the sheet music. "I've always liked that one. Catchy."

"Yes. And hard to play." Making both hands do what they were supposed to was like fighting through blackberry vines.

He scooted closer. His right hand hovered over the keys. "I'll take treble clef. You take bass. From the top."

Lina counted to four, and off they went, reeling and fumbling through the tune. They were giggling within eight measures. By the end of the piece, two minutes and several apologies later, they sounded pretty good together. They held the last chord, feet vying for the spot on the sustain pedal. Ren ended up holding it down, with Lina's foot on top of his. They let their hands fall to their laps.

"You read music," Lina said.

"We mathematicians tend to."

"A thousand talents. Quite the Renaissance man."

"Now, I don't date back *that* far."

She laughed again, tipping her head down. It nearly touched his shoulder. When she looked up, she found he had tilted his face. After a span of a moment or two, they leaned in at the same time. His lips were cool, but the tip of her tongue discovered his mouth was warm inside, as were the hands that curled around her waist. His foot slid off the piano pedal and hooked her calf, pulling her close without breaking the kiss.

"Mm." She drew away an inch. "You taste like licorice."

"Black Jack." He flicked his chewing gum forward to display it between his teeth. "Full of sugar and everything."

"Must be nice not to worry about cavities."

"Not having to see a dentist *is* one of the better things about my condition."

"I've sometimes thought you smelled like mouthwash. I guess that must have been mint gum."

"Maybe. Or the brandy."

She frowned. "Brandy? But you don't..."

"I don't drink or eat, no. Usually. But I've been able to taste that damn brandy, the one she poisoned me with, for the last seventy years."

The statement wiped out Lina's warmth. "Oh. Jeez."

"People sometimes say they smell it on me. That's the other reason for the gum. To cover it."

While Lina contemplated the dreadfulness of tasting your cause of death for the greater part of a century, a sound rang out: a thin note on the piano, repeating several times. They stared at the keyboard, but none of the keys moved. It sounded more like someone was reaching into the open piano and plucking at the strings near the hammers. In a few seconds the plucking stopped, and the last note hovered in the quiet room. Lina drew a breath.

Ren murmured, "Which brings us to our main topic."

"I thought she wouldn't act up today."

"Well, she can't do much. But I guess she's still going to try."

"Will she get angry? If we talk about her?"

Ren edged off the piano bench and stood up. "I don't get an angry feeling today. More like curious."

Lina got up too. "Then let's talk."

Ren led her to a sofa, the very one where she had fallen asleep and dreamed of kissing him, months ago. The memory kicked up a thrill in her stomach as she sat beside him. Dreams came true after all. But before succumbing to the desire to test-drive her dream again, she meant to learn more about Ren and Julia.

"You two must have been close," she said.

"Not really. That is, I never loved her."

Lina winced, expecting a vase to come flying at him. But nothing happened. "Did she know?"

He shrugged. "She does now, in any case."

"But *she* must have loved *you*. She killed herself over you."

"I believe she thought she loved me. I also believe she couldn't live with herself after what she'd done. I could see her doing it out of despair, a fit of passion."

"How long were you dating?"

"Just a couple months. It started when she slipped me a note under a saucer at Monday night dinner, inviting me to come out onto the fire escape and have a cigarette with her and Jackie."

"How unhealthy."

"Well, back then it was a luxury to have cigarettes at all. It was the middle of the Depression. But of course it wasn't really about smoking. Pretty soon, Jackie was finding excuses to leave us alone, and it became..." He shrugged. "Something of a fling."

"So that night, when everyone else went to the dance..."

"Yes, that night." Ren rubbed his eyes with the heels of his hands, as if the memory gave him a headache. Little wonder. "I agreed to stay behind and meet her after everyone was gone. She probably thought we were going to lounge around on the sofas, hang out in rooms we normally weren't allowed to be in together, stuff like that. But *my* plan was to tell her we should stop seeing each other."

"Oh."

"I couldn't see it going anywhere after I graduated, which was going to be in June—in two months."

"Did you actually break up with her?"

"Didn't get to. We met in the parlor, and she'd brought this flask. Said it was brandy—another rare treat. I wasn't much of a drinker, but I thought I'd take some, since maybe it would help me say what I needed to say." He shook his head. "Instead I pretty much stopped talking forever."

"When did you realize that you were..." Lina hesitated over the word.

Sean Reynolds did not. "Dead? Well, I don't remember anything after passing out. No floating over the room, no tunnel of light, no angels. When I woke up it was the next day, and I was with my family in Port Townsend. And they couldn't see me, and somehow I knew."

"They had been told?"

He nodded.

"That's awful," Lina murmured. She hadn't wanted to compare it to herself, but the memory of Mr. Ambaum's weeping but resigned wife and sons stole into her mind. She closed her eyes for a moment and willed it away.

Ren dragged a throw pillow onto his lap, and plucked lint off the corners. "The worst was I couldn't console them. I couldn't talk to them. It was just...over. Most horrible day of my...existence."

Lina wished their relationship wasn't so new, wished she had the confidence to wrap her arms around him and cuddle him like a child. Instead she only said, "I'm sorry," and silently screamed at herself for her inadequacy.

"I often wonder what would have happened if I'd come back to this house earlier," he said. "Before Julia killed herself."

"Why didn't you?"

"It didn't seem important. I wanted to stay with my family. I was there when the police came back to talk to them, so I heard she was beside herself, was so sorry, et cetera et cetera. I had no particular desire to see her."

" 'Sorry' doesn't quite cut it sometimes," Lina admitted.

"My folks sure didn't think so." Ren turned the pillow over and picked at the lint on the other side. "I was at my own funeral. That was the last time I saw her."

"She went to Port Townsend for it?"

"Yep. Looking very distressed, but, unfortunately, far too glamorous to gain the sympathies of a small town during the Depression."

"And the rest is history."

"Manslaughter charges. An attempt by Julia's family to buy off my parents. Their refusal. A suicide in the garage." Ren reeled off the events as if reciting the names of the first four presidents.

"Were you surprised when she killed herself?"

"Very. And then I sort of expected to see her. Even though I was angry with her, I would have welcomed the company. So I went to *her* family's house and hung around for a few days, waiting, sure she would show up. But there was nothing except a lot of weeping and wailing from her relatives. No ghosts."

"How depressing."

"Yeah. I decided I'd best get used to being alone, and spent the next year walking around, finding out what I could and couldn't do, seeing stuff I'd always wanted to see. I got on a boat down at the piers, and rode it to Alaska. Walked around Alaska for a few months, caught a boat back. Things like that."

"And you never came back here until a year later?"

"I thought of it. Lots of times. But the place where you died—well, I can't speak for anyone else, but I didn't want to see it again. Not till I started getting desperate for...what is it they say nowadays? Closure?"

"Closure. I guess you didn't exactly find that."

"Not exactly." He tossed the pillow aside and dropped his arm along the back of the sofa, behind her shoulders. "The second worst moment of my existence," he said, looking at the carpet, "was when I thought for a second that I was alive again, only to find I wasn't. I thought it had all been a dream. It was the middle of the night and I had walked into the side yard over there, and suddenly I could feel the temperature. I was shivering for the first time in a year. I could smell the grass, and the smoke from people's chimneys. I could reach down and pick up leaves. And I thought, 'I must have been sleepwalking, and I've finally woken up, and none of it happened.' I was so happy.

"Then I went around to the back door, and found a newspaper they'd thrown out, and it had the date on it—1937. I realized it really had been a year. So then I thought maybe I did die, but had been given another chance and had come back." He glanced at her, seeming shy to have wished such things. "Didn't have that right, either."

"You stepped outside the lines, and realized?"

He nodded. "Went out into the alley to run around to the front door and knock on it. But as soon as I hit the gravel, I was gone. I couldn't feel the ground. I couldn't touch anything. Went back and forth a few times, and finally understood. And that..." He let his palm fall to her shoulder. "Was when I suspected, as a descendant of Irish Catholics, that I had arrived in Hell."

Lina moved closer. Her shifting weight on the cushions tipped her chest against his. "You haven't." She leaned up and kissed him on the lips, only with an aim to comfort, not to seduce. At least, it started out that way.

His arm locked around her. She found herself melting back into the cushions. Her hand found its way up his spine and into his hair, which felt like puppy fur. What a travesty; she had known him for five months and hadn't run her fingers through his hair until now.

He broke free of the kiss, but stayed in their slanted embrace. "Why?" he whispered. "Why would you want to do this?"

"Well..." Her other hand curled against his shirtfront, luxuriating in the feel of ribs under muscle under cotton. "I never meant to fall in love with a ghost. But if the ghost is willing, I won't kick him out of my bed. Life's too short."

His surprised release of breath, and the way his eyebrows lifted and his gaze dropped, knocked a dreadful suspicion into Lina's head.

"I—I mean, if you *can't*," she said, "that's fine too. I didn't mean right now, anyway. This is—"

"I can," he cut in, blushing. "I can. And thank God for that, too. I'm just, uh..." A grin sprawled over his lips. "Surprised, I guess."

"You thought I was a prude, didn't you."

"You seemed reserved," he corrected.

"I'm not. I'm terrible. I have a filthy mind; I just never—really, you can?"

He nodded. "Which I think technically makes me an incubus."

"Nightmare?" Lina tried, groping through her

vocabulary.

"That's one of the meanings." His voice had taken on an arch, mischievous tone, and he relaxed against her. "Look up the other when you go back to your room."

"Tell me."

"Mm-mm." He pronounced the two syllables as a negative. The tip of his nose brushed hers. He teased her lips with small licorice-flavored kisses.

"Tell me."

His tongue flickered into the next kiss. "Look it up."

Lina lost interest in the English lexicon. They were on an angle headed for horizontal, lips entangled, when the piano rang out again.

Plink plink plink prrrrink!—several notes this time, as if fingernails were being drawn across the strings. Ren and Lina scrambled upright, and Lina wondered if she was insane for being relieved that it was "only" the invisible Julia, and not Marla or anyone else.

"That's so disturbing," she said crossly.

His breath skated warm along her neck. "I have the feeling that it's something we'll have to get used to."

Chapter Eleven

He invited her to the roof that evening.

Lina hesitated, a step below him in the back stairwell.

"What's wrong?" he asked.

"It seems dangerous. If she pushes people, then the roof isn't such a..."

Ren shook his head. "There are places in the house she's more active." He turned and led the way up the stairs. "And there are places she hardly ever goes. The roof is the one place I've never experienced anything."

"Strange."

"Not really. She was afraid of heights." Ren led her along the third-floor corridor toward the attic ladder. "Otherwise I'm sure she would have chosen that route rather than the garage. Would have been faster; more dramatic."

Lina climbed after him into the darkness. "You sure know when to pick your topics," she said, eyeing the shadows.

"Sorry. Here." His hand closed around hers. "Come on up and forget about it."

He flung open the rooftop door to reveal a gentle lavender twilight, and began telling her about a book he was reading. He sat down on the sloped shingles, letting gravity plant his back against a chimney, and Lina sat close to him for warmth. As they talked, the wind swirled around them, smelling of saltwater and wood smoke. When she shivered during a strong gust, he slipped an arm and leg around her, and secured her in front of him so she leaned back against his chest.

Although she had wanted to abandon the topic, she couldn't keep it out of her mind while perched three stories above the street. "What would happen to you if you jumped?"

"Think I haven't tried?" he said.

"Sorry. You don't have to talk about it."

"It's all right. Logical question. Well, when I attempt suicide, which I've tried three different ways...I die. Kind of."

"You die," Lina repeated, waiting for it to make sense.

"You know in video games, when your character gets killed, and disappears; and you get a brand new one, back at the beginning of the maze or the room or wherever you were?"

"Yes."

"It's like that. Only I was doing it long before video games."

"You disappear..."

"And reappear at the boundaries of the property. Any bloodstains I left behind are gone. I never remember anything in between. As far as I can tell it's an instant circuit. Do not pass Go; do not visit the afterlife; return directly to the house."

"Wow. That is weird."

"Yep. Which isn't to say there's no way out, but..." He shrugged. She felt it as a lift of one of his encircling arms. "I don't know how yet."

Lina huddled tighter into herself, feeling colder after hearing that story. She couldn't decide which was worse: the idea of not being able to escape even by suicide, or the image of Ren diving from the rooftop and crashing on the pavement below. *Breathe*, she told herself. *Let it go.* She did her best, turning her attention to the sunset-tinted clouds. This was a tranquil and romantic setting; she shouldn't spoil it by thinking of death.

"Did you look up 'incubus'?" Ren asked, in her ear. She heard a smile in the words.

"Yes. Let's see, 'a lascivious spirit supposed to have sexual intercourse with women in their sleep,' if I remember right."

"There. And you thought it wasn't possible. It's common enough they actually had to make up a word for it."

"Well, if you've been doing that, then you must have been discreet, because I sure haven't noticed."

"It's not my preferred method," he said. "I always wake them up first."

She laughed, turned her head, and kissed him, and they abandoned the discussion. Entwined on the rooftop, buffeted by cold wind, they kissed for the half-hour it took the stars to emerge, and at least another quarter-hour for good measure. They kissed until they were both breathing fast, until their limbs had fastened around each other in a comfortable clamp, until she couldn't separate the smell of the night air from the smell of his skin. He nuzzled her cheek with a chilly nose-tip, turning her face aside from time to time, unable to leave her ears alone for long. He nipped at them and burrowed his hands in her hair, making her shiver and laugh.

"Liiii-naaa!" Marla's voice, jolly and high-pitched, floated up through the open trapdoor. "Re-ennn?"

Ren and Lina moved their faces apart to appraise each other.

"We're being summoned," he observed.

"We're out past curfew," she said.

"Ah-ha!" Marla sounded closer now. "We've found their escape route, Mrs. B."

"Oh? Where did they go?" said Mrs. B's voice.

"Up to the roof, I reckon," Marla said.

Ren disentangled himself from Lina and crawled to the door. He leaned over it and shouted, "Boo!"

The sound echoed in the rafters.

Two shrieks from below made Ren and Lina burst into laughter.

"Lord Almighty, Ren," Marla hollered. "Would you two get down here? We've been looking all over the house for you. Time to start the movie."

Lina crawled to the opening. "Sorry, Marla. Coming."

****

"If I had any doubts about whether you took my advice," Mrs. B said after the movie, "they'd all be put to rest now."

They were in Mrs. B's room, where Lina was taking bobby pins out of Mrs. B's hair. "Because we were on the roof?" Lina smiled. "We could have just been stargazing."

"I don't mean on the roof. I mean during that movie. Sometimes when I reached over to ask you what was going on, I swear I touched Ren's leg instead."

"You really have a way of making the most innocent things sound dirty." Lina grinned, remembering how eight people had squished together into the TV room, requiring Lina and Ren to share a small space on the sofa, and how she had ended up more or less on his lap. Between his legs, actually, but there was no way to express that without sounding even dirtier.

"If you haven't kissed him by now," Mrs. B said, "then I'm just going to stop speaking to you until you do."

Lina put the bobby pins into a drawer. "Well, then I'm relieved to say we can go right on speaking."

Mrs. B's exclamation of delight was loud enough to make Lina glance to the door to see if anyone came running. "Tell me," the old lady crowed. "Is he any good? Does he know what he's doing?"

Lina sat down in an armchair, and set about assuring her that Ren did indeed know what he was doing. It was an hour of triumph and sweetness she had seldom known in her life. To be the female who had won the coveted male, the heroine of the romance, the holder of the succulent details. She even managed, for that hour, to push aside the voice of fear in her head.

But of course her triumph had a nasty twist. Unlike most romantic heroines, she ran the risk of being punished by a malicious ghost for winning the hero—or bringing punishment down upon someone else. She had never wanted a life of roller-coaster emotions, but that was what she had gotten, with even more up-and-down swing than the early stages of love usually brought.

She and Ren still met whenever they could, often talking and cuddling, more often abandoning talk in favor of kisses. When one night he pinned her to the wall in the back stairwell, his mouth so insistent against hers that they seemed to have melted together, every contour of his body tangible, she almost invited him to her room. But before she got up the nerve to ask, he let her go with a smoldering smile, and whispered, "Goodnight."

And then she had to face her room alone, and as soon as the lights were out, dread draped over her with the shadows. What would happen tonight? Would it be something bizarre but harmless, like the CDs being stacked? Or would it be frightening and messy, like the day she awoke to find her lipstick scribbled and smeared all over the mirror? She had looked for words or images among the graffiti scrawl, but there weren't any—or, at least, nothing more than any psychiatric patient would see in the average Rorschach test.

Other people felt it too. Every week there was new gossip. Dolly Tidd watched her desk drawers open and close by themselves. Betty on the second floor said all her shoes were hauled out of the closet overnight. George said the ghost must really want his hair to look bad, because his comb kept getting stolen and hidden. Most seniors believed their own stories but said the other residents were just senile. Lina said nothing, not even to Ren—not unless he asked, which he only did a couple of times, and then she played it down. Harmless pranks, she said. No need to worry.

But he did worry, and she saw it. As she came down the back stairs one day in the third week of March, she overheard him talking with Marla in the pantry below. "I don't remember it ever happening this much," Marla said.

"I don't either," Ren said. "It feels like she wants to have it out once and for all."

"Well, how the heck do you have it out?"

"I don't know."

Lina didn't want to hear any more, and went back up several steps to cough and tread heavily so they would know she was coming.

That weekend, she had Saturday off. Ren had to work, but since the weather was mild, he encouraged Lina to go out and do something fun, then come back and see him in the evening. She agreed, and said she would go downtown.

And she did go downtown, but only to catch the Bainbridge Island ferry, and from Bainbridge Island she drove out to Port Townsend.

Sean Reynolds was buried in St. Mary's Cemetery in his hometown, reported the old articles. On two different nights now, Lina had dreamed of walking into the graveyard (which she had never actually seen), and finding his tombstone. Both times it had been a massive monument, as high as her chest, with scrolls and leaves carved into the corners. Once it was red granite, and his bones were scattered on the ground before it. The other time it was white marble, and a fog had enveloped her so thickly that she couldn't see her feet or anything else except the words *Ren is dead* engraved on the stone. Whether seeing the grave in real life would make the dreams stop or not, she didn't know, but she had to find out.

The sun streamed down onto the ferry when Lina left Seattle, but the marine layer of clouds increased as she travelled west. The day had turned cold, gray, and windy by the time she drove into Port Townsend two hours later. The town had tidy, quaint, century-old façades along the waterfront, with pedestrians strolling and loitering by the shops. But when Lina got past these, following the directions she printed from the Internet, and reached the gates of St. Mary's Cemetery on top of a hill, no one was around, and all she heard when she stepped out of her car was the wind and the cry of seagulls. She entered the graveyard.

Ten minutes later she stood in front of it. *Sean Reynolds, beloved son and brother, 1913-1936*, a small plaque of weathered gray stone set flat into the ground. She should have guessed it would be modest, since he had said his family was poor, and on top of that he had died in the middle of the Depression.

Beside him on the right was an older stone, barely legible. Robert Reynolds, Ren's grandfather, to judge from the dates. On Sean's other side, in standing polished stones with clear-cut lettering, his parents William and Clara, who had died in 1964 and 1966, respectively.

She stood looking at the stones a long while, hands in her coat pockets. Her heart had jumped to her throat when she had first seen the names, but after a minute they became nothing more than words. *So it's true*, was all her mind concluded. She even felt some relief at finding the story corroborated with facts carved in stone, and couldn't conjure up much grief over it. Yes, his bones lay beneath this plot of grass, so long buried that the turf spread seamless across it. But what did it matter, since his solid, tangible spirit lived across the water in Seattle?

Still, morbid curiosity did creep into her mind. What would happen if she dug up his coffin? Perhaps his spirit would be ripped out of the house in Seattle and brought here to reanimate his corpse, in ghastly zombie-movie fashion. Or perhaps opening his casket would set his ghost free, and she would never see him again. Likelier still, nothing would happen, except she would be horrified with herself and saddled with new nightmares. She would probably also be arrested.

She turned away. Talk about crazy. She wouldn't be strong enough to dig a six-foot-deep hole by herself anyway, and she certainly wasn't going to ask anyone else to do it. She would let the dead lie.

She walked to a clump of daffodils growing at the base of a tree, picked one, and brought it back to his grave. She kissed its petals before dropping it.

Yes, she would let the dead lie, as long as one of them was still willing to be her boyfriend.

Definitely crazy. No doubt about it.

****

Lina acquired a sleep deficit before long. Nerves and despair robbed her of the peace needed to fall asleep. She stayed up reading later and later, and when the alarm clock rang at seven o'clock she had to fight through her exhaustion to get up. Night shifts were especially harrowing; Julia seemed to dance around her, flicking objects onto the floor, making them drift across the room, shutting doors suddenly so Lina would jump. The ghost came and went, acting up for five minutes then disappearing

Molly Ringle

for hours; Lina never knew what to expect. Ren, sensing the disturbances, tended to call or come up to her room to check on her, but Lina always masked her anxiety with a smile, and told him she would be fine, and that she needed to sleep. But when he left, the possibility of sleep departed with him.

She made up the time with daytime naps in the living room before or after her shifts, with a book on her chest so people would think she had happened to fall asleep while reading.

Ren caught on before long. She woke up one afternoon, blinking in a diffused beam of sunlight, to see him sitting on the arm of the sofa.

His fingers trailed along her hair. He looked troubled. "Did you always sleep out here so often?"

Lina sat up and stretched her shoulders. "I guess not."

"She's more active at night. Is that it?"

She tried a smile. "I think it's mostly my imagination. You shouldn't..."

But before she could tell him not to worry, he moved down to sit beside her, interrupting softly, desperately, "Don't; don't lie to me. Tell me."

She took his hands and looked down at them, stroking his fingers. "It's everything. Combined. Some nights it's all too much, and..." She turned a shoulder in a shrug. "I can't close my eyes."

He nodded. They watched their fingers slide over and between each other. "You're getting tired of the situation. I've seen it before. I kind of expected it."

"No. No, no." She squeezed his hands. "I'm not tired of you in the least. That wouldn't be possible. I just seem to have developed a phobia of being alone at night."

"Hm." He looked at her, a new twinkle in his eyes. "Then don't sleep alone."

****

"You're going to watch me sleep." Lina said it aloud in the hopes that it would sound less weird. It was 10:00 P.M. and she stood in her room holding her toothbrush, nightgown, and bathrobe.

Ren sprawled in her desk chair, fully dressed and grinning at her. "I'll be here while you sleep," he corrected.

"Just sitting there."

"I'll move to the floor if I get cramped."

"You could lie beside me, you know."

The sparkle flashed again. "I don't quite trust myself."

"God, Ren. What if I snore?"

"I'll turn you on your side."

"I don't look my best in the morning. My eyes are puffy, my hair's a mess..."

"You looked adorable that morning in the snow. Stop fussing."

Lina smiled, pleased. But she had to voice her one major concern. "What if you being here makes her even more angry?"

"Then at least I'll be here, and you won't have to face it alone."

"If it's really bad..."

"I'll sense it. Let's give it a try. Of course, if you want, I'll leave." He planted his feet on the floor and leaned forward.

"No," she said, and saw the satisfaction settle into his smile. "No. I want you here. Damn it."

She went down the hall, brushed her teeth, and changed into her nightshirt. When she returned, she kissed him goodnight and climbed into bed, and let him turn off the light and settle down with a book. ("I can read by the nightlight," he said. "I've always had good night vision.")

But she only lay there, uncomfortable no matter how she arranged her limbs, all too aware of him breathing and turning pages a few feet away. Finally she looked at her clock. Almost an hour had passed since she first tried to fall asleep. She grunted in dissatisfaction.

He looked up. "Still can't sleep?"

"No. Sit over here."

He pulled the chair closer.

"No; *here*." She thumped the bed with her palm. "You can put a pillow behind your back."

When he hesitated, she hauled over a spare pillow and plumped it against the headboard. "Come on. I'll feel better if you're within reach."

"Okay." He transferred himself to the bed.

She draped her arm along his knee. The fabric of his shirt tickled her nose. "That's better," she murmured, sleepier already from his warmth and scent. She had read that inhaling male pheromones relaxed women. Seemed to be some truth in that.

His hand alighted on her head and stroked her hair, hypnotically slow. She curled up closer. Her limbs became easier to arrange. Everything, in fact, improved a great deal.

The alarm clock's ring jarred her awake. She leaned across Ren to tap it off, and fell back upon him with a grunt. She yawned, blinked to clear her vision, then rolled onto her back to look at him.

He smiled in the light of dawn. The book he held had only a few pages left on the unread side. "Hi."

"Hi. Anything happen?"

"Not really."

She pushed herself up. "Not *really*? Was there anything?"

"Honestly, I don't think so. The radiator did some banging and clanging, but it's old and steam-powered, and it just does that."

"I've noticed. Used to wake me up, but now I sleep through it." She dropped her forehead to his shoulder, shy about how she must look, and hugged him. "Well, thank you for being here. I slept very well."

"Good." He folded his arms around her, rumpling the warm folds of her nightgown. "Then we'll have to make a habit of it."

Each night that week, he finished his work and came up to her room by ten o'clock. He always leaned over her and dodged past her hair-combing or face-moisturizing in order to plant a kiss on her ear. Then he kicked off his shoes and stretched out beside her, sitting up to read while she lay down to sleep. Whether or not she was on call, she always slept well, and he always reported in the morning that Julia hadn't done anything serious. One night, he said, the blanket got pulled away, but since he was there and awake, he grabbed it and pulled it back, and won the tug-of-war. Julia apparently fled the room after that and spent her wrath elsewhere. Dolly Tidd groused the next morning that a whole bunch of her books had fallen off the shelves overnight.

On the fifth morning, Lina awoke with the dawn before her alarm clock rang, and found Ren lying beside her. His book was on the bedside table. His pillow had slid down to the level of hers, and a corner of the blanket was pulled over his chest. He was asleep. Lina raised herself on one elbow, careful not to disturb him. His head was turned toward her, dark hair in a tousle against the sheets, eyelids quivering in a dream. Her hand drifted up to touch his face, and met warm skin and an emerging prickle of whiskers.

Tenderness stabbed deep inside her. What if the spell broke like a bubble, and he disappeared one day, as he should have done seventy years ago? Even if the spell didn't break, Lina wouldn't stay young forever. She might grow old here, becoming less and less desirable to him and looking more and more like a cradle robber to the outside world, and eventually she might give up and flee. Though the day when she would have to sleep without his touch could be years in the future, it made her want to cry just thinking of it.

Then Ren's breath hitched, and his eyes fluttered open, and he asked her in a confused voice if he had been sleeping. She made herself smile, told him "Yes," and teased him for being a lousy guardian.

****

What was the time-honored distraction from brooding upon death and decay? Sex, of course. It had been on Lina's mind for weeks, usually as a beautiful daydream but sometimes as a maddening need. She had never been good at initiating physical intimacy, and with Ren the situation was even more confusing. As a ghost, he might possess some quality that would complicate the matter. Even if not, he was such an old-fashioned gentleman that, incubus remarks aside, he never spoke of these things. How experienced was he? How had these customs worked back when he was alive? How would she know when the right time arrived?

Leading questions were the only tactic she thought she might successfully pull off. So that night when he settled down beside her, she rested her head on his chest and said, "I guess you probably did this with some of the others."

"No, actually." He sounded surprised at recollecting this fact.

"No? So, does that mean you've never...well, when you said you could...do things..."

Ren cleared his throat and lifted innocent eyes to the ceiling. "I submit to the jury that some activities can be performed without spending the night."

"Oh. Then how many..."

"Three. Three women, in all this time; only one

before I died, and no, it was not *her*. As for lighter stuff like kissing, not too many more. Ten. I try not to get involved if I can't be serious about it." He stroked her hair. "Therefore I'm going to be really jealous when you tell me how many have had the pleasure of being with *you*."

"I'm pathetic. Two, ever, all the way. And kissing..." Lina sighed, thinking back. "Unless you count stupid dare games in middle school, there have only been four or five. Not counting you."

Ren curled his arms around her waist and pulled her on top of him. "Then let's count me some more."

They sank into a slant across the pillows, making the best of the tight quarters in Lina's bed.

"I remember," Ren said between slow kisses, "you wearing a robe one morning, when I had come up here to look for burglars. You lifted your arms, and..."

"Oh," Lina broke in with an ashamed, delighted laugh. "I flashed you, didn't I. I thought so. It wasn't intentional."

"That's a shame. I thought maybe you were sending me a signal."

"Maybe I was, subconsciously."

"Got me thinking; tell you that." He kissed her deeper, his tongue finding its way past her teeth.

The taste of brandy in his mouth had ceased to bother her, and had even become an aphrodisiac, along with nearly everything else about him. She hooked a leg around him and her nightgown hitched up. He twined his leg around her in return.

A thumping, scrabbling sound pulled them apart. They sat up and watched a medical textbook heft itself off Lina's bookcase and flip open four feet above the ground. The pages ripped out in handfuls, faster than any normal person could manage, and sailed all over the floor until the book was completely disemboweled. The cover then dropped to the ground, landing as if exhausted upon a heap of pages.

"Well. That takes care of her," said Ren.

"That drug guide cost forty bucks!" said Lina, leaning over to see the title.

"We'll get you a new one." Ren pulled her back on top of him. "Now, I believe I was saying she's not going to bother us for the rest of the night, if you care."

"Oh." Lina smiled and wriggled herself into place. "You're right. That's worth a lot more than forty bucks."

"Fifty, at least." He looped his arm around her neck.

As they kissed, they rocked gently against one another as if slow-dancing. Through their clothes she felt him respond, and she pressed into him with her hips. He groaned. His hands gathered up her nightgown until they touched bare flesh on the back of her thighs, and he held her tight against him. Lina felt a blush pound through her whole body and flare into her face. It thawed away the last pockets of ice that had collected in her veins over the winter and sent them swirling down a warm spring flood.

This is the time. Her heartbeat went wild at the notion. He wanted it, she wanted it, Julia was out of the way, they were in bed; all she had to do was continue. And, truthfully, continuing would now be far easier than stopping. It took effort just to interrupt their kisses and ask, "Um, lame question probably, but do I need some kind of supernatural condom?"

Ren laughed and rolled her onto her back, smothering her in a kiss. "You wonderful woman. Well, now." He rucked up her nightgown and cupped a breast, and bent to take it into his mouth.

Lina bit her lip, trying—without success—to

stifle a whimper.

Ren propped himself up on an elbow. "Let's think about this, nurse lady. I step off the property, and any, ahem, *fluids* of mine left behind vanish with me. Therefore..."

"Oh. There would be nothing left to impregnate me or infect me with any diseases."

"Which I don't have, by the way. But yes, that's the idea."

"Well." Lina grinned. "Of all the creative excuses for avoiding birth control, that's pretty good. Still, as a nurse I'm not sure I'd advise a patient to believe it."

"All right." Ren sat up and slowly unbuttoned his shirt, his eyes fixed on hers. "Why don't you look me over without these clothes in the way and see what you think. Then we'll follow your final medical decision."

Lina's decision, after investigating with shy touches, then smiling kisses, then fervent strokes, was to toss his shirt onto the floor along with all their other clothes, and devote the night to hungry explorations.

As they lay skin to skin afterward, the sheets crumpled around them, she rested her ear on his chest, listening to the thud and slosh of his heartbeat. "Fully biological as far as I can tell," she said. "Not ectoplasmic in the least."

He chuckled sleepily.

She traced her nail down his shoulder. "So, if you step out into the alley now and recharge, does that mean, um..."

"I was wondering when you'd think of that." His hand slid down and squeezed her rear. "Yes, it does. But I bet I'm good for at least once more before resorting to that."

He was good for it. Quite good.

The next morning he slipped out after her alarm

clock rang, kissing her and fondling every inch of her skin within reach before he left. But she hadn't even climbed out of bed herself when someone knocked on the bedroom door a few minutes later. She put on her blue robe, kicked her discarded panties under the bed, and opened her door.

Ren regarded her shyly. He cleared his throat. "Hello. Um, the thing is, I stepped out of the lines to recharge for the day, and then, well, I thought of you, and..."

Lina hooked her fingers into the waist of his trousers and pulled him inside.

When she saw him out again, no more than fifteen minutes later, she paused to kiss him at the open door.

From down the hall George Lambert's voice thundered, "Our nurse is leaving me for another man!"

Lina gripped the front of her robe to make sure it was closed. She and Ren looked over. George stood in the hall, dressed in a red jogging suit for his morning walk, beaming.

Dolly Tidd, in a long Chinese-patterned silk housecoat, had just come out of her room and was also beaming at them. "Sure looks that way to me, George."

"What's all that?" Marla turned the corner, pencil behind her ear and clipboard in her hand. She stopped, taking in Lina's robe and Ren's flushed smile. "Oh, yeah. That's old news. You folks are behind. Ren, get your rear down to the kitchen."

The seniors laughed, Marla grinned, and Ren bowed respectfully and slipped away. Lina waved to the spectators and withdrew to get dressed, embarrassed but pleased. Compared to her other ambivalence-ridden exercises in intimacy, this one was turning out a winner.

Then, as she put on a clean pair of underwear,

the word *necrophilia* surfaced in her mind. She paused a moment, stunned. Had she just added *that* crime to her record? But after another moment she rejected the word and all its closest cousins. A lawyer might argue she was consort to an incubus, as Ren had said, but nobody could call him a corpse. He was warm, damp, salty, silky, soft, hard, supple, *alive*; and would have fooled the most practiced lover on the planet. Besides, a person only left behind one corpse, and Ren's was over in Port Townsend.

The clang of the radiator jarred her out of her thoughts. She frowned at it. It was nearly April now, and mild outside; the radiator shouldn't have needed to come on. Into her mind darted a fear she had been suppressing. She pictured the spirit of Julia stretched long and thin like vapor, sliding into the pipes and pounding icy fists on the coils in each room she passed. Lina's afterglow retracted. She hurried to get the rest of her clothes on, and twisted up her hair in a half-tucked ponytail, no longer caring if she looked like she had just rolled out of a hayloft with the houseboy.

Ren generally didn't tell her whether he felt Julia was angry on a particular day. Lina had requested to opt out of the information; she hated the paranoia it instilled in her. But she didn't require a sixth sense to guess that their recent actions may have enraged the mad dead girl.

"I'm sorry," she whispered to the ceiling. "I love him, too. I'm sorry."

Then she flung open her door, and rushed out to fetch Mrs. B's breakfast.

Chapter Twelve

Lina could forget Julia when bedtime came again, and in the glow of the seashell-nightlight she and Ren spent hours learning the feel of one another. Lina pitied the poltergeist while doing things with Ren that Julia never had, hearing him whisper how much he loved it, how much he loved her.

But she couldn't help noticing the quiet, at a time when she would have expected Julia's violence to be fiercer than ever. She bedded Ren, snagged him in the stairwells for long wet kisses, stole gropes under his apron in the pantry, and all Julia did was pound on the radiator pipes now and then? It didn't add up.

"Has anyone heard from...her, lately?" Lina asked him, early in April.

He focused on the dry rice he was pouring into storage bins in the kitchen. "I don't think so."

"You're sure? Wouldn't she be angry?"

"If you want to know," he began, slowly.

"Yes. This once, I want to know."

"She *is* angry. I've felt the storm brewing from the first day. But..." He crumpled up the empty rice bag. "There's no indication it's coming soon."

"She's biding her time? Saving her energy?"

"Could be. I don't know."

Lina leaned on the counter, stirring her coffee. "Has she ever really hurt anyone?"

Ren threw her a glance, one eyebrow cocked.

"I mean, besides you," Lina amended. "That was an accident."

210

Ren took a bunch of celery from the refrigerator and rinsed it in the sink. He brought the dripping stalks to the butcher's block, where he chopped them. "Maybe. It's hard to prove. She shoved Jackie and sent her to the hospital—maybe. I can't be sure it was her."

"Did the energy, or whatever it is, diminish right after that?"

"Yes, but that same morning she also threw your clothes around the laundry room. We *know* that was her. So did she only do that? Or did she do both, on a rampage?" Ren shrugged. "I can't tell."

"Have people been hurt any other times?"

"Things falling off shelves have left bruises and scrapes. People scared by something have run too fast and stumbled. Old people have died here; how do we know they weren't scared into a heart attack? Whether ghosts hurt anyone—well, it's not the kind of thing actuaries keep track of."

"What do *you* believe? Are we in danger?"

He gestured with the knife in helplessness. "I ask you to be careful. That's all."

"How? I'm already doing the one thing that will make her angriest, aren't I?"

His gaze flashed to her, and his voice was warmer and lower when he answered. "Yes, and I don't intend to let you stop."

"Good." She arched her back against the counter, enjoying how he glanced up and down her body. "But does this mean I should go around the house in a plastic bubble, just to be safe?"

He picked up a handful of chopped celery and dropped it into a glass bowl. "Try to stay around other people, especially at night. Don't tempt her by leaving sharp things around, or heavy things that could be toppled off high places. Stay out of the garage and the rest of the basement when you can. Open flames aren't a good idea either."

She was inclined to laugh at this cautious list. But the stern look he sent her sobered her. It wasn't wise to smirk at the idea of ghosts when you were sleeping with one.

But love made her brave, or so she fancied, as she strolled down to the basement that afternoon with a basket of Mrs. B's laundry. She needn't be afraid, especially when she was capable of filling her mind for hours with Ren kissing her, Ren's hands dancing along her skin, Ren's neck tasting like the spring breeze, Ren sighing in her ear, Ren's muscles tensing and stretching under her grip.

Yes, for the span of time it took to load laundry into the machines, Lina was quite able to put her thoughts in a happier place. She even felt brave enough to venture into the storage shelves in search of light bulbs. One had burned out in the third floor bathroom, and Lina had been meaning to replace it. Humming a love song from some musical, she walked between the shelves, swinging the empty laundry basket, dragging her fingertips along the items. Rolls of paper towels, bottles of window cleaner, boxes of candles, cases of aspirin, and, there toward the end, packs of lightbulbs.

Though old fears and new warnings nagged at her nerves, she kept her back turned to the cobwebs and the shadows, and hummed the song louder. Sunlight trickled in through the window above her head. The laundry machines tumbled and clacked from the next room. She took her time about choosing the wattage. One-hundred was too bright; twenty-five much too dim. Forty sounded good. She took a package of two, and turned to leave.

Before she got past the shelves, she heard a pair of loud metallic snaps. A sharp pain hit the side of her head and she fell to her knees, gasping. The laundry basket dropped from her hand. One of her lightbulbs slipped from its packaging and burst on the concrete floor, scattering white glass around her. Lina raised a hand to her right ear, which had gone hot, and found a hard, thin metal line along the outer ridge, and another one on the lobe. Touching them sent flares of agony all the way down to her heels. She breathed through her mouth, trying not to cry out. The bit of metal in her earlobe loosened and came away in her hand. She stared at it.

A staple. A heavy-duty staple. Blood dyed her fingertips, and a warm drop seeped down her hairline toward her neck. Shaking with shock, she looked up.

On the shelf across from the supplies, at the level where her head had been a few seconds before, a staple gun lay on its side, pointing outward. Lina dove forward on hands and knees, heedless of the light bulb glass, and scrambled out of the shelves. Behind her, something hit the wall, and she yelped a sob and looked back. It was her laundry basket, flung after her.

When she reached the stairs she jumped to her feet and ran. She didn't look back, didn't retrieve her basket, didn't try to find out whether the thumps she heard were the laundry machines or the poltergeist. At the ground floor she clamped her mouth shut to quiet her breathing, and edged around the landing with her back to the wall. She was not going to burden Ren with this.

She inched around to the next flight of stairs without anyone noticing her. Ren's voice, answering the cook, came from across the dining room. Lina swallowed upon hearing it, quashing the impulse to dash to him and hide in his arms. She fled up the stairs, her steps muffled by the carpeting.

In the third floor bathroom she set the remaining lightbulb on the counter and opened a drawer to get the first-aid kit. Only when she was ready with the sterile gauze and antibiotic ointment did she dare to turn and examine her wounds in the mirror.

Considering someone had tried to staple her ear to her head, and considering head wounds always bled more than you expected, it wasn't too bad. Holding her hair out of the way, and gritting her teeth, she yanked out the remaining staple from the upper edge of her ear. It came without much effort, but it had punctured her ear all the way through and cut her scalp.

She had suffered no worse than many a youth who had tried to pierce their own ears, she told herself, imagining what she would say to lighten a patient's qualms. She bent to the sink and washed her wounds with antibacterial soap. Thank God she had recently gotten a tetanus shot. Really, the injury itself wasn't serious. What made her stomach twist and her hand shake as she applied the ointment was knowing Julia had attacked her; knowing if it had been a nail gun instead of a staple gun, she could now be lying dead on the basement floor.

Tears spilled down her face, tears of self-pity, terror, rage; she couldn't tell exactly. She used a clean piece of gauze to wipe them away, then threw it into the trash, folded her arms on the counter, and cradled her head there. What could she do? Honestly, what could she do?

Lina arranged her hair to cover the marks, and sat for the rest of the afternoon between two old ladies in the TV room, staring with them at a game show. By the time it turned into a soap opera, her hands stopped trembling. She went up to Mrs. B, escorted her to dinner, exchanged smiles with Ren as he served them, and nodded when he leaned down to murmur into her ear an invitation to meet him that evening. Luckily, it was the left ear.

But as they stood beneath the maple tree in the moonlight, nuzzling noses and murmuring nonsense,

Ren's long fingers cupped her face and began their usual stroke along her ears. She flinched when they swiped the wound, and his touch returned there at once, feeling the scab. He frowned and turned her head aside to examine it. "What did you do?"

Lina hadn't decided yet whether she would lie to him about it. She hated lying. "I wasn't paying attention, and it got snagged on a little piece of metal," she said. Not a lie, but misleading, which made her feel guilty enough.

And he knew at once. His mouth and eyebrows set into grim parallel lines. "This morning?"

"Yeah."

"It was her." Ren didn't wait for Lina to deny or confirm it. "I felt something change, but nobody said—" He exhaled and withdrew his hands. "Were you going to tell me?"

"I'm sorry. I didn't want you to worry."

"What happened?"

Lina found a loose thread on her cuff to play with, and explained the basement occurrence, choosing the least alarming words available. They still ended up sounding plenty alarming, to judge from his reaction.

He paced, slapped both hands over his face, and paced some more, shaking his head. When she was done talking he flung himself down to sit in the grass, one knee pulled up, striking a leaf against his leg.

"I'm sorry I didn't tell you," she said again.

He waved it off.

"Say something," she begged.

"I've said 'Why me, God?' enough times in my life. Hasn't done me any good."

She knelt beside him. "That's why I didn't want to tell you. I don't want you to feel like that."

"It's fine she tortures *me*. I'm used to it, I can take it, I understand. But she has no right—" He tore up the leaf and grabbed another one off the ground. "She's the kind of enemy I can't fight, and it drives me crazy."

Lina settled into the grass with her back to the trunk of the tree. "Do you think she's waiting for you to do something that would let her go? Has she ever given any sign?"

"Not exactly." He separated and pronounced the words in a way that made Lina suspicious.

"Meaning?"

Ren peeled the leaf into small pieces, tossed aside the stem, and cast around in the grass for another. When he found one, he tilted it back and forth in the streetlight beam. "People who have claimed to be psychics or mediums have been invited here before, as a test to see what they noticed. Marla would never tell them ahead of time about me or Julia. Almost all of them made up some kind of nonsense about 'lingering spirits' and 'old memories' in the house, and had no idea they were actually talking to a ghost. It was funny, really.

"But once, just once, in the seventies, a woman visiting Marla stopped cold when she was introduced to me, and said in this Irish accent, 'Seanie, Seanie Appleseed. It's Father, Seanie.'" Ren himself lapsed into the accent for those few words, as if it came naturally to him. "My father," he explained, in his own American voice again, "was born in Ireland. When I was a kid he sometimes called me Seanie Appleseed, since the Johnny Appleseed story was one of my favorites."

"Which I doubt was in the obituary." Lina felt the flesh prickle on her limbs.

"No. I don't think I'd told anyone about it for decades. I just stared at her; Marla did too. But it was like the woman wasn't herself. She was gripping my hand and looking at me, and said, in my father's voice, that what happened to Julia and me should never have happened, and it wasn't our time, and we were locked in the house where we died. I asked, 'How do we get free?' And she said, 'The house. The house is holding you.'"

Lina shivered and folded her arms, warding off her uneasiness. "What does that mean?"

"I tried to ask, but then she said, 'Julia's here. She's angry. She wants to move on but she can't. The house is holding you both.' Then the medium came back to herself, looked at us—I'm sure we had gone completely pale—and said, 'Oh, I'm sorry! What happened?'" Ren smirked and shook his head.

"Did you find out any more?"

"No. Marla and I tried everything—ouija boards, séances, meditation. We even convinced the woman to come back, but she couldn't reach him. She said it wasn't her specialty, communicating with the dead. It was just something that happened to her once in a while."

"Then you never figured out what he meant?"

"No. Except it's beyond my control, and it's something to do with the house."

"I wonder if it was built on a burial ground or something," Lina said, then felt foolish, knowing she had provided a cliché from a horror movie.

Ren threw the leaf aside and shrugged. "Places hang onto events sometimes. They don't need to be haunted before that. Once something happens there, the place becomes..." He waved toward the house. "What it becomes."

Lina conceded with a tilt of her head. "I suppose your situation isn't totally unheard of. The ghost of Anne Boleyn doesn't roam around the entire world, just the Tower of London, where she was beheaded."

"A house in Norfolk too, I hear. Where she lived."

Lina looked at him, a sad smile pulling at her mouth. She saw it mirrored on his face. "Guess I'm not the only one who's done research on ghosts," she said.

"I looked up everything I possibly could." He found a twig in the grass to play with. "Which wasn't easy before the Internet. God, I love the Internet. My life improved immeasurably when we got that. There's one thing most ghosts can't do. Web searches."

"Maybe there are chat rooms for people like you. Do you think?"

"There are chat rooms for teenagers dressed in black who like to pretend they're like me. I suspect I'm not alone, to answer your question. But I haven't found anyone to prove it."

Lina moved closer, until their sides touched. "You aren't alone."

Ren dropped the twig and put his arm around her. "Are you okay?" His voice was husky. His fingers lifted to touch her ear.

"Yeah. I was scared, but it could have been a lot worse."

He sighed and pulled her into a hug. She felt a kiss on her scalp, through her hair. "I'll do everything I can to keep her from hurting you. But you have to be careful. I can't always be there."

"I know. I was stupid. You told me not to go downstairs alone, and I did."

"It's okay." His hand trailed up and down her spine, comfort sliding into seduction in a way she had become deliciously familiar with. "It could have been worse."

****

Lina didn't ask over the next two days whether Ren sensed Julia's impending thunderclouds or not. Lina stayed out of the basement whenever possible, and if she had to go down there she contrived ways to get other people to go with her. It seemed to work. Nothing new happened.

In the meantime she clung to Ren. It was strange, considering how awkward she tended to be with people, but she now liked nothing better than to lie naked with him, both of them trailing their fingers along the other's body as if drawing notes out of the piano. Sometimes they joked and laughed together like children. Other times they waxed thoughtful and spoke of finances, war, religion, ethics, and Ren's metaphysical observations on being a ghost.

But none of those observations predicted the ferocity of what happened a few nights later.

It was Wednesday. Ren was tidying up the kitchen after dinner. Lina was in Mrs. B's room, reading a comedic novel to her. Over their laughter, and the fitful rain blowing against the window, Lina barely noticed the clangs and hisses of the radiator. But it soon became truly obnoxious, clanging louder, hissing harder. The smell of metallic steam pervaded the room.

"Goodness!" Mrs. B turned in her chair to look at the thing. "It sounds like it's trying to bang a hole in the wall!"

"They need to get that furnace looked at," Lina said. "It's not sounding healthy."

"Well, go on—if I can hear you over that racket!"

Lina went on reading, to the accompaniment of the growing noise and sputtering steam. Finally she paused. "You know, that isn't good. There shouldn't be steam in the room."

"I think you're right. It feels like New Orleans in the summer in here."

Lina closed the book and stood up. "I'm going to turn it off, and we'll call a repair guy tomorrow."

But Lina didn't get to take more than one step, for at that moment the radiator exploded.

Steam and bits of pipe hit her in a sweeping wall of scalding noise. Lina found herself on her knees with her face against the carpet, her arms covering her head, instinct taking over as if she had lived in war zones her whole life. Books and furniture fell and shook; cries of surprise echoed from other rooms. Lina grabbed Mrs. B's arm and pulled her out of the chair. Mrs. B was limp and moaning, her eyes shut, her face contorted in what looked like anger. Lina seized her around the ribcage and hauled her along the floor toward the corridor.

The carpet was hot and soaked, and Lina's clothes were wet by the time she got Mrs. B into the hallway, where a small crowd had already gathered. Their mouths moved, but she only heard an inarticulate hum through the ringing in her ears. She laid Mrs. B on her back and leaned over her. "Mrs. B! Mrs. B, are you okay? Come on, Mrs. B, open your eyes, talk to me."

Mrs. B's brown skin had blistered and swollen on the side that had been nearest to the radiator. Alan and Marla rushed into the corridor and crouched beside her.

"Get me cold water and towels!" Lina shouted at Alan. "And you call nine-one-one," she commanded Marla. "Tell them she's got steam burns. She's still breathing. Go!"

Marla nodded and dashed away.

Steam could be inhaled. It could damage the lungs, especially in children and the elderly. That was the foremost panic in Lina's mind as she rested a palm on Mrs. B's frail chest, watching it rise and fall, willing it to keep going. If only everyone would be quiet—she needed to listen.

Alan came back with towels and a basin of water. Lina rinsed the burns gently, and when Alan tried to help she snapped at him to listen to Mrs. B's breathing instead. A moment later, she felt a cool wetness dab her arm. She jerked aside and glared at Marla, who held a dampened towel and looked at

Lina in concern.

"You got burned too, honey," Marla said. "Is it just your arms? Be sure they have a look at you."

Lina couldn't care less about her arms, snarled as much at Marla, and returned her attention to Mrs. B.

She was soon eased out of the way by the medics, one of whom took her aside despite her protestations and applied burn ointment and bandages to her arms, hands, and one edge of her jaw. At some point she felt a touch on her back, and glanced up to see Ren beside her, pale, his lips closed tight. It was pointless to say anything to him yet, while everything was still up in the air. She looked away.

As she and Marla got into the ambulance with Mrs. B's stretcher, Lina spotted Ren at the front fence, clutching the iron spikes and staring after her. Their eyes locked. The medics swung the ambulance doors shut and erased him from her view.

The doctors at UW Medical Center determined Mrs. B had multiple second-degree burns and some lung damage. Because of her age they wanted to keep her there a few days. Around midnight the nurses urged Lina and Marla to go home and let Mrs. B sleep.

Alan came and got them. Lina sat in the back seat, gazing out the window, fingers rubbing the white bandages on her arms. "I failed her," she said. "I was hired to take care of her, and instead I brought this on her."

"Don't be crazy!" Marla turned in her seat to look at Lina. "How the heck was this your fault?"

"Radiators don't do that kind of thing on their own."

"They do if they're old enough," Alan said. "We should have had that thing repaired ages ago. I wouldn't be surprised if her kids brought down a lawsuit on our heads." He drifted into a gloom.

"It was Julia," Lina said. "She was after me, and Mrs. B got in the way." She lifted her gaze long enough to see Marla and Alan exchange glances.

"Well," Marla said, "we can't prove that."

"And we sure as hell can't tell the lawyers that," Alan muttered.

Lina didn't press the point. But her mind professed the final verdict. *They know. They know it's my fault.*

Mrs. B's room was a mess. It looked like Ren and Alan had done their best, pulling things off the soaked carpet and stacking them in the hallway. But the rest would be the work of plumbers and plasterers. Steam had scarred the walls; the place smelled soggy and unfamiliar. Lina shuddered and dragged herself on to her own room.

She was not surprised to find Ren slouching in the chair there. His latest book lay unopened on the nightstand beside him, and he scrambled up at once when she arrived. The question was in his face. She answered it before he could ask.

"She'll probably be all right. As long as no lung complications set in." Exhausted, Lina threw her coat on the desk chair, and collapsed onto the bed. "She's a hardy old woman. I think she'll pull through."

"Good." It was all he said, and all either of them said, for at least half a minute. "Do you want me to stay?" he finally asked.

"I don't know."

"Tonight took a lot out of her," he said. "I doubt there'll be anything else for a couple days."

Lina closed her eyes in a throb of pain. It *was* Julia, then. As if there had been any doubt.

"But if you can't stand the sight of me," Ren said, "I don't blame you. I'll go."

"I can't stand the sight of myself," she

whispered, eyes still closed.

"Will you believe me when I say it's never been this bad before?"

"I believe you, but it doesn't make me feel better."

She heard Ren move to kneel beside her. She felt a kiss on her bandaged arm. "What about you?" he asked.

"It's nothing. Second-degree at worst. Shouldn't scar if I put the ointment on it. It's funny, though, isn't it? Burns on top of my burns."

"What? Oh. When you were a kid."

"That was my fault too." Lina didn't open her eyes. "I was twelve. Mom was out with some guy from work. Dad got mad and went out to find her. My brother and I were hungry, so I thought we should make hot dogs for everyone on the charcoal grill. A nice gesture. Maybe they'd never fight again if they came home and found we'd made them hot dogs."

Ren's cheek rested on her shoulder. His arm clasped across her.

"You can figure out the rest," Lina said. "I added lighter fluid when I shouldn't have. It flared up. I jumped, knocked over the grill, and got scarred for life. Lina strikes again."

"Lina..."

"At least that time," she said, her voice choked, "I didn't hurt anyone else."

Ren held her tighter. "You didn't do this."

"Mrs. B..." Lina winced at the flood that pushed up into her eyes. "Mrs. B never woke up, all the time we were there, so I don't know...I don't know if she blames me...if she's in pain..." Her voice was a mere squeak now.

Ren's arms lifted her and brought her head to his shoulder. While she wept he stroked her hair and said nothing until she had quieted several minutes later.

Then all he said was, "We'll make it stop. There has to be a way."

Lina was too tired to wonder how. She nodded and kissed him, and fell asleep.

****

Lina spent the next day in a variety of unpleasant tasks. When the furnace repairmen arrived, an insurance agent shadowing them, she related the incident to them, minus ghostly theories. The group clumped down to the basement to look at the furnace. Lina went along, dreading every step despite her sizeable entourage. The men shook their heads and said it sure was a weird case. A pipe must have burst, but to do it with that kind of strength, and in a mild season when the system wasn't getting overworked, well, that was bizarre. The insurance agent launched into a story of a television that had exploded on someone in a case he had examined. Lina wondered if that had been the work of a ghost, too. He would undoubtedly think her crazy if she piped up with the proposal that poltergeists were the silent killers of American households. Maybe she *was* crazy. Poltergeists were probably only the silent killers of *this* household.

She visited the other seniors, but that didn't calm her either, as they wanted to know what happened with Mrs. B, and Lina only ended up retelling the story. Not being able to tell it truthfully made it even more distasteful; and the seniors were upset, which didn't help. Some of their family members got word of the accident and called Marla and Alan to demand assurance that it wouldn't happen again. Lina found Marla slumped in her quarters, her eyes covered with one hand. Marla rambled about how one family threatened to withdraw their mother from this place, and another actually was going to, and the calls were only going to increase as more families heard about the accident; and, God, why did she and Alan ever think they could control a house like this?

"It's my fault," Lina mumbled again.

"Don't be silly."

"I'll move out." Lina felt numb as she said it. Would she really? Where would she go?

"Now that's just stupid," said Marla. "Whatever happens here, I'd rather have you around to help. Besides, Ren would only fall into a blue funk if you left, and no one would be able to stand living with him."

Lina nodded, too tired anyway to imagine having to move her stuff.

Marla slid her hands up into her hair. "At least Mrs. B wants to stay. Against her son's wishes, I ought to add. Guess she got into a holy-hell knockdown fight with him at the hospital over it."

"She's awake? And fighting?"

"Well, arguing. On a notepad. Still can't talk, with the oxygen tubes."

"Oh. Yeah."

Marla pushed up from her chair. "Come on. I was going to visit her. She'll want to see you."

When they entered the hospital room Mrs. B sat up with difficulty and smiled, but with the oxygen mask over her nose and mouth she couldn't talk to them. She patted their hands and winked, and urged them to talk by pressing her thumbs onto their palms when they paused. Lina's tongue stuck in her throat. It broke her heart to see the lively old woman reduced to this. Marla did most of the talking. Out of nowhere she conjured up some humor and regaled Mrs. B with the stories of what the repair guys said and what characters they were.

When they got up to leave at dinnertime, Lina leaned over to kiss Mrs. B on the forehead, and whispered, "I feel so guilty. I knew the ghost was jealous, and then this happens."

Mrs. B's eyes took on a disparaging look, and she waved her hand in the air to swat Lina away. The unspoken words chirped in Lina's head. *Oh, fiddle!*

She smiled despite the ache in her heart. "You're probably right. Goodnight, Mrs. B."

Marla and Lina drove back to the house, barely speaking. They parked in the garage and entered the house through the office in the basement, where they found Ren.

He shut a file cabinet drawer and stood up to look at them with a hollow gaze. For the first time, the sight of him made Lina's flesh creep. Not until now had he worn some aspect of the walking dead. Was the sparkle really dulled in his eyes, or was it a trick of the light? Were his colors washed out and tending toward gray, or did her tired eyes paint them like that? Surely his hand wasn't translucent there, resting on the filing cabinet? No, that was impossible.

She let her gaze drop. Impossible should not have been in her vocabulary anymore. It ought to have been banished along with alive, dead, and sane.

"Hey, kiddo," Marla said.

"Hello," he said. "Dinner's almost ready. About fifteen minutes."

Marla glanced from him to Lina, then trudged to the stairs. "Right. I'll see you two up there."

When the landing door had closed behind her, Ren moved again, dispelling the notion that he was nothing but an old sepia-toned photograph projected in three dimensions into the room. "How is she?" he asked.

"Mrs. B? She's okay. She's kept her spirits, at least." Then she stopped, chagrined to have used the word *spirits*. If you thought about it, language was full of idioms that wouldn't do when talking to a ghost. *I nearly died laughing. We don't have a ghost of a chance. I'll finish this if it kills me.* Ugh, why wouldn't her mind stop? In despair, Lina lifted her gaze to the walls. "So, what were you doing down here?"

"Nothing much."

She ventured forward and touched the filing cabinet. "What's in these?"

"Files on the house. Taxes and..." He sighed. "Insurance. I wanted to make sure Marla and Alan are covered. If she's going to do this much damage, and if I'm the one to blame..."

She took his hand. "You're not. I feel guilty too, but we're not the ones loosening the pipes till they burst. Or whatever exactly she did."

"I know." His hand did not move in hers, but at least it was warm. He didn't seem dead as long as he was warm.

"So are they covered?" she asked.

"About as much as they can be. Comprehensive, along with earthquake, flood, and so on."

"She can't cause an earthquake, can she?"

"I don't think so. But then, a few days ago I wouldn't have said she could make a radiator explode either."

Lina glanced around the basement room, her stomach lurching at the knowledge that Julia died about twenty feet from here. "Maybe we should go upstairs."

"Dinner's about ready. You might want to round up the residents."

He withdrew his hand and followed her up the stairs, and they parted at the landing. As Lina continued up to the third floor, she eyed everything with resentment—the carpet, the wallpaper, the overhead light fixtures, the paintings, even the doorknobs. Radiators, laundry baskets, and staple guns had already been used against her, so why not

227

the rest of the furnishings?

Lina asked so little of life. She behaved well whenever possible. She fell in love with someone who was trapped and lonely, and she wouldn't have minded living here for the rest of her life if it meant she could be with him. But Fate wouldn't even let her do that.

If Ren had been an ordinary man they could have run away together. But then, if he had been an ordinary man there would have been no need to run.

The worst was knowing that other women had found themselves in the same dilemma, and had all unanimously chosen what looked like the only wise option. Leaving this situation. Leaving him.

What began as a routine hanging up of her coat in her room ended with Lina raking the hanger at the bar until it caught, slamming the closet door, and kicking it. No! She wouldn't leave. She wouldn't be like those others. Love was rare and precious; she had to stop dumping it down the drain like a cocktail she was too squeamish to drink. She had to act if she wanted to save it. Any crazy idea was worth a try. After all, nothing could be crazier than reality.

Chapter Thirteen

That night after dinner, Ren nestled with her on a parlor sofa, the *New York Times* crossword spread over their laps. They stared at it without speaking or filling it in.

Finally Lina said, "I have an idea for putting her to rest."

"Oh?"

"I have to come clean about killing Mr. Ambaum." She whispered the sentence, not wanting to broadcast it to anyone wandering past.

"That has nothing to do with me or her."

"But it does, sort of. You're a victim of the same type of horrible mistake I made. I can't help thinking it, every day."

Ren kissed her on the neck. "Look. I've thought of it, too. But I see it as balance, justice. Maybe if we love each other, it redeems those mistakes—yours *and* hers."

"Things don't look very redeemed. Do they?"

His silence, and the way he dropped his gaze, was answer enough.

"I have to come clean," she said again.

"Doesn't the man's family already know?"

"I don't mean them." She sat up and turned to him. "Will you come with me?"

****

They walked toward the alley together in the dark. Before reaching the property line, Lina stopped and kissed Ren. "Thanks for doing this."

"My pleasure." He stroked her cheek. "Wish I could do more."

They turned and kept walking. Ren disappeared as soon as he stepped through the gate. Lina went on, car keys in her hand, purse thumping against her hip. She got into her car at the curb, started the engine, and blasted the air against the foggy windshield to clear it, giving Ren time to climb into the car. "I guess I have to take it on faith that you're there," she said, setting her purse on the passenger seat. "Here, hold my purse."

A moment later she muttered, "Sorry," and moved it to the floor, deciding it might be rude to make a ghost share space with another object even though he couldn't feel it.

She released the parking brake, peeled the Impala out of its spot, and turned toward I-5.

Forty-five minutes later she pulled up in front of her mother's house in Tacoma. The porch light and a few interior lamps shone onto the chilly night, and her mom's beat-up Buick sedan sat in the driveway. "Looks like she's home." Lina took a deep breath and closed her eyes. "Oh, Ren, don't let me screw this up."

She waited, but nothing moved or whispered in answer. She could have been completely alone.

She got out of the car and pushed through the squeaky front gate. Hoping Ren was beside her, she knocked on the door—which always felt strange, even though she hadn't lived here for over ten years and therefore couldn't just walk in.

Her mom opened the door, bathing Lina in a burst of warm air and canned television laughter. She wore her big glasses with the red frames, which she only put on when no men were around. "Lina! What you doing here, baby?"

"I'm sorry to just show up like this." Already Lina wanted to backpedal and escape. "It's not really important. I only wanted to talk for a minute."

"Well, come in, honey." Her mom let her inside,

her parted lips drooping in what Lina recognized as her anxious look.

Lina sat on the sofa and her mother muted the TV. A romantic comedy from the eighties played soundlessly on the screen. Lina watched a girl crimp her bangs and paint her lips frosted pink. "All I...all I wanted to say was..." She clutched her purse on her lap and looked down at it. "You remember at Thanksgiving, Wade told us about a nurse who gave a patient a lethal injection by mistake?"

From her seat on the edge of the armchair, Lina's mother squinted at her. "Not really, sugar. What's this again?"

Lina reminded herself that Ren was watching. She tried to behave in a way he would approve of, instead of screeching with frustration and stress. She looked directly at her mother. "It was me. I accidentally killed a patient at Everglade. That's why I left."

Horror distorted her mother's face. She gasped and put her hand to her mouth. "Oh, baby! Oh, no! What's going to happen to you?"

Lina hadn't known what to expect, but she felt a sweet comfort at her mother's concern. "Nothing, Mom. Nothing. It's okay. I mean, it isn't okay, but I'm not in any trouble."

"But that's killing someone! That's—isn't that manslaughter?"

The comfort receded. That word was not one of Lina's favorites lately. "The family didn't press charges. They understand it was a mistake. I promise, I'm not in any legal danger."

"Are you sure? Should you have told me?" Her mother twisted in the chair, pressing her knees together as if in pain. "If anyone comes asking me about what you did, wouldn't it be better if I didn't know?"

Lina felt cold now, and her voice came out that

ERROR

way. "Mom. No one's going to ask you about me. I just wanted to tell you. I hadn't told you guys, and I felt bad. All right?"

Her mother cringed and pressed a palm to Lina's leg. "Oh, sweetie, I'm sorry! God, I know, you must feel awful. I'd never get over something like that! See, honey, this is why I could never be a nurse. I'm not brave like you."

Lina's mom had always been the master of the hapless backhanded compliment. "I'm glad you understand how I feel," she said, knowing the irony would sail over her mother's head.

"You say you haven't told your dad?"

"Not yet. I will."

"Listen, honey." Her mom shifted into her "giving advice" voice. She leaned forward and planted her fingertips on the coffee table. "I wouldn't if I were you. You know how judgmental he gets. Nobody's ever good enough for him. A thing like this—God, I hate to imagine what he'd say to you!"

Lina's heart sank as she heard her own fears spoken aloud, even in a voice she tried not to trust. "But shouldn't I be honest? Wouldn't that be best?"

"I wouldn't, honey. You're braver than me, but I wouldn't." Her mother took off her glasses and pressed her eyelids with the blunt tips of the frames. "God, sweetie. How miserable. You sure no one's going to arrest you? I won't get hauled into court to answer questions, will I?"

****

Lina got back into the Impala ten minutes later. "Well. That was delightful." She imagined the amusement in Ren's eyes, and looked forward to seeing it when he reappeared at the house. "Still, I guess I feel better."

But as she sped home at seventy miles an hour, dread darkened her relief. "What if she's right about my dad?" she asked the invisible and possibly absent

Ren. "I'm not done until I tell him, but what if that's the cost? My dad despising me and never speaking to me again?"

By the time she pulled up to the curb near the house, she decided she couldn't risk waiting to find out. If the axe was going to fall, she wanted it to fall tonight, fast and clean; get it over with.

So although it was eleven o'clock in Philadelphia, she excavated her cell phone from her purse, switched it on, and dialed his number. She took shallow breaths as she waited for him to answer, listening to the clicks of the car's engine cooling.

He picked up on the third ring. "Hello?"

"Dad?"

"Hey, Lina." He sounded congenial if confused.

"Sorry it's so late. I hope you weren't asleep."

"Nope, I was up. Going over taxes. Only got a few days left to file them. Are yours done?"

"Oh, yeah. I think I get a refund. Just a small one."

"A CPA could get you more, I bet. I know some guys over there. I'll email you their names."

Already she wasn't doing enough to please him. Her mother had been right. Lina slumped back into her car seat, the safety harness still cutting into her shoulder. "Okay. Thanks."

"So what's up, missy?"

She had to go through with it. Ren was there. She had sworn to him she would. "There's something I want to tell you."

"Oh?"

"Back in September, you know I left Everglade Hospital."

"Yeah. How's that going?"

"It's all right, but...I need to tell you why I left." Her seatbelt was making it hard to breathe. She unfastened it and let it coil away. "Do you know the

233

difference between sodium chloride and potassium chloride, medically?"

"Table salt versus deadly poison?" Her dad chuckled. He was a corporate financial officer for a shipping firm, but he knew his basic science. He knew a little about everything, and a lot about many things.

"Right; more or less. Well...I switched them accidentally." Lina covered her eyes with her hand. "I injected a guy with poison, Dad. By mistake, because I'm a klutz, because I wasn't paying attention. He died. He had cancer anyway, but still, he died when he shouldn't have, and it was my fault."

"Oh, Lina." Emotion infused her dad's voice, but she couldn't tell yet what kind of emotion it was.

"I'm not in trouble," she said, miserably. "They weren't even going to fire me. But I couldn't stand being there anymore. I don't know why I thought leaving would fix things. I mean, when I didn't even dare tell you guys until today..."

"My poor kid." Sympathy. Was it sympathy? "Why didn't you tell us?"

She thumbed away a tear from her cheekbone. "I'm sure you aren't happy to learn your daughter's a killer."

"Lina." It *was* sympathy. Love, even. "How many lives have you saved? How many people have you helped? You're allowed to make mistakes, you know."

"I am?" she squeaked.

"Honey, last year I submitted a report wrong, just by mistake, and it ended up costing the company eighty grand. I felt pretty stupid, I guarantee you that."

"At least nobody died." She sniffled.

"Only because you're in a riskier profession than me. Because you're braver. And hell, I'm proud of you for that."

Finally she breathed freely again. "Mom said that, too. That I'm brave, anyway." She laughed a little. "She also said I shouldn't tell you, because you'd judge me."

"She said that?" Her dad growled his distinctive noise of irritation. "Lina, I never brought this stuff up, because I didn't want you or Wade to see any more conflict between us than you already saw. But you're a grown-up now, and I want you to know, it makes me mad as hell, the insecure crap she says to you two. Sometimes I swear she has absolutely no faith in you. That's what galls me the most about her."

Exhausted, Lina smiled through her windshield at the cloudy night sky. "I'm sorry for ever believing it."

"That's why I moved so damn far away. I couldn't stand watching her do it up close."

I must have inherited that from you, she thought. *Being tempted to leave a bad situation instead of suffering it out.* But it would sound hurtful if spoken aloud, and anyway she *was* suffering this one out. So instead she said, "Hey, here's something I haven't told Mom. I'm seeing someone."

"Oh yeah? That's great! Hope I get to meet him."

"I hope so too. I mean, I know you liked Brent, but..."

"Who? Oh, Brent. He was just fun to go golfing with, that's all. What about this new guy; does he golf?"

Lina laughed. "I don't know. I'll ask him later."

"Okay. Well, I better finish the taxes, but I'll want to hear about this guy sometime. All right?"

"All right."

"Thanks for calling. Don't feel bad."

Lina thought of the exploding radiator and Mrs. B's oxygen tubes, and her mood sank again. Not feeling bad was rather off the table. "I'll try," she said. "I love you, Dad."

"I love you, too. Bye now."

Lina turned off the cell phone and leaned back in the car seat, all her limbs heavy with relief and anxiety. "So. Is that it? Do you think it worked?"

Ren didn't answer, of course. They were still outside the property by at least half a block.

"You're there, aren't you?" Panic crept into her voice. "I didn't just let you go?"

The risk hadn't even entered her mind until now. She had thought only that by repenting for her own manslaughter she might somehow undo the ill effects of Julia's—set Julia free, or turn her into a benign ghost, or maybe even fling open Ren's prison to let him walk as a human anywhere he wanted. She hoped her own attachment to Ren might work that type of wonder. "But I might have erased you both," she whispered. "Please tell me you're there. Oh, God, Ren, tell me you're there."

A frantic tear splashed down her cheek as she dove out of the Impala and sprinted to the front gate. "Please, oh please, oh please."

She fumbled with the iron latch, wrenched open the gate, and flew forward onto the front path, then spun around to wait for him. The seconds dragged as if she were underwater and unable to breathe.

The azalea bush rustled at the corner of the yard. Ren came out of the shadows, strode over, and held her.

Lina clutched him and tried not to burst into sobs. "Where were you? I thought..."

"I'm sorry. I was there. I couldn't come in the front gate; someone might see me; so I got in through the bushes."

"You were with me?"

"The whole time."

Lina exhaled, and gulped in a new breath.

"You're still here. Good. It wouldn't have been worth losing you."

A maple branch as thick as Lina's shin swooped down, in a total absence of wind, and raked their heads with its mossy claws. She and Ren ducked and stared up at the tree. Lina sagged in dismay.

Ren said, "And we didn't lose her, either."

Lina felt too defeated to be afraid. She turned and dragged her feet up the front steps. "She can pile everything in the house on top of me. It doesn't matter. I need to sleep."

****

The next day an unremitting drizzle saturated Seattle. Ren and Lina sat on the living room floor after dinner, their backs to a sofa, gazing out the windows at the dripping maple tree. His arm draped her shoulders, his hand playing with her hair.

"How do we make her stop?" Lina asked.

Another twirl of her hair around his fingers. His gaze lingered on a faraway point outside the glass. "That, indeed, is the question."

"Let's ask her. Let's call her out."

"Could be dangerous." He sounded reluctant.

She seized his hand in mid-caress. "More dangerous than radiators exploding? Than staple guns shooting themselves at us?"

His lips flattened and he yanked his arm away. "Yes. Much more dangerous, if those were just her opening acts."

"Then what do we do?" She wanted to scream the question, but out of courtesy to the old folks in the next room she kept her voice to a clipped hiss. "Tiptoe around and never say her name? Hope she chooses something soft to fling? Wait for the next catastrophe, and pray to God it doesn't injure another old lady?"

"I don't know," he shot back. "She's never been this strong before, and nothing has ever gotten rid of her."

"Maybe you haven't tried hard enough."

"I will try *anything*. But I won't risk your life."

"Let *me* decide about my life."

They had turned to glare at one another, planting their fingers in the carpet. Lina stared him down for a few breaths, then wilted, her chin to her chest. "I won't leave you. I can't; I won't; it isn't fair. Don't make me."

He tempered his growl to a whisper. "I don't want you to. But I don't want anything to happen to you, either."

"We can't have it both ways. Not here."

Ren grimaced and let his head fall back on the sofa cushions.

Lina edged closer and put her cheek on his shoulder. "You must have come up with some ideas. There must be things you haven't tried."

"Only because they might hurt people."

"Everyone's gone tomorrow night. They're taking the seniors to the cinema." Lina watched him swallow, a ripple of his throat before her eyes. "Marla said I didn't have to go."

"Tomorrow. Saturday?"

"Yes." She sidled closer and put her arm across his waist, as much to give herself strength as to show him repentance. "I don't want to hurt anyone, either. But we have to try something. It has to stop."

He turned his head toward her. His lips parted, but he didn't speak for a few seconds. "If you really want," he finally said, "I have an idea."

A shot of nauseating fear invaded Lina's stomach. But she nodded.

She tried to make him tell her the plan that night. He would not; he was concerned Julia would overhear and act too soon. They had to stay quiet, had to wait until everyone else was safely out of the house. So Lina settled down beside him in her bed as usual; she in her nightgown and he in his ghost shirt, trousers, and socks. Neither attempted a seduction. They shared only a goodnight kiss, delicately, as if trying to touch a spiderweb without destroying it. *Kisses break a lot of spells in fairy tales*, Lina found herself thinking; and didn't dare follow that train of thought any further.

****

The next day crept by at half its proper pace. Lina ambled around the house, looking for work to keep her occupied. She tried to read the newspaper, and found it impossible to care about any of the articles. Her eyes kept wandering to the top corner of the page. April tenth. Something about the date tickled at her mind. Someone's birthday? Anniversary? Did she owe someone a card? She explored the calendar in her thoughts, and crossed off birthdays for her brother, her mother, her father, and Ren, along with her parents' anniversary (not that they would celebrate it anymore), without finding an April tenth. Didn't matter. Nothing mattered, except what would happen tonight. Probably that was what bothered her about the date. It might soon appear in her own obituary.

She had been relieved to tell her parents about Mr. Ambaum and to receive their sympathy (however tactless in her mom's case), but now she began to fear that those conversations had not been her key to peace at all. Today, walking around in a cold shadow, she feared her confession was actually going to serve as the deathbed type—a final tell-all, a repentant goodbye to her next of kin.

She went upstairs, turned on her computer, and settled chilly fingers onto the keyboard. *In the event of my death,* she typed in a new document, then sat there motionless for several minutes. She had nothing particularly valuable to leave to anyone. She couldn't write down what really happened to her, since she didn't know yet. Marla and Alan would guess the truth, but this letter was for her family, and how could she explain it to *them*?

I want you to know it wasn't suicide, she typed, *and Ren didn't do it either. We loved each other, and I was happy, but other forces—*

She stopped and erased the whole paragraph in a rattle of the delete key. She closed the document without saving it and flopped face-down on her bed, where she dragged over the pillow Ren usually rested upon. She clasped it to her nose, inhaling the scent of his cologne. He had worn it more often lately, since she had told him she liked it, and now the fragrance traced a lightning path to her heart.

There was no trace of his skin or hair in the scent, nor any way to capture that particular musk, since whatever he left behind from his own person vanished as soon as he went outside the lines. It was a sensation she had noticed a few times; a trace of moisture on her skin suddenly evaporating as, somewhere at that moment, he left the property. Though she had originally laughed at his unusual reason to go without birth control, now it just seemed macabre. She took another deep breath of the scent, then flung the pillow aside, jumped off the bed, and went downstairs, where she crammed her attention into sight-reading a Liszt concerto on the grand piano.

Chapter Fourteen

The rain gave way to a warm spring evening, in capricious April fashion. The green light of the low sun through the trees and the bewitching floral fragrance curling in through the open door only depressed Lina. Why couldn't she look forward to a relaxing walk with her lover tonight, the way couples all over town were doing? April, cruel as ever, did not have an answer for her.

At six o'clock, Marla and Alan, with the help of Consuela and one of the day cooks, got all the seniors into their lightweight sweaters, and in a slow parade bustled them outside into cars.

"The movie starts at 6:45," Marla said to Lina on the front porch, "and lasts, say, two hours, so we'll see you around 9:30. That's if we're making good time." She looked over her shoulder to the van, where George, Gertrude, and Dolly stood and waited for others to get settled in their seats. Marla rolled her eyes. "At this rate, maybe later."

"Terrific!" George hollered on the sidewalk. "I get to sit between *two* women!"

"George, you nut," Marla called. Then she looked at Lina. "You two be careful."

Lina nodded.

Marla squinted up at the house's brick walls, gaze darting from window to window as if checking for any new ghosts, then shrugged to Lina and jogged off to the van.

Ren appeared in the foyer as they drove away.

"Does Marla know what you're planning?" Lina asked.

He shook his head. "She's just concerned. Radiator thing put them all on edge."

Lina nodded, her arms folded. She stayed on the porch and rubbed the toe of her shoe against the threshold, not wishing to enter the house.

"Come on," Ren said.

She pushed herself forward, and he shut the door behind her. The sound echoed in the silent house. "Nice evening," she said. "Spring."

"Yes." He walked forward into the parlor. "Just like that other evening, sixty-eight years ago."

She followed him and made no answer, thinking it an idle comment. Then she halted and lifted her head.

He caught the surprised glance. "You didn't realize?"

"No. The date sounded familiar, but..."

"Yep." He turned, extended his arms to the ceiling, and called, "Happy anniversary, Julia!"

Something rattled on one of the upstairs floors. A series of thumps, like running footsteps, traveled north to south down the corridor, and came down the stairs. Ren and Lina turned, but the noise faded.

Lina swallowed. "Stormy weather tonight?"

"Very." Ren had let his arms drop, and now he sounded less brave. "Perfect conditions."

"For what? What are we doing?" Lina wasn't sure why she whispered the question.

Ren walked past her, scanning the walls and ceiling. "You've been replaced, Julia," he announced to the house. "You and I were over a long time ago. There's no reason for us to stay linked. I want you to leave. You hear me?"

The lights flickered. Lina heard, from the kitchen, the click and hum of the refrigerator losing electricity and then reviving. Though they stood in the middle of the parlor, with nothing but soft furniture around them, she found herself instinctively rotating, trying to watch her back at every moment. "What are we doing?" she asked again.

"She's strong tonight. Very strong. I almost think she's trying to answer me."

"Has that ever happened before?"

"Never." He took a few steps toward the kitchen and called, "Show us what you want, Julia. Answer me when I've got it right. Do you want this woman to leave?"

"Ren—"

"Shh."

They waited.

Nothing. Lina felt relieved for a moment.

"Do you want *me* to leave?" he asked then, and panic hit her. "You want me to stay off the property from now on? Will that set you free?"

"Don't," she whimpered, but he shushed her. She held her breath. When nothing moved after several seconds, she exhaled and seized his elbow. "Ren, don't. What good is it? Haven't you asked before?"

He took her hand, but kept his gaze on the room around them. "All the time, but tonight—you have to believe me—tonight feels very different. We might actually get an answer." He raised his voice. "All right, Julia. Is there any way to set you free? Is there anything we can do to make you leave this house?"

The row of paintings on the wall in front of them, landscapes of seashores and forests, swung on their hooks one after the other in a succession too quick for a living hand. The air throbbed with a strange cold breath; the word *yes*, like a trick of the wind, echoed from all corners at the same time.

Ren drew closer to her, the two of them pressing their backs together. "Did you hear that?" he said.

"I did."

"She spoke. Oh, my God, she spoke. Julia! Is there something we can do? Can you tell us?"

The pictures swung again, this time more violently. One of them fell to the carpet. A keening cry reached Lina's ears, starting soft from upstairs, then sweeping down the stairs and growing louder. A female voice sobbed and shrieked, and between the hysterical gasps Lina caught words.

"Sean! Oh, God, no...no no no...wake up, Sean, wake up! Oh, please, Sean!"

"Julia," Sean Reynolds answered, pressed to Lina's back. "Julia! I forgive you, for God's sake!"

The sobs faded out quickly, as if someone had turned down the volume knob and then switched it off. The quiet now hung like a guillotine blade above them.

Mastering every impulse she had to rush outside into the gentle, free night air and sprint as far as her feet would take her, Lina turned around to face Ren. He was pale. He tottered backward a step and sat down on the nearest sofa. She sat too.

"I never heard her say that," he said. "I was unconscious. I never knew what she said, what she did..."

Even then, the colder logic in Lina's mind reasoned that Julia had hardly said anything unusual for the situation. But the words themselves were not the important factor. "She spoke," Lina said.

"And she thinks there's a way. A way out of this."

"But how?"

He looked at the ceiling. "She's always stronger on this night, the anniversary of *my* death, not hers, because that's what started it all. So I think...I think we have to erase it."

"Erase it?"

"Tape over it. Go through all the steps. Reenact

it. I've always guessed that if she saw it happen all over again, on this night in particular, she'd go mad—probably knock the place to pieces. So I haven't dared. Besides, I'd need someone to help me, someone to play her part. Never wanted to ask anyone to do that." He lowered his face and smoothed his trousers at the knees. "And if it were someone who was similar to her in one crucial way; if it were someone who had..."

"Also killed someone accidentally," Lina murmured.

"Yeah. Then it might work even better. I don't know."

Though he still avoided her eyes, Lina composed her features into something like courage. "I'll do it. If that's what it takes."

Now he looked at her, and his appearance gave her a strange flash of fear. Once again, he looked pale and eerie enough to be a ghost. "You can still run, you know."

The words, his voice, the touch of wry humor, the love and understanding beneath it, filled her with grief at everything they were risking. But she stayed where she was, and shook her head. "Not this time."

He took her hand and looked down at it in silence. At last he said, "Shall we begin?"

Her throat felt like it was coated with rust, but she managed one word. "Sure."

He led her to the back staircase. "It started here. The rest of the girls all went away to the dance. The other houseboys were out, too. I came up from the basement to wait for her." He released her hand and hopped onto one of the stools at the breakfast bar. "Julia," he said, laying emphasis on her name now, "pretended she didn't feel well, and stayed. She came down when the others were gone." He tilted his chin toward the stairs.

Molly Ringle

Lina understood it was her turn. She climbed up a few steps, then swiveled. Feeling a fool, and a frightened fool at that, she came back down and tried to imagine herself as an elegant blonde from the 1930s. She paused at the landing to view Ren, who sat there looking exactly as he must have that night—the same outfit, certainly, and perhaps even the same angle of light, from the bulb above the sink.

"What do I say?" she asked.

He bowed his head to grimace at his nails. "She said, 'Oh, houseboy, I seem to have a headache. Would you help me to the couch?' " His mimicry of Julia's flirtation might have been funny any other night.

Now, Lina felt sick. But she repeated the line, in a pathetic echo.

A door slammed somewhere on one of the upper floors. They both glanced up.

Ren slid off the stool and took her hand. "So. To the couch."

They returned to the parlor beside the dining room and sat down on a sofa. "This couldn't be the same couch," Lina pointed out.

"No, but it'll do."

"What next?"

"Well...I let her kiss me." Even now, in the middle of all this, Ren found a roguish smile for her.

Lina, in turn, found a laugh, and kissed him. The scent of his skin brought tears to her eyes, but she blinked them away, and settled her arms around his neck. "I guess now I offer you a drink?"

A crash came from the darkened dining room behind them. They looked over the back of the couch. Several of the chairs had been knocked over. The sound of angry, fast breathing gusted toward them, and stopped.

Shaking, Lina looked to Ren.

He pulled a flask from his back pocket, swung it between finger and thumb, and placed it in her hand.

She removed the cap with unsteady fingers, and sniffed at the flask. "Brandy. And presumably something else."

"Yes. The drug."

"What kind of sleeping pill did she use?"

"You can't get it nowadays. It was found to be too unsafe in too many people. Imagine that."

"So this is..."

"Prescription pain meds. Strongest I could find. Scrounged it from Gertrude's room."

Lina winced, knowing the pharmacopeia the residents took. "Yeah. That should do it." She lowered the flask to her lap. "Oh, God, Ren. Don't."

"Why? What'll it do? Kill me?" His mouth twitched in a dry smile.

"But what if it works this time?"

"It worked last time, technically." He plucked the flask from her. "What do you think, Julia?" he said to the dining room. "Shall I have a little brandy for strength?"

An enraged growl zoomed toward them. The curtains on the nearest window, along with their rod, came down in a rip of fabric and squeak of drywall screws. Fine dust sifted over Ren and Lina, who shielded their heads. Quiet settled in, with the faint background sound of labored breathing.

Lina ventured to lower her arms and glance around, though every primal instinct screamed for her to run.

The rooms were starting to look a mess. Ren noted it as well. "We'll have a lot to answer for tonight when Marla gets home." He held up the flask in salute to Lina. "To you, my love." He pivoted to toast the air beside the couch. "And to Julia, whom I never loved, and who must leave tonight." As he swigged the brandy, another frustrated shriek rippled around the sofa. Lina, sure she was caught in a nightmare, watched Ren's throat pulse as he swallowed the poison; one, two, three gulps; and then she couldn't count them anymore, because the floor lamp tipped over and went dark. Seconds later, all the remaining lights flickered and went out too. The hum of the kitchen appliances died. This time nothing came back on.

Lina squeezed her eyes shut.

Ren's arm slipped around her, and his lips, damp and rich with the scent of brandy, kissed her forehead. "Don't be afraid."

A laugh, which would have been charmingly girlish in other circumstances, danced away from them toward the staircase.

"She's still here," Lina whispered.

"Of course."

"We don't have much time. The drugs will work fast. You'll pass out soon, and it's dark, and..."

"Come on." He rose from the couch, guiding her by the shoulders. "Candles."

Just enough light leaked in from outside, from the city, for them to get into the kitchen without tripping over the fallen dining room chairs. Ren, who knew all the contents of the cupboards, led the way to one of them. Lina heard the waxy click of candles being drawn out of their box, and the papery rattle of a matchbook. Then came a brilliant yellow flare, and Ren lit a white taper. He jammed it into a candlestick and handed it to her.

"Now what?" Lina asked. "What happened next?"

Ren steadied the candle by closing his hand around it, just above hers. "She invited me up to her room. Said she had something to show me, but we all know what that means." A row of hanging pans rattled and banged, their copper bottoms flashing.

Ren turned and raised his voice. "Yes, we know what that means, don't we, Julia? Come up to my room and *die*."

The pans lifted from their hooks and flew every which way. The clatter was deafening. Lina ducked, shielding the flame. Ren stumbled. A heavy saucepan fell at their feet. When she lifted her head, she saw him gripping the edge of the counter, one hand covering his eye. She reached for it. "Are you all right?"

He let her draw the hand away to reveal a curved cut on his cheekbone. Blood oozed up dark in the candlelight. She yanked a clean dish-towel from a shelf, but he stopped her before it touched his face. "Doesn't matter," he said. "Doesn't matter."

"Step outside the lines," Lina begged. "Make yourself well again. Forget all this."

"So we can wait for it to happen another night?"

She looked about at the scattered cookware, and crushed the towel into a tight ball in her hand. He was right, of course. It would not end here if they chickened out now. She flung the towel across the butcher's block, where it unraveled after one bounce and rippled to the floor. "It makes me so angry," she burst out.

"Good. Be angry. It's better than being afraid." His hand slipped onto her shoulder. "Now let's go upstairs."

As they climbed the steps, whispers and moans and scrapes sounded from all sides of the house. It could have been the wind; leaves swayed outside the windows. But when the intercom sputtered and crackled with static despite the electricity being gone, she knew the poltergeist was still with them. "To her room, you said?" she asked.

"Yes. Your room."

Lina paused on the stairs and looked at him. The candle flame made his shadow jump and quiver.

His right cheek was a reddish smear, smudged where he had dabbed at the blood. "Wait," she said. "You died in my room?"

He tilted his head reluctantly. "I didn't want to scare you, but..."

"Good Lord," she moaned, and resumed the climb. "I thought it was the parlor."

"I'm sorry. It just seemed..."

He didn't finish the sentence, and she heard a sliding sound like cloth against the wooden walls. She spun around. He had halted, his two feet on different steps, and now leaned his shoulder against the wall, blinking as if disoriented.

Terror and grief sprang up in her heart. She dove under his arm and hooked it around herself. "The pills?"

He nodded. "Starting to kick in, I think."

"Come on." Her voice wasn't quivering, at least. If she just viewed this as tending to a patient, maybe she could get through it. "Let's get you to my room."

"Girls are...always saying that to me." He smiled.

As they walked slowly down the dark third-floor corridor, a rumble shook the house. Lina felt it in her feet, and heard it in the jingle of wall ornaments and light fixtures. "What's she doing?" she asked. She prayed it wouldn't be something as bad as the exploding radiator.

"Don't know. Tearing down the...cabinets...in the kitchen?" He had begun blinking and giving rapid little shakes of his head, as though unable to focus.

Don't panic, Lina told herself, pressing her lips together to fight down a scream. His weight heavy on her shoulders, they made it into her room and fell to their knees. Lina set the candlestick on a hardback book lying on the floor. Ren collapsed onto his back and closed his eyes with a sigh.

Lina ran her hand over his puppy-fur hair. "How

you feeling?"

"Oh...just fabulous." His eyelids lifted, and he reached up to brush her face with his knuckles.

She tried to smile, but tears filled her eyes. In a floor below, something heavy smashed into something solid and structural. The house rang with the vibration. "Ren," Lina squeaked. "If you pass out, and she's still here, what do I do?"

"Tell her...to do what she has to do...to end it."

"But..." A tear fell down her face, and sparkled in candlelight on the back of his hand. He smoothed his thumb across her cheek. "What if...what if her leaving makes you disappear, too? What if she takes you with her?"

"Lina," he soothed, faint but warm, tired eyes shining with reflections of flame. "I should have been gone a long time ago."

She knew that. She had thought it many times, and steeled herself against the possibility. Or, at least, she had tried to. She pressed her face against his hand and choked down sobs. Now was not a good time to cry, not now, when the floor was shaking and the books scudding along their shelves from whatever destruction Julia was wreaking downstairs.

"I'm glad it's you," he said, "I'll finally get to die for."

"Don't say that." She wiped her eyes. "If you're dying, I'm dying right next to you."

"No, no. Listen. Promise me..."

"What?"

"If she tries to trap you, promise me you'll run."

She gave him a twisted, affectionate smile. "And leave you here? I'm a nurse. I can't abandon a patient."

"Run." He closed his eyes again. "You have to run. Promise me."

A tremendous boom rang out, accompanied by a

glare of light from her window. The whole house shook. Glass shattered on the lower floors, and a strange and awful roar advanced.

Lina scrambled to her window and looked down. Horror silenced her, though her mouth opened as if to scream. Fire poured out the broken doors and windows on the ground floor, licking upward toward her along the brick walls. She flew back to Ren, who lay with his eyes closed, his fingers splayed on his forehead. "Fire!" she shrieked, her voice returning in force. "She set the house on fire! Get up; please get up!" She tried to tug him upward, but he was heavier and limper than before.

"Run," he breathed, through lips that barely moved.

She had both arms under him now, and pulled his torso up, but his head fell back and his arm drooped to the carpet. "Wake up!" she screamed. "Oh, no, no, no...oh, God, Ren, please wake up!" She felt a gust of hot air, and looked at the doorway to see an orange glow lighting the hall. It brightened even as she watched. "Oh, God," she whimpered, then pulled Ren as hard as she could. "Come on, baby. You're coming with me."

The glow from the encroaching fire lit the hallway well enough that she didn't need the candle, so she left it. Fire hazards were a moot point now, she thought; and as she hauled Ren out into the corridor she wondered how on earth Julia could have caused such a massive burst of flame from a mere book of matches, which was the only firestarter Lina recalled seeing.

Then she remembered the gas stove. The crashing noises must have been Julia breaking through a wall and into a gas line, and flooding the kitchen with natural gas so she could strike a match and set off an explosion. The horror of this thought gave Lina a burst of panicked strength, and she managed to drag Ren past her own doorway and halfway to Mrs. B's.

The orange glow came from the back staircase, the one they had just used. That was also the direction of the fire escape, but if the flames were coming from that direction, she didn't dare try it. Besides, carrying Ren down the iron ladder would be almost impossible. In the other direction, toward the wider main staircase, the hall was still dark. Though the idea of venturing into that darkness unnerved her, it was the safer of her two options. She prayed for a clear passage down the stairs and out to the street. It was dangerous to stay in the house any longer. If the fire didn't trap her, Julia would. Lina just needed to get outside, drag Ren to safety...

Something tugged him the other direction. She stumbled, and his arms almost fell from her grasp. As she looked at her unconscious lover, he slid a few inches away from her. Someone unseen was pulling his feet. Lina was done with fear; now anger flooded through her. She seized Ren around the torso and pulled. It worked for a second or two, but then the opposing force recovered and yanked him back. She squinted at the yellow-lit hallway. Were the wisps of smoke playing tricks on her, or did a translucent figure actually stand there? Was that a slender, curved body; a flutter of a skirt below a knee?

The figure, if there was a figure, moved again, and Ren's body slid another few inches away from Lina. Lina's fingers, wrapped around his wrist, felt instinctively for a pulse, and found none. She pressed a kiss onto his hand and held his wrist tighter, willing the pulse to come back.

But instead his arm melted into nothing; he dissolved and vanished into the smoke. Lina stared at the empty carpet in amazement and anguish. A few yards away, the air rippled again, stronger now, as if trying to coalesce into the solid form of a woman. Ren was gone. Staying here to fight a partially-invisible ghost was pointless. Lina turned and bolted into the darkness.

It would be okay, she tried to believe as she turned a corner and stumbled down the pitch-black corridor, one hand on the wall for guidance. He said he had tried suicide before, and still came back. He would come back this time, too. But she also remembered that he—or rather his father, through the medium—had said *the house is holding you.* If the house was destroyed, its ghosts might be set free. He should have been gone long ago, he had said, and now this escape began to look like it had been his plan all along.

The thought that she had just left him forever was too painful. She halted and looked over her shoulder, her mind clamoring idiotically that she should at least *check* that he was really gone. She took a step that direction, but something wooden (a beam between floors?) squealed and crashed nearby, and the roar of flame amplified. Smoke stung Lina's nose and filled her lungs, hot and choking. She leaned on the wall.

Perhaps, after all, she needed to do nothing more. She had always counted death her bitterest enemy, whether she had been a fearful child or a nurse or the lover of a ghost, but now she saw that death was also sweet release. She had long dreaded her final hour on Earth and what shape it might take; but now it was not hard to face. It might even be the honorable thing, to stand here in the suffocating smoke, go down with the ship, let Julia destroy her along with Ren and the house and all the residents' possessions.

"See you on the other side," she whispered, dizzy from the fumes. She was certain Ren heard her.

A draft of cold air swirled around her, clearing a space for her to breathe. Ren's voice came from behind her, from beside her, from within her head. "Live. Promise me. Run!"

She gasped a breath, and the clean air brought with it the reminder that she was still young, that the world was still out there, that happiness and beauty still existed. She turned and plunged into darkness and smoke, and flew down the stairs. She made it to the second floor without collisions or falls, despite the murky, un-breathable blindness. She felt along the wall until she gripped the handrail of the stairs leading to the ground floor, and began jogging down them. Here there was light, but it was a dangerous light; yellow and orange throbbed in a screen of smoke; and as she descended, thin flames poured out from where they licked the first-story ceiling. She ducked to avoid them.

She was almost to the ground when the blow hit her. A body, slender and fast, jumped onto her back. Arms wrapped around her throat. Lina, her scream choked off, fell the last two steps and rolled on the carpet at the foot of the stairs, embroiled in a wrestling match with someone she could not see. But when she gripped one of the arms and pried it off her throat, she found, with shock, that she *could* see it. A lady's arm, dusted with downy blonde hair, fingernails neatly pared and painted red.

"No!" Lina coughed, struggling. "You. Will. Not. Kill me!"

Furious breathing blew against Lina's ear as Julia tried to regain her chokehold. But with a twist, a kick, and a jerk of the elbow, Lina knocked Julia away, and heard the ghost-girl cry out. Lina got her feet beneath her, but a glance up convinced her to crawl instead of run. The ceiling was a mass of smoke and flame, and bits of burning plaster were falling. She bolted ahead on hands and knees. She needed only to reach the front door.

A line of fire raced across the carpet, cutting her

off from the foyer. She stared in horror, and knew at once she could not attempt one of those jump-through-the-flames tricks people were always doing in movies. She turned wildly. Was there a window anywhere near? Or—

A female figure emerged from the smoke, crawling, flickering between transparency and opacity. Her short blonde waves were in disarray, and her jade-green skirt dragged on the carpet beside her knees. The malice in her eyes, fixed on Lina, was hard, glittering, and thoroughly determined. It was enough to reanimate Lina. She turned and leaped through the wall of fire.

Crashing on the slate floor of the foyer hard enough to leave bruises on her hip and shoulder, she thought only of whether or not she was on fire. With amazement, she discovered she was not. Furthermore, she was only a yard from the front door. She lunged for it, burned her palm on the knob, yanked her hand away and wrapped it in her shirt, and was about to try again through the cloth, when the window beside the door shattered. Lina curled away, covering her face. The glass fell in shards around her shoes, and she looked at it. That was odd: why would the glass break inward?

Then an axe smashed the remaining shards in the window frame, and a yellow-coated arm reached through. Flashing red and blue lights colored the smoke. She had not even heard the sirens until now. A firefighter wearing a clear-shielded helmet stuck his head in and grabbed her by the arm. "Come on! Get out! Take my hand. Put your foot here."

Something hot fell on Lina's shoulder as she climbed onto the windowsill, and the firefighter batted it off. Slipping through, she cut her ankle on a piece of glass, and paused out of instinct to press her sock against it. The firefighter hauled her farther away, down the front path, telling her they would take care of her as soon as they got her away from the house.

A fire truck blocked their street; hoses snaked all over the pavement. Barriers had been set up at the nearest intersections. Men in fluorescent yellow coats and fireproof boots jogged up to incoming cars and curious pedestrians, telling them they had to stay back.

"Is anybody else in there?" the firefighter holding Lina around the ribs asked. "Listen to me. Is anyone else in there?"

"No," she rasped. "I don't think so." And then she dared to turn around and look at the house. The sight brought her to her knees.

Above the neighbors' roofs and treetops, flame-lit smoke billowed and plumed. The beautiful century-old house was burning; roaring and crackling and blistering. All three floors and the basement and the roof and the maple tree, windows shattering, steam hissing in the wake of fire hoses. She thought she heard a high-pitched scream from within, but it might have been the wail of a staircase collapsing.

And so the spell is broken. She sat back on the wet pavement and put her face in her hands.

She heard Marla asking a firefighter, "Did you find anyone else inside? We have to know! Did you? Have you found anyone?"

"No, ma'am," the firefighter said. "Nobody except this lady."

Something in Lina's mind snapped, and for a time she had no notion what was happening around her.

After a while she discovered she was sitting across the street on the curb, being given a cup of something bland and sweet to drink. Her ankle was bandaged, and a portable oxygen mask sat beside her. Tears stung her face, especially the steam-burn along her jaw. She glanced up to see Gary, who offered her a sympathetic smile and said something meant to be comforting. She made no sense of the words.

Marla, Alan, Consuela, and some of the seniors' family members milled on the sidewalk, tending to the elderly residents and talking on cell phones, writing down where each person was going to stay that night.

Lina hoped no one would try to assign her a hotel room, or send her to her mom's house in Tacoma. She was determined to stay here until the last ember was cold and everyone else had left, and then maybe Ren would reappear on the blackened, vacant property. If he did, it would be enough. Even if he had to haunt the ruins of the house instead of the house itself, and even if she couldn't touch him this time, it would be enough to see him again.

Behind her, Gary's voice emerged from the clamor. "What about your houseboy? He wasn't in there, was he?"

She clapped her hands to her ears so she wouldn't hear whatever lie Marla or Alan responded with. After a while she got up and stepped across the obstacle course of hoses. The rest of her acquaintances stood in a knot under a cherry tree, talking and shivering. She didn't attempt to make eye contact with them, and no one stopped her.

She stumbled past onlookers, people she had never seen before who had congregated in excitement to watch a giant house burning down. She kept walking until she turned a corner and the street grew darker and quieter. The concrete retaining wall of someone's front yard loomed over the sidewalk, higher than her head. It felt dank and pebbly to her fingertips. Her feet came to a stop, and she turned and leaned her forehead on the wall. "I don't know how to go on without you," she said. "You told me to live but I don't know how."

The sound of sobs, moving closer, brought her head up. They advanced with unusual speed, and around the corner came a young woman, moving fast but not exactly *walking*. She glided as if on silent roller skates. Lina recognized her and stepped back in alarm—then paused, because this was not the same Julia she had wrestled at the front staircase. This Julia was still pretty, still had wavy fair hair cut to her chin, still wore a tea-length dress in jade green. But she carried no malice in her eyes, no cruelty. She looked merely like a heartbroken girl. She stopped in front of Lina, imploring her with a look. The scent of Oriental rose-vanilla perfume and cigarette smoke drifted to Lina's nose.

"Tell Sean..." The woman gulped. "Tell Sean thank you. Tell him thank you."

An icy feeling skittered over Lina's skin. "What?"

"Tell him thank you," Julia insisted, clutching a handkerchief up in front of her chest. "Tell him."

Lina managed to nod. It seemed to appease the young woman, who lowered her head and moved past, skimming along the sidewalk. Lina turned to watch her. The white of her graceful neck disappeared a few paces away, dissolving into the night air. The sound of her sobs ceased. The scent of perfume, which smelled like one favored by the richer old ladies at the house, lingered a moment before blowing away on a gust of wind.

Chapter Fifteen

Lina returned to the scene when she had collected herself, before anyone came looking for her. Alan, Gary, and Consuela had left to take the seniors to other facilities, where they would stay until they found a new residence. Marla, her eyes swollen, stood watching the blaze dwindle under the efforts of the firefighters. A few uninhabitable slabs of charred brick remained, housing two-story-high piles of ash and rubble.

"I'm sorry, Marla." Lina's lips felt dry and dulled.

Marla looked at her for a moment before returning her gaze to the dying flames. "Not your fault, honey. And I'm not letting anyone think it was."

Wasn't it, though, in some sense? Lina stood beside Marla and watched the firefighters spray down the remains of the living room. The grand piano, the carpet where she had danced with Ren, the ceiling where the mistletoe had hung—all destroyed. And Ren...

"They haven't found anyone," Marla said, as if divining Lina's thoughts.

"Didn't really think they would." Lina wouldn't cry here. Not yet. Not until she knew. But how would she know?

The fire crew hauled blackened maple branches to the side of the yard, clearing a path for the hoses. The grand old tree was ruined too. Mr. Ambaum, a mansion, two ghosts, and a maple tree. Someone had to lock up Lina before she killed anything else.

"I called your mom," Marla said. "Told her about this. She said she'll get the guest room ready, and you can go on down whenever you want."

Lina folded her arms. "I won't go tonight. Tomorrow maybe."

"Yeah. I won't be sleeping either." Marla sat down on the curb. Lina joined her.

They stayed there for another hour, until the fire was out and the onlookers had gone home, and only one fire truck and one police car remained. Then Marla got up to talk to the police, leaving Lina to wait. Lina looked at her watch in the red glow from the trucks. Only midnight. Only four hours since she had seen Ren. Four days since they had last made love. Just over two months since their first kiss, that half-drunken pounce at the breakfast bar; unless you counted the mistletoe, in which case it was a bit under four months.

Lina hugged her knees and hid her face against her lap. When would she stop counting? How long would it be before she went a whole day without calculating the hours? Would she ever see a pack of gum again and not think of him? Would she ever remember him and smile, rather than wanting to wail and tear things apart?

Marla's footsteps came back. Lina lifted her head. "They say it looks like a gas main broke," said Marla. "Happens now and then."

Lina's eyes trailed over the wreckage, and she nodded. She faintly remembered, now, telling Marla what had happened, in a hysterical ramble, when the Drakes had arrived.

"Someone mentioned the houseboy, so they asked about him, but I..." Marla's voice weakened. "I said he was out of town tonight. That you were in the house alone, taking a nap." Perhaps seeing the emotion in Lina's eyes, Marla crouched and took her elbow. "Come on, kiddo. We got things to do. Got to get the seniors settled, and tell Mrs. B."

Lina resisted, not wanting to rise.

Marla's grip held firm. "God knows I wish he'd come back too," she whispered, "but if he was able to, he would have by now."

With that death knoll reverberating in her ears, Lina closed her hand around Marla's, one finger at a time, and got up. Together they walked away from the empty, smoldering property.

****

Some of the seniors went home with their families. The Drakes found arrangements for the rest in other facilities. Lina rode beside Marla as they drove to one of these houses in the middle of the night and helped the graveyard-shift staff get the bewildered seniors into their new rooms. Of course it was harder for any of them than for herself, Lina tried to believe. They had all lived in that house longer than she had. As for possibly losing Ren, well, Marla and Alan had known him far longer.

Yes, but I loved him. They have each other. He was all I had.

They arrived at the hospital at five A.M., and Lina collapsed on a bench in the waiting room, unable to keep her eyes open, though also unwilling to sleep and face the certain nightmares. Marla marched to the nurses and asked them to check if Mrs. B was awake, and demanded to see her if she was.

Mrs. B was asleep. Marla grumbled, walked off, and came back with scones, a pair of apples, and cups of coffee. Lina sat up and accepted the coffee. *My first breakfast since he died.* She scowled, irritated with herself. *Not really; he's been dead since 1936.*

Marla left again and this time came back with T-shirts and sweatshirts from the gift shop. "Don't know about you, but I'm tired of reeking of smoke," she said.

Lina took the clothes to the restroom. She stripped off her long-sleeved T-shirt—the same one she had worn when she had first kissed Ren at the breakfast bar—and used the pink liquid soap to scrub the smell from her hair, face, and arms. Cloudy gray water dripped into the drain. She dabbed her skin dry with paper towels, and wrung out her hair over the sink. She put on the white T-shirt with the Seattle Seahawks logo, and the navy blue sweatshirt with a ferryboat and an orca on it, but she still smelled the smoke on her jeans. She imagined she would be smelling that smoke for months, no matter how clean she got.

A little before six o'clock, a nurse told them Mrs. B had woken up. They went in. Mrs. B's happy smile at seeing them, eyes crinkling under the oxygen mask, changed quickly as she saw that something was wrong. She hummed an inquiring sound.

Lina sat in a chair beside the bed and took Mrs. B's hand. Marla sat on the other side and began talking. Mrs. B's eyes widened and her heart monitor beeped faster, and she uttered cries as she learned what had happened to the house.

"And we..." Marla flashed a distressed glance at Lina. "We can't find Ren. He was probably in there."

Mrs. B gasped; her arms, dragging their delicate IV tubes, went around Lina, bending Lina's head to her chest. It was impossible for Lina not to burst into tears at such kind treatment. She heard Marla start crying, too.

Ren had told her once about the worst day of his existence, along with the second-worst. At the time, Lina had thought about her own life and tried to decide what her worst day was, and couldn't have said in certainty—the day Mr. Ambaum died, or the day she burned herself when she was twelve, or the day her parents announced their divorce? They were all contenders. But now she had a winner. No question.

I hope you're still going to come read to me, no matter where I end up, Mrs. B wrote on a pad of paper, after their flood of grief subsided. Lina nodded, gave the old lady a kiss, and excused herself to wash her face.

She sat on a couch with aged purple upholstery in the hospital's waiting area, staring out an east-facing window and watching the dawn break on this landmark day. As the water on her face evaporated, it left her skin taut and dry, as if she were aging and shriveling already.

Marla stood nearby, looking out at the sparkling city, the evergreen-swathed hills, the Cascade Mountains silhouetted by the yellow sunrise. "Everything's so beautiful," Marla said.

Lina wasn't sure if irony lay behind the words or not. She could have made a case for agreement either way.

Her eyes drifted shut, and soon she found herself walking down the hallway at Everglade Hospital, her high heels clicking on the tiles. The shoes were the same jade green as her dress, whose tailored fabric hugged her ribs and waist in a perfect fit. The glass of a fire extinguisher cabinet reflected the gleam of her blonde curls as she passed.

Rounding a corner, she collided with Sara, another nurse. Lina apologized and pulled herself to her feet. After dusting off her skirt, she made sure none of the medicated brandy had spilled, then carried the flask into her patient's room.

Ren, an ancient man, lay in his bed, frail and shrunken. His hair, entirely white, grew in patchy curls like a baby's. He wore a blue-dotted hospital gown, the same type Mr. Ambaum and most other patients wore. His room's window was a rectangle of glassy black, as if the hospital lay engulfed in a dark forest rather than in the middle of Seattle. She looked at it and shuddered. The blackness pressed on the windowpane as if it wanted to get in. Her hands shook as she imagined being swallowed up in that eternal night.

She turned to her task at hand, focusing on work to bring herself back under control. She leaned over his bed and placed the flask at his lips.

He opened his eyes and smiled. His hand, flecked with liver spots, stopped the flask before the brandy could flow into his mouth, and lowered it to the bedspread.

Gasping at her mistake, Lina dissolved into tears. "I killed you," she wept. "I should have been more careful. I was trying to help, that's all, I swear. Oh, God. I want to die."

He shook his head. "What you gave me was better than any afterlife. Come on. Discharge me, nurse lady. We need to get out of here."

She lowered her face to his arm, sobbing. "No. I'm scared. I can't let you go out there. Please come back."

A breeze stirred her hair and cooled her skin. She lifted her head in a panic, but soon calmed down. Rather than the inky dark forest, sunshine and fresh air surrounded them.

She recognized the place. St. Mary's Cemetery, Port Townsend.

Ren looked young again, and wore an Edwardian-era black suit jacket and bow tie over his usual shirt and trousers. He gazed curiously at the ground ahead. "Hmm," he said. "I think you better have a look at this."

She turned to see, but then a warm wind howled across the hill, stealing his voice, tearing off leaves and knocking over an empty flowerpot on a gravestone. Even as Lina reached for him, the gale hauled her off, tore her free, pulled her back to

Seattle.

Lina opened her eyes with a jolt.

Marla still stood there. The sun had risen a mere inch above the horizon; Lina could only have slept a few minutes.

"Marla."

Marla turned. "Hmm?"

"I know this is crazy. But we have to go to Port Townsend."

****

Puget Sound sparkled in the morning sun as Lina and Marla rode the ferry from Edmonds to Kingston. They stepped out of the car for the short journey and leaned on the upper deck's railing, the chilly wind whipping through their hair.

"What is it you reckon we'll find?" Marla's spine slumped with exhaustion, but kindness still emerged in her voice.

"I don't know. I just have to see the grave again."

When the boat docked in Kingston, Marla and Lina drove off the ferry and onto the peninsula. They passed white clapboard churches in the countryside on the way to Port Townsend. Flowers and ribbons and purple banners decked their front steps, and families in suits and pastel-colored dresses emerged from cars in the gravel parking lots.

"It's Sunday morning," Lina remembered aloud.

"Easter Sunday," Marla said.

"Is it? Oh, that's right."

Lina thought of chocolate bunnies and egg hunts, innocent childhood joys she would never feel again. Did growing up break every adult this way? Or had her dalliance with a dead man pushed her too far past any normal person's limits for peace of mind?

The Olympic Mountains to the west, usually a ragged silhouette from Seattle, loomed high and

266

clear now. Snow gleamed on the blue slopes. Wildflowers flashed along the roadside in pink, yellow, and purple. Between the fir trees, Lina glimpsed wide, rippling saltwater, sunlight scattered on it like broken glass. The beauty acted as a balm to her grief, but her mind refused to settle down from its racing circles. Something awaited her over here; she sensed it like a taste in her throat. But would it be a horror greater than before? And was that even possible?

In Port Townsend they parked on the silent street outside the hilltop cemetery. The sea-scented air, warmer today than on her previous visit, embraced Lina as she walked through the gates. Marla hung back several paces, inspecting other tombstones, probably to give Lina some time alone with Ren's grave.

The stone still lay there. The sight of it, solid and gray and engraved with his name, bruised Lina's heart, suffocating her timid hopes. She knelt, staring at it in agony. "That's it?" she whispered. "You're dead, you always were, nothing changed?"

The tombstone stared back blankly, the sun blazing upon the name *Sean Reynolds* and the death date from seven decades earlier.

She glanced over her shoulder helplessly. Marla had wandered away, far off to the western wall of the cemetery. Lina could crumple and sob if she wanted to.

But crying would solve nothing. What she yearned for was an explanation. Had the dream meant anything beyond wishful thinking? Had someone sent her here, and if so, why? Could nobody advise her, at least, which direction to steer her life now that he was gone?

She sank to her knees. Dew seeped through her jeans and touched her skin, but she didn't care. If she sat here long enough, perhaps that wind from

267

her dream would blow her back to Ren's side, to whichever alternate existence he now resided in.

A strand of dead grass landed on the second letter of his name, thrown down by the breeze. Automatically Lina reached out to flick it away. When her finger touched the grave marker, the stone cracked soundlessly, like a mud flat drying in the sun. As she pressed her hand to it in distress, hoping to halt the damage, the cracks multiplied and splintered. Within seconds the stone fell apart into gray dust as if it had been made of wet sand.

Lina rose, astonished and horrified, eyes fixed on the heap of dust. Had she just destroyed the last trace of him?

"Well," said his voice, behind her. "I guess that means I'm really back."

She sucked in a gasp and spun around, almost falling in the slick grass.

Ren stood in the sunshine, grinning, wearing the same old-fashioned suit he had worn in her dream.

"Oh, my God," she squeaked.

He held out his arms and she threw herself into them.

He chuckled, staggering backward with the force of her embrace. "Hey, darlin'." He spun her around; the sunlight flashed past them counter-clockwise.

"Who the...*Ren?*" Marla yelled from across the cemetery. A moment later Lina heard the thumping jingle of her keys as she jogged over to them. She felt Marla's arms fold over hers as the hug expanded to encompass all three of them; then Marla dropped away, lauding the miracle in nonsensical words while Lina held him tight.

She buried her face in his chest, crying and laughing at the same time. Her dazed mind proclaimed that this was really happening; it was not just another cruel dream. The thought resounded and repeated until it became solid enough to believe. And why not? Here he was in the flesh, smelling of wet grass, sea air, and warm sleepy male. She kissed his neck and tasted skin and dirt, healthy and outdoorsy.

When she blinked the tears out of her eyes and focused, the first thing she saw was a smear of green and brown on his shirt collar—grass stains and dirt. The spotless white ghost shirt would finally need to be washed.

"What happened?" she asked.

"What are you doing way over here?" Marla asked.

"Why didn't you call us?" Lina added.

Ren held up his hand, buying a space in which to answer. "I'm sorry. I just woke up. I know you must have worried."

Marla whacked him on the arm. "Hell, yeah. We thought you were dead. Deader than before, I mean."

"I don't think that's a problem anymore. I, uh..." He squinted in the sun, looking around the cemetery. "I slept all night, I guess. I woke up a little while ago. On my own grave, in the suit they buried me in." He tugged at his bow tie, unraveling it into a kinked ribbon of black that shone in the sun.

Awakening on his own grave, whose tombstone had now collapsed into dust? Eerie and chilling, yes, but also phenomenal, wondrous, perfect. Did it mean what she hoped? Lina grasped a fold of his jacket between her fingers, rubbing it, half expecting it to fall apart like the tombstone had. But the fabric was good as new, not a speck of mold or decay.

She looked up at him. "How on Earth..." she asked, unable to articulate the entire question.

His eyes twinkled, tea-brown in the daylight. "I'm guessing our ritual did the trick. We worked some kind of serious magic—with a little help from the rest of the dead."

"Wait," said Marla. "So you're here, outside the house, and you can touch stuff? Walk around like a normal guy? Just like everyone else?"

He stood taller, his chest expanding with pride. "Evidently."

Lina's legs had gone weightless with joy. "It worked? You're alive?"

"According to my folks, yes. I thought it was a dream at first, but..." Ren's voice turned husky. He thrust his hands into his pockets and gazed down at his parents' graves. "I was in the garden in our old house. It looked just like it did when I was a kid. They hugged me and said they were happy, even though they'd have to wait another lifetime to see me again."

Lina wobbled, and planted her feet wider to support herself. "I knew it. I dreamed about this place. Marla, that's why I said we had to come out here."

Ren slid his arm around Lina. "Connected, are we? Always figured as much."

"I'll be damned." Marla looked him up and down, fist on her hip. "Well, it sure is good to see you, kiddo, but does this mean Julia's out here too?"

"I doubt it," he said. "My guess is, she moved on. After putting in a good word for me, or so she said."

Lina hugged him around the chest, her heart beating a wild and joyful rhythm as the magical pieces fell into place, constructing a new and beautiful reality for the two of them. She could tell him later about the horrors of last night, about her struggle with Julia in the fire. They could theorize later about how it happened; perhaps the enchantments broke down as the house burned, malfunctioning and letting the two ghosts switch places for a short time, Ren becoming ethereal and Julia becoming tangible. Later, Lina could learn if he had really been there, telling her to run; and she could tell him about seeing Julia in tears afterward. She would pass along the thank you, and then find out all the details of his own strange, mystical night.

They could make sense of it later, if sense could be found in a miracle. But for now, holding him was more than enough. She lifted her head for a kiss. Ren, ever obliging, tilted his head and locked his mouth to hers. Recalling her bleak tally of final kisses and embraces, she melted in euphoria to realize that from today she could ditch those dates and start counting forward again.

They both stumbled sideways as Marla shoved them. "I'm mad as hell, you know."

Ren lifted his face, keeping his arms around Lina. "I know. I'm so sorry."

"Like hell you're sorry. You're going to build us a new house. We're taking you out of that kitchen and putting you to work with a damn hammer."

"Absolutely. It's the least I can do."

"Who are you going to pretend to be?" Marla added. "You thought of that? Did you get a magical Social Security number along with your new life?"

"Not that I know of." He sounded amused, if anything. "But we'll find ways. You figured out how to hire a ghost all these years. I bet you're up to the challenge."

Lina nuzzled her temple against his chest, smiling at Marla.

Marla still tried to scowl. "Everything looks great to you *now*, but life's not going to get easy all of a sudden, you know."

"I know," said Ren. "But at least it'll be life."

Marla regarded the two of them, then shoved his arm again. "You're both nuts. Anyone hungry?"

"Very," Lina said.

"Starving," Ren admitted.

"Come on." Marla turned and walked to the car.

Ren and Lina stumbled a few steps that way,

271

trying to kiss at the same time.

"We need to get you into some new clothes." She took hold of his loosened, outdated tie.

"Funny." He slipped his arm around her waist and hitched her close. "I was thinking we needed to get you out of yours."

"Hmm, really? You know, we'll need a place to stay tonight. Perhaps a hotel."

"The honeymoon suite might be appropriate." He paused under the cemetery's entrance arch for another kiss.

"What are you saying?"

"Well—"

Marla blared the car horn and stuck her head out the window. "Get *in!*"

They smiled sheepishly at her, and Lina pulled Ren toward the car. He hesitated at the door. Lina looked up at him.

"In a safety-deposit box," Ren said, in a rush, "I've got an engagement ring that an old woman left to me, at the house, when she died. I haven't lost everything; I've saved some things; I have accounts, under other names, and—never mind. It's yours if you'll have it, the ring. If you'll have me, I mean—"

Half a minute later, Marla was forced to shout out the window at them again, because Lina had thrown her arms around Ren and tangled him in another kiss.

A word about the author...

Molly Ringle grew up in the Pacific Northwest and currently lives in beautiful rainy Seattle with her husband and son. Her studies include a Bachelor of Arts in Anthropology (University of Oregon) and a Master of Arts in Linguistics (University of California, Davis). She was a Tri-Delta in college, in an old sorority house that was supposedly haunted, which inspired some of the central ideas for *The Ghost Downstairs*. When not writing, she can often be found experimenting with hot chocolate recipes and indulging in odd blog projects.

She loves to hear from readers, so please visit her at: www.mollyringle.com.

Thank you for purchasing
this Wild Rose Press publication.
For other wonderful stories of romance,
please visit our on-line bookstore at
www.thewildrosepress.com.

For questions or more information,
contact us at info@thewildrosepress.com.

The Wild Rose Press
www.TheWildRosePress.com